Benjamin B. Comegys

A Tour Round My Library

And Some Other Papers

Benjamin B. Comegys

A Tour Round My Library
And Some Other Papers

ISBN/EAN: 9783337241490

Printed in Europe, USA, Canada, Australia, Japan

Cover: Foto ©Andreas Hilbeck / pixelio.de

More available books at **www.hansebooks.com**

A

Tour Round My Library

AND

SOME OTHER PAPERS.

———

BY

B. B. COMEGYS.

———

.

PHILADELPHIA:
GEO. S. FERGUSON CO.
1893.

To

THE PHILADELPHIA BANK,

The Oldest Bank in the City Chartered by the Commonwealth,

An Institution which for Ninety Years has held a most
conspicuous place among the best of the Banks in our
City, second to none in presenting a model of
sound conservative Banking; whose Directors have always been
distinguished for their wise and liberal support of all
Public Measures for the good of the Nation, the
State and the City, as well as for their just
and generous treatment of those employed
in their service; whose methods of
business and system of training
have graduated an unequalled
number of men into higher
positions—

A TRUE ALMA MATER,

this book is dedicated
by the

PRESIDENT

(iii)

BOOKS are the windows through which the soul looks out. A house without books is like a room without windows. No man has a right to bring up his children without surrounding them with books, if he has the means to buy them. It is a wrong to his family. He cheats them. Children learn to read by being in the presence of books. The love of knowledge comes with reading and grows upon it. And the love of knowledge, in a young mind, is almost a warrant against the inferior excitement of passions and vices. . . . A little library, growing larger every year, is an honorable part of a young man's history. It is a man's duty to have books. A library is not a luxury, but one of the necessaries of life.

—H. W. Beecher.

Were ready comrades whom he could not tire—
Of whose society the blameless man
Was never satiate.   Their familiar voice,
Even to old age, with unabated charm
Beguiled his leisure hours, refreshed his thoughts ;
Beyond its natural elevation raised
His introverted spirit ; and bestowed
Upon his life an outward dignity
Which all acknowledged.   The dark winter night,
The stormy day, each had its own resource :
Song of the muses, sage historic tale,
Science severe, or word of holy writ
Announcing immortality and joy
To the assembled spirits of the just,
From imperfection and decay secure.
                              —*Wordsworth.*

(vi)

PREFACE.

THERE are few lives so busy that some intervals cannot be found for the indulgence of a taste for art, science or literature. For most of my life I have been engaged in an occupation laborious, exacting and full of responsibilities. But from my early youth I have been a lover of books, and though I make no claim to scholarship, the cultivation of a taste for general literature has been one of the chief pleasures of my life. The companionship of books has been, and is, among my most cherished companionships, and I love them as I love my friends.

The love of books has led me to the gathering of some such as I cared most to have, and which were within my means ; and the "intervals," which have always been the evenings, have given me opportunities for reading and sometimes for writing.

It is the merest fancy to call these informal sketches, most of which were written in the form of letters to an old friend, "A Tour Round my Library," for a whole life might be spent in such a journey. The "Other Papers" are some of the articles I have written on Religious, Literary, Financial and other subjects—and, whether printed heretofore or now for the first time, will perhaps best show the course of reading and study which I have pursued through my long life.

Some of the chapters have to do with religious truth and duty or the interpretation of the Scriptures, and grew out of lessons to a Bible class which I had the honor to teach for several years in the church to which I belong : and in these there is probably much in the way of Scripture illustration for which I am indebted to the writings of others, for I have spared no reasonable expense in supplying myself with the works of the best commentators, in English, on the Bible.

In so few chapters, I can notice only a few of my "friends," those whom I know the best and love the most : anything more than this would swell this volume to an unreasonable size.

CONTENTS.

A TOUR ROUND MY LIBRARY.

THE THOUGHT OF THE LIBRARY.

A LIBRARY is a collection of books for reading or for reference. So common are books nowadays that every dwelling-house, containing more rooms than are absolutely necessary for living-rooms, has one which is called the Library. It may not have many books ; it may be used as a family sitting-room and work-room, where the children have their playthings and study their school-lessons in the evening ; but all the books belonging to the family are gathered in this room and it is very properly called the Library. It ought to be, and generally is, one of the cosiest, most comfortable rooms in the house, so attractive from its books, pictures and objects of art that the family prefer it to any other common room in the house. It is quite proper in small houses to combine the uses of the library with the parlor or reception-room, or even with the family-room, where the daily meals are taken ; but every dwelling-house where the father and mother and children are able to read and write ought to have its library, whether large or small.

I have nothing to do now with professional libraries. The physician, the scientist, the architect, the lawyer, the theologian, must each have his own library, for books are the tools of his trade ; nor am I dealing with the library of the specialist, which may have hundreds and thousands of volumes, treating of certain special subjects or branches of

1 (1)

knowledge of any kind, but I am thinking of a general
library for the household. A business man of cultivation,
who had gathered four or five thousand volumes of general literature, and who had built a beautiful room to con-
tain them, but who died before he had enjoyed them as
much as he had expected, once said to me that his idea of a
library for the family was such a collection of books as
would give one information, and answer any questions on any
subject within the range of ordinary inquiry or discussion.
In other words, that one need not go outside of his own
library to obtain any knowledge he seeks.   My friend's large
fortune permitted him to fill his shelves with everything
necessary to this thought.

A library bought for the purpose of filling a room, large
or small, with books, even if well selected as to authors,
subjects and binding, is not a library in the truest and best
sense. A library for the family should be the growth of
many years.   Begun with a few books over the mantel shelf,
and growing to fill a cupboard or two, then overflowing to
some temporary shelves, it grows until a bookcase is needed;
then another and another, until the room itself scarcely contains its treasures.   Children must be provided with books,
picture-books at first, then stories well chosen, then histories,
such as the admirable series of histories and biographies by the
Abbotts ; then large histories, then fiction, then poetry, then
books for Sunday reading, of which there is a vast field most
attractive : for a household that is brought up to make a distinction between Sunday reading and every-day reading, will
be none the worse for it when the children are grown, even
if some people do sneer at such a distinction ; then polite
letters generally, then books of reference, never intended to
be read, then dictionaries, then encyclopædias.

A library formed on some such plan, the needs of the
family being the motive for getting the books, may be years
and years before its accumulations are large ; but every book

so purchased will have a history of its own, every book will be loved for its own sake, its author will somehow become as a personal friend and visitor in the house—and no book, the reading of which would bring a blush to the cheek if read aloud, will find a place in that library.

The value of a library does not depend upon the number of books it contains. The readers of "Ten Thousand a Year," Dr. Warren's charming novel, will not fail to recall the attempts of Tittlebat Titmouse to gather a library. This ridiculous character was, in this quest, a type of man whom some of us have seen in our country. ·

II.

A Preliminary Glance.

As we agreed the other night that "a library is not a luxury, but one of the necessaries of life," you asked me what writers I would recommend to a young collector of books. Come and let me present you to a few of my friends —first, the Historians.

If one wants to study the history of England, he can get all he needs for general purposes from Hume, Macaulay, Froude and Green; if the history of Greece, Mitford and Grote; if the history of Rome, Arnold, Gibbon, Merrivale and Milman.

Of France there seems to be nothing entirely complete and satisfactory, and the same may be said of most of the other countries of Europe. Prescott, Motley and Freeman are most important writers. When you come to our own country, Bancroft and McMaster bring the story down as far as it is worth while to bring it, for it is too soon yet to write the history of the civil war.

One does not need to have all the poetry that has been published in England in the last five hundred years. Some of Chaucer and Spencer, Milton of course, old George Herbert, Pope and Dryden and Parnell, and in later times Scott (selections only from Byron and Burns), Wordsworth, Southey and Tennyson, the Brownings, and Matthew Arnold and Sir Edwin, and of our own poets, Bryant, Longfellow, Lowell, Whittier and others.

(4)

Of dramatists it is hardly too much to say that Shakespeare is all that the general reader needs or cares to know.

When you come to fiction, the field is boundless; but all that one cares to know has appeared within say one hundred years. This period includes Scott, James, Bulwer, Thackeray, Dickens, McDonald, Buchanan, the Brontés, Mrs. Oliphant, Stevenson, Blackmore, Thomas Hardy and many others in England; and Cooper, Irving, Hawthorne, Marion Crawford and Howells of our country. I do not refer to the poets and novelists of other tongues than the English, though, of course, one cannot afford to be ignorant of Goethe, Victor Hugo and many others.

When we come to books of a serious character—religious literature, so called—the field is, indeed, boundless. If by the selection of a few books or by the accumulation of many we could have answered, as my good friend thought, any theological question without going outside of one's own library, happy, indeed, would he be who had such books. But, alas! "of making many books there is no end"—especially on this subject.

Yet in a well-selected library that part ordinarily is the most valuable which contains books written to interpret the Holy Scriptures.

In our many conversations upon theological and religious subjects how often we have referred to the Epistle to the Romans, as one of the most difficult to understand of all the writings of the great Apostle! Here is Lyman Abbott's Commentary on that book, and in some important respects it is most satisfactory. This is especially so of the full introductory chapters. Here, too, is Dean Alford, who has made a commentary on the whole of the New Testament; two, indeed, one for Greek students, the other for English readers. And here is Dr. Addison Alexander on the Psalms, on Matthew and Mark, and the Acts. He modestly calls them "The Acts, etc., Explained," and truly they might have been written with a lexicon in one hand and a grammar in the other. Good Albert Barnes ! my friend and neighbor (how often he has sat where you are now sitting). See that shelf of his "Notes"—so he called them—notes on all the books of the New Testament and on Job, the Psalms and Daniel. For many years Mr. Barnes was the most popular and most satisfactory of all modern writers on the Scriptures.

George Bush was in his day, a generation ago, among the clearest and simplest of all the writers on The Pentateuch, but in later life he became a Swedenborgian, and although there is no tinge of this school of theology in his commentaries, many readers ceased to care for them.

Do you see this shelf of little volumes in grey cloth? They are the "Cambridge Bible for Schools," written by many authors and supervised by the Bishop of Worcester, though he is careful to say that he is not responsible for every statement. As a whole, I hardly know where a commentary can be found with so much to approve and so little to push aside. What a blessed day it would be for our schools and colleges if we could have some such systematic and scholarly study of the Scriptures as is implied in these volumes !

Of course you know Samuel Cox of Nottingham. He is a Non-conformist and one of the ablest living expositors of the Holy Scriptures. His works on Job, Ecclesiastes and some other books are the best of all. For many years he was the editor of the *Expositor*, a monthly paper in England of great value to Bible students; but his "higher criticism" did not suit the views of the owners of that periodical and they dispensed with his services. Bishop Ellicott, the late Bishop Lightfoot, of Durham ; and Westcott, the present Bishop of that Diocese, Davies, Farrar, Jowett, Dean Stanley, Trench, Wordsworth, and other Church of England men have made splendid contributions to the literature of Scripture interpretation, while Morison, a

Scotchman, has written Commentaries on St. Matthew, St. Mark, and on certain chapters of Romans, not excelled by any written in English, and our own Dr. Schaff, in his translation of Lange's great German Commentary by many writers, has done a great work in this direction.

Matthew Henry is perhaps the only man who ever wrote a Commentary on the whole Bible, and did it well ; but David Thomas, an English Non-conformist, who has rare gifts in this direction of homiletics, if he should live long enough, will approach him as a homilist or expositor nearer than anybody else, for his work upon the Acts, the Psalms and the Proverbs has been admirably well done.

But I think I have given you enough for one evening.

III

THE THOUGHT OF THE TOUR.

UNDER the title of "A Tour Around My Garden," a French writer, a quarter of a century ago, told the story of two friends who were separated by the departure of one of them on a journey of foreign travel. The other, whose circumstances or inclination did not permit him to accompany his friend, remained at home and beguiled the weary hours by exploring his own garden and writing frequent letters to his absent friend—describing the incidents of his daily walks and the objects of interest which lay in his paths, from the great tree to the spider's web ; from the birds that sought shelter in the deep shades to the tiny insect that made its home under the leaf of the smallest bush ; from the vast tropical plants which his conservatories developed to the smallest wild flower that sought and found life in the clefts of the rock. Into these letters the author wove a pleasant story of love and flowers and poetry ; and sometimes a profound philosophy, though often of a decidedly French cast of thought, bubbled up through his brilliant sentences.

Another French writer, Xavier de Maistre, in the early years of the present century, wrote a pleasant little book of forty-two chapters, which his translator has called, "A Journey round my Room." It was an instance of "enforced leisure," when under a military arrest in Turin, which confined him to his room for forty-two days, he amused himself by writing a description of his chamber and the articles of furniture and art contained in it, with no idea, though, of

(8)

publication. His brother, however, to whom he sent the manuscript, thought better of it, and surprised the author by the return of a printed volume containing the brilliant little chapters. The book was very popular, for it touched just at the edge of many agreeable subjects, affording the author an opportunity to discuss very briefly, in his own quiet way, some things which instruct us all.

I, too, am a prisoner. A severe cold, threatening serious consequences, has shut me up in my home, and, after a few days' confinement to my bed, I am allowed to move about the house. I naturally find my way to my own cozy sitting-room, and here, left to myself, I sit, and, looking into the cheerful fire (for it is midwinter), call up the scenes of the past.

I will not deny that the books referred to, though read many years ago, have suggested the writing to you of a few letters, which may be called, in a very plain and humble way, "A Tour round my Library"—

Not that I have much of a library to travel round, or that the tour will be a very long one. But I have thought that some things which I have gathered would interest you, and possibly you would like occasionally to hear from one whom you once saw a good deal of, and who, like yourself, is a lover of books.

I need not remind you that we began life not very far from the same time and the same place. The first fifteen years of life we spent very much together. We attended the same school as boys ; we engaged in the same sports ; we read the same books ; we had mainly the same experience.

Since then our lives have been separated—you sought your fortunes in another part of our land, and have achieved a character and position of which you may well be proud, while I have remained nearer the place of my beginning, and am only a plodder in the great highway of life.

We have both traveled far, though never in each other's company. We have crossed oceans, and visited the old world, and seen society as developed among the surroundings of an old civilization. We have looked into those venerable seats of learning which are the sources of our best literature. We have heard men, in languages strange to our youth, discourse in academies of the profoundest mysteries of our nature. We have looked on the broad plains of Germany and of France, the latter so lately, alas, soaked with blood. We have climbed Alpine heights and trodden the fields of perpetual snow. We have gone down into Italy, breathed her balmy air, and rejoiced in her glorious sunshine, reveled in her wonders of Art, and reproduced in imagination, as we looked upon her hills, her plains and her blue sea, her venerable and wonderful history.

Our days of travel are probably over—at least, in foreign lands. But we need not go far from home to see grand things, or to recall the greater and grander things of the past ; and I propose to make one more tour, and to give you an account of its incidents, if you care to hear it. My field is a small one. You have never seen it. A few steps, if you are in a hurry, will take you through it. But years may be spent in it, if you seek for pleasure and profit, and are not driven by steam. In fact and in short the "Tour" contemplated is "round my Library."

I propose to talk to you in a chatty way about my books (they are mine in a double sense, by possession, which is common enough, and because *I love them*) and about their authors ; and if I go somewhat into detail about such of the books as I particularly love, or whose authors I know, or have met, you will excuse me, for the tour will not be a long one.

IV.

THE LIBRARY.

BUT first let me describe the room which I call my library. An irregularly shaped room with a deep, wide bay-window on the south and another window down to the floor: a deeper alcove and two windows on the north : the shelves on the west side broken by a wide fire-place and a mantel reaching almost to the ceiling, and a fine old German cabinet: a room wainscoted throughout with wood ; no plaster, paint or paper ; the ceiling of dark yellow pine set in deep panels, with pendants of dark walnut.

The spaces between the windows and all the rest of the wall are covered with shelves—the highest range being within easy reach, and over the shelves are placed busts of some of my favorite authors. In the middle of the room is the broad, strong table, that can bear any load of books —so firm that it does not shake under its sometimes heavy load. Across one corner of the room, quite away from the doors and the fire-place, is a most tempting lounge, with its pillows, the other furniture being the easy arm-chairs, all leather-covered, and the chair without arms, but with nearly straight back, which is always drawn up to the table, and which is my work-chair. I must be indulged for a moment here on the subject of chairs. Cowper sang of the sofa, and who can forget that picture in the "Winter Evening?"

> "Now stir the fire, and close the shutters fast,
> Let fall the curtains, wheel the sofa round,

> And while the bubbling and loud hissing urn
> Throws up a steamy column, and the cups
> That cheer but not inebriate, wait on each,
> So let us welcome peaceful ev'ning in."

But I do not sing—I only talk of my friends and chairs.
Some chairs are frauds—they do not serve the purpose for
which they are made—they are unsightly in appearance, uncomfortable in use.   They are either too straight in the back
or incline too much—too hard or too soft—and the legs are
too stout and heavy or too slight and frail.   Then if covered
with horse-hair you are slipping out of the seats ; if covered
with plush you can't move without rising to your feet.   Next
to the bed, and not always with this exception, the chair is
our most constant companion, and how important that we
should be on the best terms with our next friend !   On the
whole, my judgment is, that a chair of the height which will
rest you most, with capacious arms embracing you not too
closely, with casters on the front legs only, and covered with
strong leather, will do pretty well until something better is
invented, which, however, is not unlikely to be the case, for it
may be said of chairs as of lamps, they are not yet perfect.
There are wide, deep arm-chairs which invite to rest and
meditation.   They are not for study : they are too comfortable for that.   Drop into one, touch the spring, and let the
back incline gently until you find yourself in a posture that
is so restful that forgetfulness steals over you and you are
asleep.

Poor Tom Hood, in his immortal "Miss Killmansegg and
her Golden Leg," has helped us to appreciate the bed, but
who has thought it worth while to commend the chair?   We
have chairmen and chairwomen, who preside at public meetings when Mr. So-and-So or Mrs. So-and-So assumes the
chair.   We have the chair of state, the sedan chair, the
chair or chaise with two wheels and one horse ; the chairs
that Grandfather Smallweed and his amiable wife lived in

(in Dickens' story of "Bleak House"), which they converted into hostile forts, from which missiles were hurled from one to the other. We have the gig-top chairs, such as one sees on the beach at English and Dutch watering-places. Then we have the professor's chair, the curule or ivory seat on a car in classic times, the chairs which hold the iron rails of our roads, and last and least, Jenny Geddes's three-legged stool.

Now, I leave my chair and go to the window. I look out to the north. The ground is covered with snow ; the sun is bright but it seems to have no power. The polished surface of the snow glitters with a brilliancy which is almost blind-ing. The grand, old trees, which for generations have stood as they now stand, greeting the morning sun, and sighing good-night as he sinks in the west, leaving his golden flush on their trunks—the grand, old trees now throw up their bare arms into the clear, blue sky as if reaching into the very heavens.

I turn and walk to the south window. What a change ! The same sun is shining and the snow lies on the ground, but not so abundantly. In the middle of the day, and protected from the north winds, little pools of melted snow form in the hollows, and soon flow into streams which run down towards the valley, increasing by their own influence the volume of melted snows. The fine old cedar standing so near the win-dow, which for so many years has protected us from the sun's fierce rays in summer, is now so closely invested by the ivy that soon the question will be raised, shall we give up the cedar or the ivy? For one or the other must die. Through this window I get a glimpse of the little conservatory which, filled with brilliant flowers, is bringing the glory of sum-mer every day of the long, cold winter into our home and hearts. Blessings on the flowers, and on Him who sends them, and who permits us to enjoy them, not only in their own natural sweetness, but who has taught us how to repro-

duce them even in the cold winter, and thus gladden the
sick chamber, and brighten the darkest and gloomiest days.

The English papers come to us full of notices of Lord
Lytton (Bulwer), whose recent death was announced by
telegraph.   Some time I may tell you of a visit I once made
to him.

V.

THE AMERICAN FIRST-CLASS BOOK.

I HAVE been turning over the leaves of an old school-book. It has been a fancy with me to collect the books which I studied at school in my early youth, in the hope (vain hope) that I might reproduce the impressions which such books made upon me then. My school-days were not days of terror, but pleasant days. I was never overburdened with a multitude of subjects of study, never overworked, and never punished. In fact I was always at the head of my class; but truth compels me to add that the "class" was numerically a very small one.

The book which I cared most for—which had most to do in creating a literary taste, and was most suggestive in leading me to further reading and study—was the "American First-Class Book, designed for the highest class in public and private schools," by Rev. John Pierpont; published in Boston. The copy that lies before me is a book of 480 pages, small type, bound in leather, very much worn and stained. The selections are from "moderir authors of Great Britain and America," of prose and verse, alternating through the volume.

My connection with the public schools of our city, as well as with two very large Institutional schools, has given me opportunities of examining, more or less carefully, many reading-books; but I have never seen any that was equal to the "First-Class Book." If I could copy its table of contents it would be evident that the whole field of English literature, up to the date of its publication, had been laid

under contribution to make the selections. None but a
poet or a man of the highest literary culture could have
made such a book. At that time schools generally had
depended on Lindley Murray's "English Reader," with its
"Introduction" and "Sequel," three books which were
hammered into the brains of all scholars until they loathed
the very names. Yet these books were not without real
merit ; only the compiler was a grammarian simply, having
no poetic taste and little imagination. His divisions were
arbitrary; his prose selections, entirely from English authors,
were heavy, didactic and dull ; and his poetic selections,
very few in number, often deficient in taste and placed at
the end of the several volumes.

Dr. Pierpont changed all this by mingling selections of
prose and poetry throughout the volume, by a much smaller
proportion of "didactic" pieces, and by a very generous
selection from American authors. In fact, there is hardly
any American author of note at that time who is not represented by one or more selections.

The book is extremely valuable for its suggestiveness.
The interview between Edward Waverley and Fergus
MacIvor in Carlisle Castle, on the morning of Fergus' execution, sends the reader at once to the book itself for the whole
story, giving a glimpse of one of the Scotch rebellions; the
story of Old Mortality etching the letters on the old grave-
stones provokes the reader to look up the book, where he sees,
as in pictures, old Balfour of Burleigh, Claverhouse, the
slaughter of Archbishop Sharpe, the battle of Drumclog,
and the charming love story of Henry Morton and Edith
Bellenden, and the never-to-be-forgotten Lady Margaret and
Guse Gibbie ; the two extracts from Rob Roy, so well
chosen, are glimpses of Scott in his prose writings ;
while his vivid description of the battle of Flodden and the
death of Marmion, as well as Rebecca's hymn in "Ivanhoe,"
give a taste only, of his wonderful poetic power.

Wordsworth is seen in his "Deaf Man's Grave," and "A
Natural Mirror," from the "Excursion," and in "Goody
Blake and Harry Gill," a pathetic poem of the country-side.

Professor John Wilson is well represented by characteristic
tales of Scottish life, such as the "Headstone" and "Gilbert
Ainslee" and "Shipwreck;" and Graham, the Scotch poet,
by an extract from his "Sabbath."

Nothing could be finer than the selections from Shake-
speare, such as the scene from "King John" of Arthur and
Hubert; and from "Macbeth" of Malcolm, Macduff and
Rosse, and the street scene and dialogue between Brutus and
Cassius, and the tent scene at Philippi between the same,
and, of course, Antony's address over Cæsar's body.

Some of Washington Irving's best things are here—"The
Widow and her Son," and "Midnight Musings," and
"Forest Trees;" two speeches of Daniel Webster; Wirt's
"Blind Preacher;" Bryant's "Inscription on an Entrance
into a Wood," and "The Waterfowl," and "Thanatopsis,"
and "Green River," and "A Winter Scene;" and Per-
cival's "Coral Grove;" and Everett's "Alaric the Visi-
goth;" and many very choice selections from Sir John
Bowring's "Russian Anthology;" also Campbell's "Loch-
iel's Warning" and "Hohenlinden;" Burns' "Winter
Night;" and the Park Scene from Hillhouse's "Percy's
Masque;" Byron's "Address to the Ocean;" Milton's
"Lycidas;" and Southey's "Alderman's Funeral;" "Gil
Blas and the Archbishop;" Coleridge's "Mont Blanc;"
Thompson's "Castle of Indolence;" Beattie's "Minstrel;"
Channing's fine articles on "Daily Prayer, Morning and
Evening;" and many, very many other extracts in prose
and verse from American authors, not forgetting "The
Son," by Richard H. Dana.

The compiler was too modest to give extracts from his own
writings (was any other compiler ever so modest?) or we
should have had glimpses of his own "Airs of Palestine"

2

and that most touching and pathetic poem on the death of
his own son:—

> I cannot make him dead !
> His fair, sunshiny head
> Is ever bounding round my study chair ;
> Yet, when my eyes, now dim
> With tears, I turn to him,
> The vision vanishes—he is not there !
>
> I walk my parlor floor,
> And, through the open door,
> I hear a footfall on the chamber stair ;
> I'm stepping toward the hall
> To give the boy a call ;
> And then bethink me that—he is not there ! *etc.*

The fine old book is forgotten now: it has disappeared from
the book-stalls ; the compiler himself has passed from the
recollection of all but his own descendants; other reading
books, prepared with far less care and taste, have come to the
front, full of selections for declamation, as if the chief end
of a reading book were to make public speakers ; but I
doubt if there was ever a school-book so well adapted to
cultivate a fine literary taste as Pierpont's "American First-
Class Book."

VI.

SIR WALTER SCOTT.

WHEN I come to the shelves which hold Sir Walter Scott's works, I seem to be back again in my school-days. For the Waverley Novels were the first novels I ever read. I began to read them just as the author was passing away. Each story, as I read it, became a picture gallery of men and women whom I seemed to have known personally. The characters were real. The mountains, the valleys, the lakes, the rivers, the cities of Scotland, especially the Border land, became to me almost as familiar as the landscape about my own home. Every novel, from the first to the last, I read as I could lay my hands upon it, and long before I was able to count them as my own books. The poetical works fell in my way after I had read most of the prose tales.

It was but natural that when in Scotland a few years ago I should desire to see some of the localities made famous by the life and writings of Scott. So in the early morning of a day in June I set out to seek the place of his birth, in the old town of Edinburgh. I found the College Wynd, where the house had stood in which Scott was born. The house itself had disappeared years before, though my guide tried to persuade me to the contrary ; but this was undoubtedly the narrow street, and this the spot, where Walter Scott was born. There was little need to spend much time there, but one could not help being interested in the thought that here the young boy learned to talk, to walk, to play.

(19)

At noon I was at Abbottsford, the house of his own creation, where he hoped to found a family and spend the evening of his days, reproducing in a modest way the atmosphere
of the feudal days which he knew and described so well, and
then passing it on to his eldest son as so many others had
done before him.   The house is finely situated on the slope
of a range of hills, and almost at the edge of a meadow, on
the farther side of which is the Tweed.

At the beginning I said to the guide, or custode, that I
had come three thousand miles to see Abbottsford, and
stipulated, by promise of double fee, not to be hurried
through as others had been.

Through a narrow passage and up a winding stair I
reached the great entrance hall and armory, in which Scott
had gathered the many kinds of arms and armor that grateful and admiring friends had presented to him.   And along
the cornice was this inscription :

**"These be the Coat Armories of the Clannis and
Chief men of name wha keepit the marchys of
Scotland in the auld time for the Kings. Trewe
ware they in their tyme, and in their defense God
them defendit."**

Then I was shown into the study where he did his work.
This was not a large room.   The ceiling was high enough
to admit of a gallery round the room, so that the walls, from
floor to ceiling, were covered with books.   A circular stair
led from this room to his bed-room immediately above, so
that if he desired to work far into the night or in the early
morning (not often the case, I believe), he could do so without disturbing his family.   On the mantle over the fire-place
in the study was the engraving of Stothard's Pilgrimage to
Canterbury ; the bay window was low to the floor, so that
the dogs could jump in and out at pleasure, and in a glass
case was the plain suit of clothes he wore towards the end

of his life. Here was the large, plain, old-fashioned desk with a lifting lid, and on this desk he wrote most of his wonderful works. A large leather-covered chair faces the desk, protected by a guard to prevent visitors from abusing it, but I was graciously permitted to sit in it and lean on the desk. Ah! if I could have caught some of the inspiration which filled the soul of the great magician!

Through a door, on each side of which was a suit of armor mounted, I passed into the library. Here was indeed a splendid room—large, well lighted, with a huge bay-window overlooking the Tweed, the walls covered with books (twenty thousand, it was said), more than one hundred of which being from his own pen. Here was a large table with many precious gifts from friends; here was the famous bust by Chantrey; and over the mantle was a portrait in oil of his eldest son, in the uniform of a Hussar; and near the door which led to the dining-room was a picture of Mary, Queen of Scots, taken immediately after her execution, most sad, most touching.

The dining-room is not shown, although I had a glimpse through the door, which for a moment was ajar. It is only of interest as the room in which Sir Walter died; a scene so admirably pictured by Lockhart and others. Standing by the library window in that beautiful day in June, the air perfectly still, the sun shining in unclouded brightness, I could easily imagine the scene in the adjoining room when Sir Walter passed away, for I, too, heard the Tweed as its clear waters rippled over their pebbly bottom beyond the meadow.

In the evening I stood by his grave at Dryburgh Abbey. The old ruins seem almost to have been preserved that they might be a resting-place for him who had made those valleys and hills so famous, that pilgrims from all parts of the world throng there. The spot had been chosen centuries before as the seat of a great religious house by those who knew how to select the best sites.　It lies in a broad meadow land, with the Tweed sweeping round it on three sides and the Eildon hills looking down on its beautiful slopes.　Just at this hour in the evening the long, solemn procession passed over the plain, pausing a moment at a house in the near distance, and then in a great company gathering about the ruins, where was an open grave, into which the remains were tenderly lowered. Then the service of the Church of England was read, the earth covered the coffin, and the great crowd dispersed.

As I stood there, how could I help recalling some of the lines in which a writer had endeavored to reproduce that funeral occasion : when, instead of the noble, the rich, the great and the common people who followed in that long procession, he causes to appear some of the principal characters whom Scott has created, and makes them the chief mourners as they follow the body to the grave !

There was wailing on the autumn breeze, and darkness in the sky,
When with sable plume and cloak and pall a funeral train swept by !
Methought (St. Mary shield us well) that other forms moved there
Than those of mortal brotherhood, the noble, young and fair.

Was it a dream?　Methought the "dauntless Harold" passed me by,
The proud "Fitz-James" with martial step, and dark, intrepid eye ;
That "Marmion's" haughty look was there, a mourner for his sake :
And she, the bold, the beautiful, sweet "Lady of the Lake."

With coronach and arms reversed, forth came "McGregor's" clan,
Red "Dougall's" cry pealed shrill and wide ; "Rob Roy's" bold brow
    looked wan ;
The fair "Die Vernon" kissed her cross, and blessed the sainted ray ;
And "Wae is me," the Baillie said, "that I should see this day."

On swept "Bois Gilbert," "Front de Bœuf," "De Bracy's" plume of woe,
And "Cœur de Lion's" crest shone near the valiant "Ivanhoe,"
While soft as glides a summer cloud, "Rowena" closer drew,
With beautiful "Rebecca," peerless daughter of the Jew.

And so on in many stanzas.

As a writer of fiction, whether of poetry or prose, Scott

has been more to me than any other writer. I do not mean to say that he wrote the best poetry or the best prose romances ever written, but I mean that on the whole I like him best of all. If you will look around the Library, you will see that this is not said without knowledge of other writers.

Some years ago it occurred to me that it would be a pleasant work for winter evenings to illustrate the poems and the novels of Sir Walter. So I secured the Abbottsford edition of the novels, originally in twelve thick volumes. This edition, you know, has some two thousand engravings on wood made especially for it, besides a few steel engravings. It was not difficult to obtain sets of the embellishments that had been made for the many other editions. The work grew on my hands : some old book collectors, knowing my quest, supplied me with additional material until my twelve volumes grew to twenty-eight volumes, and might better have been thirty, and the steel engravings to more than a thousand. There they are on those shelves, a goodly array. Open some of them. Is it not a fair setting of the precious jewels ?

Then, as to his poems. I found a set of the original editions in royal quarto, in five volumes, in very large type, with broad margins. These five volumes I have expanded to nine, and have added more than three hundred full-page engravings on steel, copper and wood. See " The Lady of the Lake " and " Marmion," each in two quarto volumes—no photographs, so unsightly in a bound volume.

If Sir Walter were now living and within my reach, how I would delight to bring him into my Library, and show him my treasures, and say, " What you have done for me can never be measured. My life has been made far happier by you than it would have been without you : this is what I have done for you and your works ; and it has been a labor of love."

In one sense Sir Walter Scott died too soon, at the early

age of sixty-two; in another and sadder sense it would have been better had he died earlier. The pecuniary reward which came to him as an author was marvellous; no other writer had ever received so much. His publishers proposed to increase still more rapidly his gains by taking him into partnership. At first, things went well, and the returns were almost fabulous, but there came commercial distress. The firm failed and Sir Walter was deplorably involved. The liabilities were so large that the effort to liquidate them was almost hopeless, and few men would have made the attempt; hardly any other man would: but Sir Walter determined to pay all these debts. Then began those heroic labors, which have no parallel in authorship. He never spared himself after this, but month after month and year after year he produced an amount of matter for the press which was almost incredible. And almost all of it, until towards the last, was matter of the best, of the highest literary quality. It is noticeable, however, that it was all prose; the Muse seems to have left him. These works, produced under such circumstances, under the lash, as it were, were most abundantly rewarded. He could not write too rapidly for the public; and they repaid him handsomely. Money came to him by the thousands where other authors were content with hundreds; payments large and liberal were made to reduce his indebtedness, and the work went on, the mind wrought up to the highest tension, taking no rest. Sometimes the author was writing two books at a time, driven as a trained racehorse continuously at the very top of its speed. But this could not endure forever: his powers began to give evidence of the excessive strain; his family, his friends, his physician urged him to abate somewhat of the relentless drive; but all was of no avail, until Nature herself protested against the mad struggle. Then began the decline and the decay of his mental vigor; then some of the things he wrote added nothing to his literary fame; then his friends became more and more anxious.   Still he worked and worked, until he could do no more.   Then it was hoped that entire withdrawal from work and from home might restore his overworked powers ; and the King placed a frigate at his disposal, in which he went to Gibraltar, to Malta ; where the fever of writing seized him again, and he began two more novels.   He landed at Naples, spent weeks there, was shown all the sights, but he took little or no interest in anything.   He lingered in Italy.   There was no improvement.   He went to Bologna, to Venice, up through the Tyrol, to Heidelberg, down the Rhine to Rotterdam, thence by steamer to London, where he remained a few days, waiting a steamer to Edinburgh, hardly conscious most of the time ; landing at Newhaven, he was conveyed in a carriage to Abbottsford.   Before he reached his home the familiar scenery aroused him.   At a turn of the road he looked out and said, "Gala water surely !"   And so after an absence of many months he reached his dear home.   But it was only to die, and the tired, wasted brain, the worn-out body, soon yielded to the claims of Nature.*

There is nothing in authorship more pathetic than the decline and death of Sir Walter Scott.   His sun went down too early, in the afternoon ; and no wonder that an examination by his physician disclosed the fact that his death was caused by softening of the brain.

---

* Once he insisted on being seated at his desk and having writing materials placed before him. His family could not but indulge him. He smiled, and said, "Now give me my pen, and leave me a little to myself." The pen was put in his hand ; he tried to hold it in his fingers, but they could not close on it—the pen dropped on the paper. He fell back, the tears rolling down his cheeks. He never wrote another line.

VII.

BULWER.

IN the earlier part of this century, following close upon Sir Walter Scott, there appeared a new writer, chiefly of fiction, who gave promise of great popularity—Edward Bulwer. He was of noble family, finely educated, of splendid imagination, and a man of the world in every sense. The moral tone of some of his earlier tales was more than questionable. I could hardly count them as among my friends, in the best sense; but no one can read without deep emotion the description of the eruption of Vesuvius and the story of the widow of Nain's son, pieces of unusually fine writing, in the "Last Days of Pompeii;" and the most pathetic conversation between William Waife and his wretched son, Jasper Loosely, in "What Will He Do With It?"—the contest between mental power and brute force, as depicted in the library scene between the same Jasper and his father-in-law, Guy Darrell—nor the conversation, so reproachful, so sorrowful, between Guy Darrell and Lady Montford, once Caroline Lyndsay, in the same charming and powerful novel.

Among my earliest recollections of Bulwer are "Pelham," "The Disowned," "Devereux," "Paul Clifford," etc., and others following in rapid succession. Further on in the series, and of a better, more wholesome character than these, came "The Last Days of Pompeii" and "Rienzi," historical novels of the most absorbing interest. From that far-off

(26)

period until the publication of "The Parisians" I have highly enjoyed the fictions of the great master, for in certain features of his works, his brilliant imagination and his profound philosophy, he certainly had no peer.

If, in his later works, high moral teaching can atone for the want of this in his earlier fictions, it has been accomplished in his novels of society, especially in "The Caxtons," "My Novel," and "What Will He Do With It?" There is nothing in our language finer than these, and they will live and make their impressions long after some of his other works are forgotten, for the reason that the pure, the true, the good, will outlast the evil in all things. It was but natural then, with my high appreciation of the genius of Bulwer, that I should embrace the opportunity of a personal visit to one whose pen had charmed my boyish fancy and also instructed and moved me in later years.

It was about noon of a bright day in July that I made my call on Lord Lytton. I had a note of introduction from Dr. R. Shelton Mackenzie, of our city, a man of letters who had known Bulwer in his younger days so well that he now addressed him as "My Dear Lord Lytton." The house was in Grosvenor Square, a plain four-storied building, facing south. I was shown into a reception-room while the servant took my introduction and card. · He soon returned with his master's regrets that he could not see me at that time ; he was preparing to go out; but hoped it would be convenient for me to call on the following Monday, at 2 o'clock. This was Saturday. At the appointed time I called again, was met at the door by another servant, who, on receiving my card, asked if I had called by appointment. On my replying in the affirmative he showed me into the reception-room while he went to announce me. While he was gone I made my observation of the surroundings. The house, as I said, was plain, whether his own town home (it did not answer to his address in the city directory) or a hired furnished house I could not know.   The front door opened into a large square hall, from which the stairway led to the upper rooms. On the left of this hall were, first, a small drawing or reception-room, and back of that, through a wide doorway, now open, I could see the ordinary furniture of a well-appointed dining-room.   The furniture in both these rooms was that heavy, almost clumsy kind, of which the English seem so fond, as if it were to last from one generation to another, and as if the fashion were never to change.   On the mantel-piece were some good bronzes, and on the pier-table large, heavily chased platters, standing on edge, with classic figures bas-relief. Presently the servant returned, a tall man in livery, and asked me to walk up-stairs.   We ascended to the third story (the second being occupied by the drawing-rooms), where was the study, and so on to the landing at the top, the door opening into it.

With no little embarrassment I found myself, when the door opened, face to face with the great author. He was in a working-jacket, sitting at a table in front of a fire-place where, earlier in the day, there had been a fire.   In his mouth was a pipe, with a stem so long that the bowl rested upon the hearth.   Whether it was lighted or not I cannot say, but there was no smell of tobacco in the room. He took the pipe from his mouth, rose, and came forward to meet me—holding out his hand and giving me a very cordial reception.   I thought, however, that there was upon his countenance a very slight expression as if he expected to be bored. I sat down in the chair he offered me, and he very quickly put me comparatively at ease by his conversation.   For myself, my eyes were fixed upon his face so closely that, somewhat to my regret, I failed to take a full survey of the room itself.   It was a moderate sized apartment, with shelves on two or three sides, filled with books ; and with books, pamphlets and papers in heaps and groups lying about.   Like his own person, the room was rather untidy, showing the condition

of things where a man will have his own way, or where he
has no one near enough to him to attempt to keep things
in proper order.   The only book on his table, among heaps
of writing paper, whose title I remember, was Miss Edwards'
story, "Barbara's History," in 3 vols.

Sitting within a few feet of this great man, his countenance was strongly impressed upon my memory.   His face
was that of a man of seventy years at least, and those years
not all spent in the open air.   It had a worn and tired expression, as if he had seen all there is to see in this life, and
enjoyed all that this world can offer to the man of fashion
and society.   The hair was thin, its natural color restored by
the aids of art.   His beard also thin, straggly, and also indebted to extraneous help for its concurrent tint.   His figure
was slight, much bent as he sat, though quite erect as he
stood.   There was not much expression in the countenance
while he listened, but there was a bright lighting up when
he spoke or laughed.

The conversation turned on America, and first as to his
friend, Dr. Mackenzie, who had given me the note.   I said
he was chief editor of one of our most popular and influential
daily papers.   We then turned to political matters.   What
would we do with the question of universal suffrage?
"Ah," said he, "you Americans are teaching us a sad
lesson."

"What is that?" said I.

" Do you not see," said he, " that men cannot be trusted
with the open ballot?"

"We do not see that yet," said I.   "We hope that our
system of public schools will prepare our people for the safe
use of the ballot."

"So it might possibly," said he, "under your form of
government; but your danger is from emigration.   The
hundreds of thousands of people that we and other countries
of Europe are sending you every year counteract, in great

measure, the influence of your public education.   These
people are ignorant—many of them depraved and semi-
criminal." .

"Yes," I replied, "but their children go to the same
schools as ours, and while we may be able to do no more
than keep quiet the fathers of those who come to us, the
sons will be as our sons, and they will imbibe the principles of our free institutions with their daily lessons."

"But you are teaching these lessons to our people, too,"
said he, "and we do not want your republicanism, your free
suffrage."

"It seems to me, however," I rejoined, "that whether the
question is pressed upon you from us, or whether it springs
up from among your own people, you cannot escape it."

"It is so," said he ; "the movement in Parliament toward
household suffrage is a step in that direction."

And I thought as I sat there, how could you look on it in
any other light? You, the head of an aristocratic family;
you, who have been bred in the lap of luxury; you, who
have never known what it is to toil, except for pleasure or
for fame; how can you be expected to sympathize with the
poor, when you know that if ever the time should come
when manhood suffrage prevails in England, down will go
the law of primogeniture which holds together the immense
family interests; down will go the hereditary House of
Lords; down will go the church establishment, and if the
monarchy itself remains it will probably be elective, or
stripped of its immense emoluments. Less power it can
hardly possess. Of course I did not express these reflections,
but they came naturally to my mind.

The conversation then turned towards books, and I felt
that it was only just to assure him how he had laid all English-
speaking people under obligations for his charming works.
To such remarks he would bow very profoundly, and as I
went on he resumed his pipe, but not to smoke—the task or

the habit of holding it in his mouth in his study overcame
his sense of the presence of a stranger.

"I cannot help saying to your Lordship that the last
book I read before leaving home was 'The Last of the
Barons.'"

He bowed.

"I read it aloud to my family—the entire four volumes."
Again he bowed.

"And," I added, "my youngest child, a boy of eleven
years, would sit up until midnight, wide awake, to listen."

Again he bowed—this time with a hearty laugh.

Finding that he was not insensible to compliment, I went
on.

"You can hardly be aware how great is your popularity
in my country."

He smiled, and said that he was aware of it, but that it
was of no pecuniary advantage to him.

I asked if he could not make some arrangements with
American publishers, as other English authors had done, by
which he could receive a royalty on a new and revised edition of his works.

He did not know.

I ventured to suggest the name of Ticknor & Fields, of
Boston, as a firm of high character, that would probably
make such an arrangement.

"They publish for Dickens, do they not?"

There was something in the tone with which he uttered
this sentence that satisfied me that he did not want to be
associated with Dickens in any way.

I said, " I hope you will soon give us something more.
The last works from your pen have been so admirable
and so universally popular that we hope the series is not
finished."

"I believe," said he, looking on his table and around the

room at the heaps of papers, "I believe there is a novel lying about here now somewhere."

It was shortly after this that "The Parisians" appeared in successive numbers of Blackwood, and this was doubtless the "novel lying about here somewhere," of which he spoke indifferently.

I felt that I had no right to stay much longer, so I said :

" Before I go, may I tell your Lordship a story ? "

" Certainly," said he.

" There were two friends in Philadelphia, one a distinguished banker, the other one of the most eloquent and popular preachers in America.   It was Sunday, and the clergyman was dining with the banker.   After dinner, while sitting in the library enjoying their cigars, the banker used some expressions which caused the clergyman to say ' Caxtoniana.'

" ' Do you read Bulwer?' said the banker, turning with some surprise upon the preacher.

" ' Do I ?' said he.   ' There are three books—the Bible, Shakespeare and Bulwer.' "

As I said this his Lordship took the pipe from his mouth and, making a very low bow, laughed, " Haw—haw—haw."

" ' I am delighted,' said the banker, ' to learn that you are an admirer of Bulwer, though I fancy it is not usual with men of your profession.'

" ' The man,' said the clergyman, ' who can preach such a sermon as that which " Parson Dale," in " My Novel," preached ; the man who can talk as " George Morley " talked to " Guy Darrell " in " What Will He Do With It ?" has the root of the matter in him, and I honor him as a man and a Christian.' "

Lord Lytton again took the pipe from his mouth, made a most profound bow, and broke into his " Haw—haw—haw."

I now arose to leave, feeling that my call was already probably too long.

"What can I do for you?" said he.

"If your Lordship can give me an order for admission to the House of Lords, I should like much to hear the debates on the disestablishment of the Irish Church."

He sat down, took half a sheet of note paper, on which was his coronet, and wrote :

"Admit the bearer to the House of Lords.

"LYTTON. July ———."

He handed me the note and shook hands cordially, and I turned and left the room. The servant met me in the passage and showed me the way to the street. I need hardly say that while a few shillings judiciously used will admit any one to the House of Lords, I did not waste Bulwer's note for that purpose, but retain it as a memento of my visit.

3

VIII.

John Todd.

In one corner of the library are gathered the books which I like most, and which have had the most to do with my life. Among them are three by one author—John Todd. They are "The Student's Manual," "The Sabbath-school Teacher" and "Lectures to Children;" and although Todd wrote many books, these, probably, will survive all the others. "The Student's. Manual" was written for college students, and has been most widely circulated and read. More than 150 editions of this book have been published in English; while it has been translated into German, Welsh, French and many other languages. Its influence could not be, and was not, limited to college students. Many a boy, many a young man, never enrolled as a college student, has read and studied that book over and over again. It has the distinction of being not only the pioneer in the field, but of having no successor or imitator. It stands alone. While a young pastor in the city of Philadelphia, Mr. Todd wrote and delivered weekly to the teachers in his own Sunday-school a series of addresses, which were so popular and useful that they were immediately collected and published here and in England; and if I were asked to name the book which is well adapted to give the teacher a large and liberal view of the work, and which would fill his mind and heart with vast conceptions of the good to be accomplished by this means, I should say, "Todd's 'Sabbath-school Teacher.'" There have been many followers in the path of this pioneer, and

(34)

some most worthy, but none have excelled him in magnify-
ing that office which he did so much to illustrate. His
" Lectures to Children " were the first sermons of a popular
character to children ever published in this country. They
were translated into most of the languages of Europe, includ-
ing modern Greek, and have been printed in raised letters for
the blind. There is nothing superior, in their various lines,
to these books of Todd.

Who was the Rev. John Todd? In the year 1836 a few
men and women of New England birth or parentage, connected with the Presbyterian church on Arch street, near
Tenth, Philadelphia, having become dissatisfied with some
things in their own congregation, and desirous of introducing a New England church into Philadelphia, withdrew
from the Arch street church ; and having hired a hall on the
northeast corner of Eighth and Chestnut streets, they began
at once to have public worship, and gathered a Sunday-
school. They called their organization "The First Congregational Church of Philadelphia." New England Congregationalism was unknown in Philadelphia, except as represented by the "First Unitarian Church," of which the Rev.
Dr. Furness was pastor, and the people separating from the
Arch street church were determined to have an orthodox
Congregational church. Their next thought was to get a
pastor. Mr. Todd was somewhat widely known even at that
early age as an author, but especially as the founder and
organizer of churches. At that time he was pastor of " The
Edwards Church," Northampton, Massachusetts, which he
had gathered and organized. He was invited to come to
Philadelphia and take the pastorate of the new Congregational church. This invitation, after much hesitation, he
accepted. The new congregation was duly organized ; Rev.
Albert Barnes' church having been offered for the services of
organization, and Mr. Todd was installed as pastor. Their
next need was a church building. This they erected on

Tenth street, below Spruce, depending almost wholly on promises of the members to pay for it. The persons who had so pledged themselves to pay for the church building when it was finished, found themselves—towards the end of 1837, when the building was ready for dedication—unable to fulfil their obligations. The panic of 1837, which swept away the Bank of the United States and many other institutions and firms all over the land, was felt very severely in Philadelphia, and some of the people who had pledged themselves largely towards payment of the church building were overthrown in the common distress. The church was finished, however, and dedicated in November. The night of the dedication was one of violent rain, but the house was filled. The musical services were most attractive, and the pastor had thrown his best thought into the sermon, which was undoubtedly able and strong; in fact, the best presentation of Congregationalism that could be made in a city that was distinguished as the headquarters of Presbyterianism. But, unfortunately, in setting forth the distinctive characteristics of his own church, the new pastor thought it necessary to indulge in sharp criticism of almost all the other churches, the result of which was that the sermon was thought to have done far more harm than good.

The church was heavily mortgaged, and it does not take long for a church under such a condition to become disturbed in its internal arrangements. It was so in this instance. The people fretted and worried under the burden of the heavy incumbrance, and finally, after five years of heroic effort on the part of the pastor and those who stood by him, the church was obliged to disband, and the property was sold under foreclosure.

During the short pastorate of Mr. Todd—less than six years—he had succeeded in gathering more active, intelligent, educated young men about him than could be found, perhaps, in any other congregation in the city. He had the

best equipped Sunday-school. He taught the teachers, regularly and faithfully, during the week the lesson they were
to teach their scholars on Sunday. He organized the first
Young Men's Christian Association ever organized in this
city, limiting it, however, to the young men of his own congregation ; and he inaugurated a series of cottage prayer-
meetings, which up to that time had been practically
unknown here. He had the best volunteer choir to be
found in the city, and one of the most accomplished organists, a musical composer of acknowledged ability, Mr. George
Kingsley. But all these things availed naught. The church
was doomed, and its life soon came to an end.

In 1842 Mr. Todd was called to the First Congregational
Church in Pittsfield, Massachusetts, where he spent the rest
of his life, holding the pastorate of that congregation until
he was seventy years of age ; he having previously determined that should he live to that period he would resign
pastoral work. He was my first pastor, and I count it one
of the privileges of my life—my early life, for I was not
much more than a boy—to have sat under his ministry. I
heard almost every sermon he preached while in this city,
and took notes of very many of them. In a sense—the general sense of seeking to catch every word that fell from
his lips—I was his pupil. I was very much attached to him,
and from the time he left Philadelphia, in the midwinter of
1841-'42, until his death, in 1873, I kept up an uninterrupted
correspondence with him. His life and instructions were of
more value to me than I can express in words.

Mr. Todd was educated at Yale, and received his theological training at Andover Seminary. He was a Calvinist of
the sternest, strictest character, and yet holding these views
in theology, he had the rare faculty of availing himself of
the methods used by the New School of Theology, for his
ministry in Philadelphia was characterized by revivals of religion and large ingatherings of converts from beginning to

end.   He was the strongest and most impressive preacher I
ever listened to.   He had the fire and the fearlessness of
Jonathan Edwards himself.   Once in a conversation I had
with Oliver Wendell Holmes, Mr. Todd's name was mentioned, when Dr. Holmes said, " I always told Todd that he
ought to have been a Puritan colonel so that he might slash
the enemies of the Lord."

Dr. Todd was tall and straight.   His short, black hair
stood on end.   He wore glasses always, for he was near-
sighted, but his eyes were very keen.   His voice was rough
to harshness, but his pulpit power was great.   His style was
sometimes highly pictorial and even dramatic, and his sentences always short.

The general effect of his preaching (his sermons were
almost entirely written and read) was that of a man who was
talking to you as an individual, and this style of composition
led him to think that his sermons would not read well : at
least he always refused to publish a volume of his sermons,
though often urged to do so.   He said he "could not bear
the thought of being the father of a dead child."

IX.

DEAN STANLEY.*

OF all the shelves in my library, none is more attractive for serious reading than that which holds the works of Arthur Penrhyn Stanley, the Dean of Westminster. No writer in the English Church in our time has made so large and so valuable contributions to religious literature as Dr. Stanley. The Church, whether Christian or Jewish, is rich in historical literature, but its readers have been mainly theological students, whose curriculum has compelled them to wade through turbid streams with little satisfaction. It has been a common saying that church history is the least attractive of all historical studies, but no one can now say this if he has read any of the Dean of Westminster's lectures on the Church, whether Jewish or Christian.

The man who has done more than any man who has ever lived to throw a flood of light on the history of the church, from the days of Abraham to Christ, and who has reproduced with marvellous beauty the scenes and the characters of the old time, is Dean Stanley. It is not merely the fascination of his matchless style, clear and pure and pictorial beyond parallel, but there is a magnetism in the spirit of his teaching which sends his hearers and readers to searching their bookshelves to learn more of the subjects on which he has thrown, if only in flashes, the light of his vast learning and eloquence.

Who is this man whose life devoted to sacred studies, whose splendid genius cultivated in the best schools and

---

* October, 1878.

chastened by deep sorrows, have made him foremost of all
Christian preachers ?

Arthur Stanley is the second son of an English Bishop,
Edward Stanley of Norwich, one of the most gentle and godly
men who ever wore a mitre.   When fourteen years old he
was sent to Rugby, not long after the appointment of Arnold
as Head Master.   Here he spent the full course of six years,
acquitting himself admirably, and winning the full confidence of the Master.   The relation between the young boy
and the great teacher was not merely that of pupil and
master, it was rather that of son and father.   It was a true
affection ripening into full communion as the years passed,
and the Rugby boy became the Oxford student.   Of the
many graduates of Rugby who have achieved distinction,
such as Hughes, Vaughan of the Temple, Lord Stanley, now
Earl of Derby, the Bishop of Rochester, the Bishop of New-
foundland, Professor Cunnington, Mr. Göschen, Matthew
Arnold, none have written their names so high or in lines so
deep as Arthur Stanley.

He went from Rugby to Oxford, having obtained a scholarship in Balliol College, where his course was, as might have
been expected, eminently successful.   In his second year he
recited his prize poem in English, "The Gypsies," "took
a first class in classics, gained the Latin prize essay in 1839,
and the English essay and theological prize in 1840."

He has held most important positions in the university and
in the church.   He was a fellow and tutor of University
College.   He was Secretary to the Oxford University Commission, where he did most essential service.   He was made
Canon of Canterbury, some say as a reward for these faithful
services.   He succeeded Prof. Hussey as Regius Professor of
Ecclesiastical History at Oxford.   He was examining chaplain to Dr. Tait, Bishop of London, Arnold's successor at
Rugby, and now Archbishop of Canterbury.   He was
chaplain to the Prince of Wales, and having declined the

Archbishopric of Dublin, was, in 1864, made Dean of Westminster, the place he now so worthily holds.

His literary labors have been great, and have made his name more widely known than that of any other living preacher. The first course of sermons which he published is that on the Apostolic Age—a work not so generally known here as his subsequent works—but full of interest and those graces of style which seem to be his natural expression.

It is in the preface to this book that he makes that singular acknowledgment, "If there are fewer references than might naturally have been expected to the name of one to whom, though not living, this, as well as any similar work which I may be called to undertake, must in great measure be due, it is because I trust I may be allowed to take this opportunity of vindicating, once for all, for the scholars of Arnold the privilege and pleasure of using his words and adopting his thoughts without the necessity of specifying, in every instance, the sources from which they have been derived."

This work was followed by his lectures on the Eastern Church, of which the most brilliant perhaps are those on the Council of Nicæa. Then his lectures on the Jewish Church —first, second and third series—three volumes not equaled by any other three in our language from one mind, in grace and beauty of style, in vividness of description and in pictorial coloring.

Then follow, not in chronological order, but as they stand on my shelves, his lectures on the Church of Scotland, which so stirred up the "Auld Reekie" people and which brought a swift rejoinder from Principal Rainy, of the Free Church. Rutherford, Burns, Scott, all sources and authors are laid under contribution for illustration in these lectures, which are preceded by a sermon preached in the Old Grey Friar's Church as an introduction to the course "On the Eleventh Commandment:" "A new commandment I give unto you,

that ye love one another," which is a splendid specimen
of the preacher's broad and liberal Christianity.

Then comes that charming book, Memorials of Westminster
Abbey—which is complete and exhaustive—done as no other
man could have done it ; then his Memorials of Canterbury
Cathedral of equal interest ; then his grand work on Sinai and
Palestine, only excelled by our own Robinson, and by him in
certain respects only ; then his sermons preached before the
Prince of Wales while traveling in Egypt and Palestine, etc.;
then his essays on Church and State, a selection of his
articles from magazines and reviews, a few of which, some
of his friends think, ought not to have been reproduced ;
then his modest but excellent memoir of his father, Bishop
Stanley ; then his Commentary on the Epistles to the Corinthians, which, for its clear exposition, its admirable para-
phrases, its most satisfactory dissertations and discussions, and
especially for its splendid introduction, placed it in the front
rank of all works on these grand epistles ; and, lastly, except
some smaller books, occasional sermons, etc., his really grand
"Life of Arnold," probably the finest biography in our
language.

It was my good fortune in the summer of 1869 to spend
some time in London.   On the first Sunday I went to Westminster Abbey.   Having been told that in order to hear the
sermon distinctly one must be very near the pulpit, I went
as early as half-past nine o'clock, and had to wait a little for
the gates to be opened.   Quite a company had already
gathered at the gates.   But I was fortunate enough to get a seat
within a few feet of the pulpit, where I could not only hear
every word the speaker said, but could see the minutest expression of countenance.   The music was good, though hardly
so good as that at St. Patrick's in Dublin or at York Minster.
The text was from Matthew v. 22, the Gospel of the day :

" But I say unto you, That whosoever is angry with his
brother without a cause shall be in danger of the judgment,

but whosoever shall say to his brother, Raca, shall be in danger of the council, but whosoever shall say, Thou fool, shall be in danger of hell fire."

"I propose to speak of the words," he said, "after explaining their meaning, in their application to individuals, churches and nations." He went on to say that the words "Raca," "council," "judgment," "thou fool," "hell fire," implied thoughts and images familiar to the people of the day, but not so familiar to us. Our Lord is speaking of sins of the thoughts and of words. He speaks of causeless anger. Anger is sometimes justifiable and right. No character is perfect without it. The Lord Jesus was himself angry more than once. But, never quarrel if you can possibly help it. Keep from quarrels, which, if unchecked, may ultimately lead to murder. But, under the feeling of anger, angry words are spoken, such as "Raca," meaning "shallow, thoughtless," a contemptuous expression and another step in the scale of offence; and then, just as the law of England years ago regarded mere words as not treasonable, another form of words is adopted still more mischievous, such as "Thou fool!" In the original this is not a Greek word, but Hebrew or Syriac, "Moreh," and should have been so rendered. Its proper meaning is rebel or heretic, and it is the same word that Moses used when he said : "Hear, now, ye rebels, must we bring you water?" for which offence he was so severely punished. Though this word and others of like character are beyond the reach of any earthly tribunal, they may be so used as to convey the greatest reproach. Hell-fire is, more properly, fire of the funeral pile—the burning furnace of that dark accursed valley, the draught-house of Jerusalem, whence the smoke of a continual burning was always ascending. All such words as "Raca," "Moreh," may have had a religious use once, but are now irreligious and equivalent to cursing and swearing. So far the explanation of the words of the text.

In the general application, the Dean proceeded to say that it is not the outward act merely, but the inward spirit which God judges. Sometimes we are tempted to use strong language ; we should check and restrain ourselves. We have given up duelling and feudal barbarities in dungeons, as abhorrent to the spirit of this enlightened Christian age ; but so much the more should we give up the use of those insulting words which set the soul on fire. We have given up putting people to death for differing from us in religious opinion ; and racks and tortures and the fires of Smithfield are among the things of the past ; but so much the more do we need to be reminded that they who say "Moreh," "rebel," "heretic," have no other object than to break up Christian fellowship. The Valley of Hinnom was the proper type and emblem of such views and words.

This warning of Christ, spoken first against individuals, refers also to nations and churches. Look at the Christian churches in their fulminations against each other. "Raca," "Raca," Presbyterians against Prelatists, Prelatists against Non-Conformists. Nations invent words of stinging reproach, such as it is not proper to hear in this sacred place. The check to all this is in the Saviour's words, "Thy brother." Thy fellow-man is thy brother. Each man in common life has such relations. Each church has brotherly or sisterly relations to other churches, which should induce kindly feelings and a determination never to quarrel.

"One application, and the last which I make of this subject," continued the dean, "is this : This is the Fourth of July, the anniversary of American Independence, the day which separated the Colonies from the Mother-country. On such a day our Lord's warning has a peculiar meaning. The sons of that Great Republic are our brothers in such a sense as can be said of no other people—the same in race, in language, in faith, in literature.

" During the fierce days of the Revolutionary struggle, such bitter words as 'Raca,' 'Raca,' 'Rebel,' from one side, 'Tyrant,' from the other, were hurled across the Atlantic. But those days are past, and we know how promptly and cordially the new Ambassador was received at the court of the old sovereign. And what American is there now, who does not glory in our old English history, and feel that it is his own! What Englishman does not feel proud of the once dreaded name of Washington! Woe! woe! to those, then, on either side, who would stir up the ashes of the old dissensions, and blessed be the peace-makers who come forward with the firm determination neither to give nor to take offence."

It may readily be supposed that such sentiments are not often heard from the pulpit in England, and probably were never heard before in Westminster Abbey. The time and the place alone repressed the applause which would certainly have broken forth from the audience, for there were many Americans present. While these notes of the sermon are brief and disconnected, and give a very bare and incomplete outline of it as a whole, the reference to America is about as literal as could be taken without the aid of stenography.

During a brief interview with the Dean after the service, when I expressed my great gratification at the pleasure not only of hearing him, but of hearing such sentiments from him, he said that it seemed the most natural and proper conclusion to such a sermon on such a day, and he was most happy to know that there were any Americans present to hear him.

Such is the man who is so tenderly loved and so bitterly hated in the English Church ; loved for his broad Christian charity, comprehending " all who profess and call themselves Christians," no matter what other name they bear ; loved for his own love of all that is good and true, wherever found; loved for his magnificent contributions to that literature which is most worthy of study ; loved for his chivalrous advocacy of what he believes to be right ; and hated for his liberal views of the interpretation of Scripture, for his independent position in the church (he being the only Dean who is not under a Bishop) and his bold assertions of that position ; hated for his courageous course toward Colenso in that unfortunate controversy ; hated because he shut the doors of his grand old Abbey in the face of the Pan-Anglican Council and opened them for an address from the German layman and philosopher, Max Muller.

X.

Jacob Abbott.

THERE are four books that I have read over and over again, and always with unabated interest ; and it is of very few books I can say so much. They are not much known now, having passed somewhat out of view ; but with a more or less extended acquaintance with this kind of literature, I can frankly say that I have never read anything so good. They are : " The Young Christian, or a Familiar Exposition of the Principles of Christian Duty ; " " The Corner Stone : a Familiar Exposition of the Principles of Christian Truth ; " " The Way to Do Good ; or the Christian Character Mature ; " and " Hoaryhead and McDonner."

These are works of the Rev. Jacob Abbott, a clergyman of the Congregational church, who was born about the beginning of this century, and who died in Maine in the year 1871.

Mr. Abbott wrote more books, so far as I know, than any other man. There is a catalogue of at least 180 distinct books, some of them, in fact most of them, very small books intended for children and young people.

Besides this he was joint author and editor of many more volumes. His life was devoted to making literature for young people, after he ceased teaching school as a principal. He was the founder of the Mt. Vernon school in Boston, and one of the most successful and distinguished teachers of his time.

The book by which Mr. Abbott was most widely known, in this country as well as in England, was, " The Corner. Stone." When he came before a council of the Congrega-

(47)

tional church for ordination to the ministry of that body, there was some hesitation on their part as to whether he should be ordained or not. Certain of the views of Christian truth which he had presented in that book were believed not to be in strict accord with the orthodoxy of that day, and for some time .it was very doubtful whether he would pass a satisfactory examination for ordination. He did so, however, and at once entered upon a pastorate in Roxborough. In England this book made quite a stir, and attracted extraordinary attention, especially from two sources—Thomas Arnold, the famous head-master of the Rugby School, and also from a writer in the Oxford "Tracts for the Times." This writer was supposed to be Dr. Pusey, and he criticised Mr. Abbott's views of religious truth with the most positive objections. Indeed the writer classed Mr. Abbott with the well-known Thos. Erskine, of Linlathen, a Scotch writer, a layman, who was supposed to be quite far away from the strict lines of orthodoxy. The title of the tract in which the criticism appeared was, "Rationalism in Religion ;". and it was a most severe criticism of Mr. Abbott's book. Some time after the publication of this article Mr. Abbott was in England, and he went to Oxford for the purpose of seeing and talking with Dr. Pusey. Not finding him there, but hearing that Dr. Newman was at Littlemore, two or three miles out of Oxford, he walked out to that village, and went into St. Mary's, where Dr. Newman was holding the regular morning service. From the hotel, immediately after service, he wrote Dr. Newman a note, stating that he was passing rapidly through England, and would be very glad if he might be permitted to call upon him at some hour before noon of the following day, when he intended to leave Oxford. This brought a very prompt reply from Dr. Newman, asking Mr. Abbott to call at once, if it were convenient. In the interview which followed, which was an hour or more in length, Mr. Abbott discovered that Dr. Pusey was not the author of the tract in question, but that it had been written by Dr. Newman.

With great frankness, towards the close of the interview, Mr. Abbott admitted, that possibly some of the expressions in the statements of truth as presented by him were unguarded, and if he could have had such an interview as this before he had written the criticised book he probably would have put some of his statements in a different form ; while, however, he held very firmly to his views of the truth essentially. In return Dr. Newman expressed regret that possibly in his treatment of the book, in the tract referred to, he might have gone beyond the lines of prudence, and have said some things which were personally offensive ; and if such were the case he would be very glad to withdraw them. The interview was extremely interesting, and very creditable to both parties, although neither one was drawn to the views held by the other. Dr. Newman, however, was so much impressed with the candor and Christian character of Mr. Abbott, that when the interview ended, and Mr. Abbott rose to leave, Dr. Newman not only followed him to the door, but, taking his hat and cane, walked across two or three fields with him, as he said to show him a shorter road to Oxford, but in reality for the purpose of prolonging the conversation. A newspaper of the day got hold of a part of this story, and published it, very much to the embarrassment of Dr. Newman, and not entirely to the credit of Mr. Abbott. Dr. Newman very promptly came out over his own signature, in the next issues of the paper, and corrected the misstatements ; expressing his sincere regret that Mr. Abbott should ever see the paper which so misrepresented the interview, and be pained by it.

The other English author who was attracted by Mr. Abbott's books was the distinguished head master of Rugby, Thomas Arnold. In the autumn of 1833, on the publication of the "Young Christian," Arnold had written to

4

Abbott, expressing great admiration of the little book, and as they are both engaged in the work of education, he hopes Mr. Abbott will forgive the liberty a stranger takes in addressing him. He goes on to speak of the importance to the welfare of mankind that the people of the United States should be a God-fearing people. And he concludes by sending Mr. Abbott a volume of Rugby School Sermons, and another little book of his, for no other reason than the pleasure of submitting his views on great questions to the judgment of a mind, furnished morally and intellectually, as Mr. Abbott's must be.

A year after, writing to Chevalier Bunsen, he says, "I have been much delighted with two American works which have had a large circulation in England, 'The Young Christian,' and 'The Corner Stone,' by Jacob Abbott, of New England. They are very original and powerful, and the American illustrations, whether borrowed from scenery, or the manners of the people, are very striking."

But some time after this, probably, is a footnote to an appendix to one of his sermons, speaking of "The Corner Stone" again; he says "the writer is so anxious to repel anthropomorphic notions of a monarch on a throne of marble and gold, with crown and sceptre, and sitting in a fancied region which we call Heaven," that he ventures to describe "the all pervading Power which lives and acts throughout the whole universe."

Dr. Arnold thinks Mr. Abbott's language is not sufficiently guarded here, and fears that, from such expression, some erroneous opinions have been entertained concerning the Divine Nature.

Three or four years after this, Arnold, in writing to a friend, says: "Jacob Abbott's last work, 'The Way to Do Good,' will, I think, please you very much: with some Americanisms, not of language, but of mind, it is yet delightful to read a book so good and so sensible, so zealous for what is valuable, so fair about what is indifferent.''

It was a long time ago, and I was not much more than a lad. I had recently connected myself with the church, and had formed the habit of spending many of my evenings in my own room. I was away from my father's house, and living in a small family of non-church-going people.

One of the members of the family was a lady in middle life, a fashionable dressmaker, who rarely, if ever, went to church, but who spent her Sunday mornings in resting and her afternoons and evenings in reading novels. In the late winter and early spring she was so driven by the exacting demands of her patrons that it was her habit to work far into the night, and every night. ·

Either her sympathy for the lonely youth, or the desire that her labors might be lightened by the entertainment of reading, perhaps both considerations, led her to ask me to sit in her work-room in the evenings, surrounded as she was by her young apprentices, and read to her. I complied without hesitation, and she gave me properly the choice of books. There was lying on a table in the parlor a copy of "The Corner Stone," by Jacob Abbott. How the book ever got there is a marvel. .It was a strange book to me and I knew nothing of the author. The first chapter interested the reader almost as much as the listener. The interest deepened as the reading went on. No question was ever raised or thought of being raised as to the orthodoxy of the book. We were simply led on from chapter to chapter, and from evening to evening, until the book was finished. Some weeks, because of many interruptions, were consumed in the readings, and at the end the evenings had become shorter, and the readings were not resumed until the following autumn. Long before the readings ended, however, I observed that the lady began to go to church. I do not now remember that she ever spoke a word to me concerning any change in her feelings until once she expressed a desire to have a conversation with my pastor. An appointment was made with him. I took her to his house, introduced her to him, and left them together. At the next communion season she made a profession of religion, attributing the beginning of her change of heart to the reading of Abbott's "Corner Stone." It was a real change. The poor woman, working day and night with small remuneration; living for this world only; the future of this life hopeless, grinding toil, with no light from the next world to brighten it—becomes suddenly a child of God, a follower of Christ, bright, cheerful and hopeful; and living ever afterwards the life of a humble disciple of Him whom she found to be the chief "Corner Stone."

XI.

HENRY ALFORD—ALBERT BARNES.

THE intelligence has reached us (January, 1871) by the ocean telegraph .of the death of Henry Alford, the Dean of Canterbury. All that we know is, that it was a sudden death.

All over England this announcement will produce profound sensation, not only because he was a high dignitary of the Church, but because of his place in the world of letters, and of his pure and exalted personal character. In the year 1857 he received the appointment of Dean of Canterbury, and since that time his pen has never been idle. The later volumes of his Greek Testament have been given to the world in this time—a work deservedly occupying the highest rank. This was followed by his " New Testament for English Readers," which " was undertaken with a view to put the English reader, whose knowledge is confined to our own language, in possession of some of the principal results of the labors of critics and scholars on the sacred text." How well he succeeded in that undertaking is known to those who use that invaluable work. It may well be doubted whether any commentary on the whole of the New Testament has ever appeared in England which for conciseness without obscurity, for solid learning, for clearness of statement, for honest admission of difficulties, for soundness of criticism, for that happy medium between advanced principles of interpretation and sound orthodoxy, is the equal of this " New Testament for English Readers." Ellicott and Lightfoot and Davies and Trench and Stanley and Jowett may have brought a profounder learning to certain portions of the New Testament, but Alford has covered the whole volume with light. Nor should it be forgotten that the little volumes, "How to Study the New Testament," gathered from monthly contributions to the *Sunday Magazine*, are among the most valuable aids that have ever been given for this purpose. Most clergymen and all Sunday-school teachers would do well to avail themselves of these little books.

Probably no man in England has done as much to stimulate and encourage the study of the Scriptures, and make the Bible plain to the comprehension of plain minds, as Dean Alford. And what higher praise can there be than this? He has published many volumes of sermons—sermons, too, which were worth publishing ; not striking, startling or sensational, but sound, practical and Scriptural. In his college days at Cambridge he was somewhat addicted to poetry. Some beautiful hymns and one or two volumes of verses attest his interest and success in this direction. At this time he was in close intimacy with Tennyson, to whom he has dedicated the latest collection of his poems. There is a very playful vein in some of these pieces, and especially in one which he calls "A Letter to America," addressed to his friend Hale, in February, 1862, in the height of our war, in the course of which he says, playfully, some things which we could not well bear to hear then, but which strike us as more tolerable and truthful now.

There appeared in Dr. Guthrie's *Sunday Magazine*, a most valuable periodical, a series of papers called "Fireside Homilies" by the Dean of Canterbury. They are supposed to be familiar talks on Sunday evenings with his children on certain passages of Scripture. One was on that passage, "Master, we saw one casting out devils in thy name, and he followeth not us, and we forbade him because he followeth not us," in which he teaches most lovingly the doctrine of

Christian charity, toleration towards those who differ from us in our views of Christian truth if they follow Christ. The familiar homily 'was suggested by the storm of indignation which raged in certain quarters in England because, at the first meeting of the Commission now in session at Westminster for the revision of the authorized version of the Scriptures, a Unitarian clergyman, a member of the body, partook of the Sacrament of the Lord's Supper with his colleagues preparatory to the commencement of that work. No better lesson was ever more kindly given than the rebuke which Alford administered to that feeling of jealousy and intolerance which the Saviour himself rebuked so plainly. Another homily was on the subject of the words : "Why was this waste of the ointment made ? For this ointment might have been sold for more than three hundred pence, and given to the poor." But the Saviour rebuked the complaint, and commended in the very highest terms the poor woman who broke the alabaster box of ointment, and said : "Wheresoever this gospel shall be preached throughout the whole world, this also that this woman hath done shall be spoken of for a memorial of her," thus teaching that nothing is too costly or too valuable to be given to Christ and his cause.

A little more than a year ago I spent a Sunday in Canterbury. There were but two Sundays left of my long vacation, and I determined to spend one in the old city of Canterbury, that I might, if possible, see and hear Dean Alford ; and the other in the city of Chester, that I might, if possible, see and hear Dean Howson, the author of that great work, "The Life and Epistles of St. Paul." The Cathedral at Canterbury is very old and grand. Its history is the history of England from far back in the middle ages ; for it was here that St. Augustine, a prior from a convent in Rome and sent by Gregory the Great, landed and preached the Gospel nearly thirteen hundred years ago. The little

Church of St. Martin's, on the hill overlooking the old city, is built of Roman bricks, probably as old as the second century, and is said to be the spot where Christianity was first preached in Great Britain.

In the Cathedral the famous Thomas á Becket was assassinated, and here for many years hundreds of thousands of weary pilgrims trod their way to his shrine and offered their devotions. And here was the first Archbishop's throne set up ; here was the first connection of Church and State, which for more than 1,200 years, Roman Catholic and Protestant, has continued the established Church of England.

I went to the Sunday morning service at the Cathedral, but Alford did not preach. In the afternoon I went again. His sermon was very plain and simple. The text was from Isaiah : "There shall come forth a rod out of the stem of Jesse, and a branch shall grow out of his roots." It was an Advent sermon, and was appropriate to the time. I remember being struck with his modesty in giving another rendering of the passage when he said that "those who are familiar with the original, say that this passage might perhaps more accurately be translated," etc., etc.

I had a note of introduction to him from the Bishop of British Columbia—a fellow-passenger in our ship—but it was mislaid. I sent in my card, however, after the service, with a word of explanation. He came out of the Chapter House and greeted me in the most cordial manner. I shall never forget his appearance. He was above the middle height, full set, with a countenance expressing great dignity and kindness, full gray eyes, regular features, and the lower part of his face covered with a heavy flowing beard, quite un-English, slightly mingled with gray. Neither can I forget the kindness with which he pointed out the beauties of the Cathedral (one of the finest in England), nor his leading me across the Close to his residence, the Deanery, adjoining the Cathedral, and into his library. Oh ! such a library !—his work-

shop as he called it—a large, square room, full of books—
books on the walls, books in alcoves, book-laden tables, and
lounges covered with books ; with a blazing fire of sea-coal
in a grate (it was late in November), and the whole room
flooded with gas-light—the most beautiful room, except one,
that I ever saw ; nor can I forget his reference to Mr. Barnes
and his " Notes," which were on his shelves, nor his taking
down a volume of his own " Sermons on Christian Doctrines," and presenting it to me as a memento of my visit,
with my name written by him with his own on the fly-leaf.

It seems hard to realize that he is dead ; that a man so vigorous in appearance, so full of life, so solid and substantial,
so full of good works, with ten years yet before he had fulfilled his threescore and ten, should so suddenly have been
called away, when in our poor judgment he is so much
needed.   In the early days of the new year, while full of
plans for the coming year (he was a leading member of the
commission for the revision of the Scriptures), God sends his
messenger, and the summons must be obeyed.

So in the last days of the old year our own Mr. Barnes was
called from us.   His work was finished.   He was gathered
as a shock of corn, fully ripe.

There are some circumstances which closely associate these
two distinguished men in our minds.   They both died suddenly ; they both had spent their lives in the service of Christ,
in preaching his gospel, and in writing commentaries to unfold his word and make it plain to others ; they had both
suffered severe and harsh criticism, and both had endured it
in the spirit of their Master ; they were both engaged in
doing good to the very last, and died in the full possession of
their faculties.   The one ascended from the sacred precincts
of the venerable Cathedral ; the other passed away in the
house of a friend a moment after entering it.   " He went out
about as far as to Bethany, and while they beheld He was
parted from them and was carried up into heaven."

Dean Alford was not a High Churchman, nor a Low Churchman, nor a Broad Churchman, in an extreme sense, nor did he anathematize those who were ; he was a sound, conservative preacher and writer, always holding forth the doctrine of free grace and salvation by faith in Christ. Sharp and bitter things have been said of him because he dared to say that in the advanced state of modern learning, and Biblical science and Oriental researches, and the discovery of ancient manuscript copies of the Scriptures, a better translation of the Scriptures might now be made than the authorized version ; but he held on his way unawed until he began to draw all scholars to his views.

Mr. Barnes was persecuted almost unto death because he preached the doctrines that all who would, might repent and be saved ; that Christ died for all ; and that men were lost, not because there was any necessity for it, but because they would not come unto Christ and be saved.

He lived to see the day when almost a revolution has taken place in this respect, when all pulpits hold forth the doctrines of free grace, and when the statements of a limited atonement are confined to quarterly reviews, which few read.

Dean Alford's crowning work is his Commentary on the New Testament, a work which is not likely to be supplanted for many a day ; the only drawback to which is, that it is so costly that it cannot be in everybody's hands.

But the man who has done more than any other one man in our own time, or in any other time, to make the study of the Scriptures comparatively easy, reducing them to the comprehension of plain, uneducated minds, is he who so lately walked in and out among us—Albert Barnes. He was the pioneer, and therefore the most original in this, the most important of all the fields of literature. His notes on the New Testament, written in the midst of the duties and trials of a most laborious pastoral charge, have been scattered far and wide wherever the English language is spoken, and have

been translated into many other languages ; and thousands
of Sunday-school teachers are at this day preparing their
lessons with the help of these admirable volumes.   Their
circulation is not limited to the Presbyterian Church.   I
have seen them in the study of one of the most learned and
critical commentators of the English Church, an Archbishop,
and in the hands of plain mechanics, teaching in a humble
school in a Methodist church in the ancient city of York ; and
not many years agò the rector of one of the most ritualistic
Episcopal churches in this city said that he had put a copy
of Barnes' Notes in the hands of all his Sunday-school
teachers.

Almost all the commentaries on the Sacred Scriptures that
have been published within the last thirty-five years have
been modeled on Mr. Barnes's plan, and he is therefore en-
titled to the credit of originating that plan.

The Cathedral of Canterbury was filled with a vast crowd
while the service of the Church of England was said over the
body of the honored and beloved Dean.   High dignitaries
of the church followed in the long procession that wound
through the narrow streets of the quaint old city to the
grave-yard around St. Martin's on the Hill, where after singing his own hymn,

Ten thousand times ten thousand,

they laid his worn body to rest, and on the stone which is
to cover the grave, will, by his own direction, be engraved
these words :—

DEVERSORIUM VIATORIS HIEROSOLVMAN PROFICISCENTIS,

i. e., The Inn of a traveler on his way to Jerusalem.

The stormy day and the bad condition of the streets did
not hinder a vast crowd from filling the First Presbyterian

Church, at the funeral of Mr. Barnes, to testify their respect and affection for the man, most of whose life was lived in this city and in this church : a life of singular simplicity, beauty and devotion.   Clergymen of all the Protestant branches of the Church were present.   Bishop Stevens in tender and appropriate words expressed to the great congregation his sense of the loss the whole community had sustained.   The simple funeral service of the Presbyterian Church was most impressive and tender, and the body was borne to Laurel Hill for its final resting place.

Henry Alford—Albert Barnes—how can the church afford to lose such men?   How can the great head of the Church make up to us our loss?

"My Father, the chariots of Israel and the horsemen thereof!"

XII.

FREDERICK D. MAURICE.

THERE is hardly any better testimony to the life and writings of one who has been dead for twenty years or more than the fact that Macmillan & Co. have brought out, in an unusually beautiful style, six volumes of sermons preached in Lincoln's Inn Chapel by Frederick Dennison Maurice. The pages of these volumes are so attractive that in turning them over, one lingers as if unwilling to let them pass without reading them entirely. But why should not these beautiful volumes be illustrated by a portrait of the author? and with some prefatory note as to why they are published now? The title-page says it is a new edition; but the admirers of the author in this country (not very many possibly) are not familiar with the sermons in this form. The list of the sermons in the first volume is particularly attractive, the first five being called Eucharistic sermons; the others on practical subjects from texts chiefly from the New Testament.

I am indebted to a friend in London for an engraved likeness of Mr. Maurice. It represents a man somewhat past middle life, with clearly defined features, and eyes full of earnestness and tenderness that seem to be looking for something we do not see. It is a remarkable face. Sweetness and purity, strength and beauty are most strongly impressed on those features. Frederick Dennison Maurice was one of the foremost men of his time; one of the best known yet the least known of English churchmen. He was a broad churchman, one of the leaders, if not the founder, of that school of theology. If he did not himself originate that school, he was at heart regarded as the most original of that class of men which included Archbishop Whateley, Arnold of Rugby, Jowett of Balliol, Dean Stanley, Robertson of Brighton, Charles Kingsley, Rowland Williams and Dean Alford in the English Church; whose counterparts in the Kirk of Scotland were Principal Tulloch, Robert Lee of Grey Friars, Norman McLeod, Story of Roseneath, John Service and Robertson Smith.

He was a professor for many years at King's College in London; principal of the Working Men's College there; chaplain at Lincoln's Inn for a time, holding when he died the chair of moral philosophy at Cambridge. He was a laborious worker and indefatigable and patient thinker, the almost unconscious possessor of enormous mental power, the leader of a school of thought as diverse as the poles from the Oxford heresy, yet not entirely free from another form of heresy himself.

If he may be said to be the founder of a school of theology, he hardly knew it, for his mind and heart were so entirely engrossed in lecturing and preaching, so thoroughly in earnest in communicating truth as he understood it, that he did not stop to inquire what use his pupils and hearers would make of his views, only he was anxious almost to distress that they should receive liberal views of religious thought. He did more, perhaps, than any other man in England to stimulate activity of thought and independence of expression. He did not rise to high preferment in the English Church, for his teachings in some important respects were not considered orthodox; but he lived a life of most extraordinary beauty and purity, a life of unusual labor, and has left behind him a score of volumes of teachings, which have helped to mould some of the brightest minds in the Church of England.

I refer to Maurice to show how a man thoroughly in earnest could leave the impression of his mind on all who came within his reach not only, but who by the force of his character as a teacher actually, though unconsciously, developed and enlarged a school of religious thought which has been a most potent factor in theology.

His views of theology have hardly yet found a large following in America, but the materials are not wanting and may be discerned in the teachings of such men as Professor Briggs, Lyman Abbott, Beecher, Newman Smyth, Munger, Bishop Brooks, and others.

A life so laborious, so self-denying, so hidden with Christ in God, had its appropriate ending. As long as he had strength he preached from the pulpit of his own church, St. Edward's, Cambridge ; a living to which he was presented the last year of his life ; a parish with no salary ; and when no longer able to go out he gave a lecture at home.

During his last illness he hardly ever awoke in the night without repeating aloud the Lord's prayer, and "the grace of our Lord," or "Praise God from all whom all blessings flow." When, in answer to the question asked of his physician whether his life was a question of days or of hours, he was told "not days," he prepared at once to receive the communion. Afterwards he talked much and very rapidly, as if he still had much to say ; when one said, "Speak slowly," he went on speaking, but more and more indistinctly, till suddenly he made a great effort to gather himself up, and after a pause he said slowly and distinctly : "The knowledge of the love of God, the blessing of God Almighty, the Father, the Son, and the Holy Ghost, be amongst you, amongst *us*, and remain with us forever." He never spoke again. In one instant all consciousness was gone.

It may indeed be true, that while at least in his larger and more philosophical works, or even in his theological essays, his style was obscure and not easily comprehended by very plain minds, yet this can hardly be said of some of his books which were intended for plain people, and which have done so much to make him read now so long after his death. His

"Family Worship," a dialogue between a layman and a clergyman, the latter speaking his own thoughts; his "Sermons on the Lord's Prayer;" his little "Manual for Parents and Schoolmasters," being very short talks on the Lord's Prayer, the Creed and the Ten Commandments, the language of which he hopes "will be intelligible to any child;" his discourses on the Prophets and Kings of the Old Testament, and perhaps some other volumes, are surely not liable to the charge of obscurity and indefiniteness.

These are the books which I love to recall, and one of which, at least, I have read more than once.

Stanley speaks of him as "the noble-hearted man, who, whatever may be thought of the obscurity of his style, the insufficiency of his arguments, or the erroneousness of some of his conclusions, is perhaps the best example that this age can show of that deep prophetic fervor, of that power of apostolic sympathy, which awakens not the less because it often fails to satisfy; which edifies not the less because it often fails to convince."

XIII.

A Memory of the East.

I HAVE drawn my chair up to the fire, for it is winter weather. It is too early to light the gas. The red glow of the anthracite coals throws a deep crimson light over such parts of the room as are within its range, illuminating the large San Sisto Madonna on the opposite wall, while the shadows are very deep. The wind, which has been high all day, has not " gone down with the sun," but roars through the leafless branches of the trees and beats against the windows, as if it too wanted to get near the fire. Alas for the poor wretches who are exposed to the wind on such a night. I think of the car drivers, the post men, the messenger boys, the many workers in offices, shops and mills going home at the end of the day's toil, through the slippery streets, and of all the people who are compelled to be out in such weather.

And my thoughts go further. The blazing coals suggest figures. I seem to see a ship in the Mediterranean, rolling and plunging on her way from Italy to Egypt. There is a gale from the northeast, such as drove St. Paul's ship to her doom. But this ship is crossing that path going southeast. I look more closely ; and in the early morning I see two persons on the deck. They have just come up from below. No comfort there, for the ship is rolling heavily.

One is a young man of slight form and dark complexion ; the other is past middle life, and both apparently uncomfortable from yesterday's storm. In the older person I recognize myself. I am leaning towards the young man as we sit on the bench and with that desire for companionship which

5

even seasickness, except in a violent form, does not entirely destroy, I. ask the young man if he speaks English. He replies that he does. We enter into a conversation, which, to me at least, becomes very interesting.

From the long ago come the echoes of our voices—will you listen to them?

I learned that he was an East Indian who had spent three years in England and now was on his way back to Calcutta. He had been at Oxford, and while not a member of the University had had the advantage of the laboratories in his studies of Physical Science. He had paid his fees, he said, but had attended few or no lectures and had not submitted to any examination. His real education had been in Calcutta.

To my question whether Christianity was making any progress in India he replied, "Numerically, yes; in real religious power, no."

"But I do not believe in Christianity," he continued, "although I believe that Jesus was a Prophet. The missionaries come among the common people, but they are so far above them in the social scale, live in so much better style in their fine houses,. etc., that the people are not drawn to them."

"You mean the English missionaries," I said, "for surely this is not true of all."

"The English and Scotch," said he. "I see no difference."

I spoke of the American missionaries as being of another stamp, but he did not seem to know of them.

"When your missionaries come to us," he said, "we ask, 'What message do you bring us? What can you tell us that we do not already know? What is your gospel? How is your religion better than ours?' Then they begin to preach discourses on the Father, the Son and the Holy Ghost. But we do not want the doctrine of the Trinity, we do not want theological discourses, we want practical religion. We look and we see that the Christian missionaries live above us, and not amongst us, not *with* us. We look to see some of the self-denial that their Saviour came to introduce. Buddhism has its Trinity, so has Brahma its Trinity : we want something better if you can give it,—self-denial, suffering for the good of others.''

"Have you read the Christian Scriptures carefully?" I asked.

"Yes, more or less, especially the New Testament. But the Scriptures are written in Eastern metaphor and are not to be interpreted literally.''

"But the Sermon on the Mount," said I, "that is more didactic than figurative ; you must approve heartily of its teachings.''

"Yes," said he, "I do, and what is needed is that believers in your faith should live according to those teachings.''

"They do," I said ; "there are many, very many, whether you have met them or not, who are trying to live just as the New Testament teaches.

"Do you believe in God?" I continued, "a first great cause who created all things, a personal God?''

"I do not know. I can form no conception of God. I cannot give him form or shape.''

"God is a Spirit: he can have no shape or form.''

"Then how can I conceive of a Spirit?''

"But you can think of Christ as coming into the world, sent to save sinners.''

"Yes, but is he God? His character and life were most beautiful and his teachings were noble and grand. Even Renan, the French writer, could say all manner of beautiful things about his life and character and teachings, but I cannot conceive of a God such as Christians worship. After all, what is there beyond this life?''

"Does not Jesus most distinctly teach," I said, "that the soul is immortal?''

"If you take his teachings literally, yes," said he, "but I do not know whether they are to be taken literally. Besides, what is the soul?"

And then he went off into metaphysics where I could not follow him. He seemed to be familiar with Haegelism, Kantism, Darwinism, Spencerism, Huxleyism and all the other modern isms of which I have heard.

"Your philosophy is a sad one," said I, "if it gives you no hope of another and better life than this."

"Perhaps it is," he replied, "but I am not sure whether there can be another life."

"Have you no dread of death?"

"None whatever; in fact, it is a matter of indifference whether I live or die. I rather think I should prefer to die. What is there to live for? Before I left Oxford I started a night-school into which I had gathered twenty-six plain, poor people. I told them I would give them my time, but they must pay for the lights, fuel, etc., so I charged them two pence a week. Now I am called away to undertake some educational work in India. Why could I not remain and work with my Oxford people? What is life to me or to any one?"

So we talked from time to time as we sat or walked up and down the deck. I tried in my poor way to show him a better faith than he knew of.

Once as we talked he related the following incident: "I was at a company one evening at Oxford. There was music which I did not understand and could not enjoy, and the time was passing so heavily with me that I took up a book to amuse myself, when a young lady sat down at the piano and sang the following. And then he recited these words:

> Seated one day at an organ,
>   I was weary and ill at ease ;
> My fingers wandered idly
>   Over the noisy keys.

I know not what I was playing,
  Or what I was dreaming then;
But I struck one chord of music
  Like the sound of a grand Amen.

It flooded the crimson twilight
  Like the close of an angel's psalm;
It lay on my feverish spirit
  With the trust of an infinite calm;
It quieted pain and sorrow
  Like love overcoming strife;
It seemed the harmonious echo
  Of our discordant life.

It linked all perplexed meanings
  Into one universal peace,
Then trembled away into silence,
  As though it were loth to cease.

I have sought, and seek it vainly,
  That one lost chord divine
That came from the soul of the organ,
  And entered into mine—
It may be that death's bright angel
  Will speak in that chord again;
It may be that only in heaven
  I shall hear that glad Amen.

"While she was singing and as the song ended," he said, "my eyes fell upon a picture on the wall which I had not observed before. It was a head of the Christ crowned with thorns, and, although the eyes were really turned upward, they seemed to be fixed upon me. I could not escape their look, and twenty times that night I asked myself the question, 'What have you been doing with your life these twenty-three years? How have you been living? What good have you been doing to your fellow-men?'"

I was not familiar with the words of that song, though it is so well known in our country as well as in England, so I listened with great interest as he recited it from memory. I asked him to give me a copy, and he said he would write it for me when he went to his cabin.

"I am reminded," I said, "of one of our hymns," and I recited to him that beautiful but now somewhat neglected hymn of John Newton :

> In evil long I took delight,
>   Unawed by shame or fear,
> Till a new object met my sight,
>   And moved me to despair.
>
> I saw One hanging on a tree
>   In agony and blood,
> Who turned his failing sight on me,
>   As near his cross I stood.
>
> Sure, never till my latest breath
>   Can I forget that look ;
> It seemed to charge me with his death,
>   Though not a word he spoke.
>
> A second look he gave, which said,
>   "I freely all forgive ;
> This blood was for thy ransom shed ;
>   I die that thou mayst live."
>
> Thus while his death my sin displays
>   In all its blackest hue,
> Such is the mystery of grace,
>   It seals my pardon too.

The young man listened with fixed attention as I slowly recited that hymn. When it was finished he asked me for a copy, which of course I gave him. He was apparently much impressed.

It was the last day of the voyage and just before dark, the great sun having gone down into the sea. He and I were walking up and down the deck.

"To-morrow," I said, "we shall see Africa, and we shall part; you to go on your way to Calcutta and to your work there ; I to make a short visit to Egypt and Jerusalem, and then soon after to return to my native land and to my work ; but I shall never forget you, and the conversations we have had. You have told me much that I never knew, and that I wanted to know, especially about India, and also about yourself.''

" Yes," he said, "and I shall never forget you ; but may I show you my picture ?''

He went to his cabin and brought me, most carefully packed in cotton, a small framed oval photograph of one of Guido Reni's heads of Christ, crowned with thorns.

" This was given me," said he, "by the lady at Oxford who entertained me the evening I heard the song.

"When I get home," he added, "this picture will hang on the wall of my bed-room ; it will be the only picture in my room, and on the back I will copy your hymn :

I saw One hanging on a tree
In agony and blood.

XIV.

ATHENS AND ST. PAUL.*

"To describe Athens aright one should be an Athenian.
He should have long looked upon her soil with a feeling of
almost religious reverence. He should have regarded it as
ennobled by the deeds of illustrious men—his own ancestors.
The records of its early history should not be an object of
study, a science, but should have been familiar to him from
infancy. Nor should the period of its remote antiquity be
to him a land of shadows, a cave in which insubstantial
forms flit before his eyes as if he were in a dream. To such
an one the language of its Mythology should have been the
voice of Truth. The temples of Athens should not have
been to him, as to us, mere schools of art. They should not
have afforded materials only for his compass and pencil,
but for his affections and his religion. We see Athens in
ruins."

Most modern travellers approach the city from the east and
north on their way from Constantinople to Italy. The place
of landing now, as in St. Paul's day, is the Piræus, and the
tourist on leaving his ship lands probably where the great
Apostle landed; but instead of pushing his way on horse-
back or on foot, he steps into a railway carriage and is
whirled along over a plain, the undulations of which are
full of the ruins of the old time. At the railway station he
steps into a cab, as in any other city, and is driven over

---

* A Bible-class study, 1872.

roughly paved streets to a modern hotel, where he registers. his name as he would on going to one of our cities. That part of the city at present inhabited is built up of houses few of which are fifty years old. The total number of inhabitants is less than 25,000, one-half of whom, on any occasion of unusual interest, will be in the street at one time. The streets, with few exceptions, are narrow, crooked and filthy, and one must forget the present very much, if one would enjoy the history of the past. But there is a king's palace and a royal court, a nobility and an aristocracy, a small army and an inefficient police. The city has its streets of shops in which the curious may find many things to tempt them to purchase, with the result of sometimes carrying away, as specimens of a past age, articles made to look like antiques, but manufactured in the present day.

Athens is situated four or five miles from the sea-coast in the central plain of Attica. It is a wide plain enclosed by mountains, except on the south, where it is bounded by the sea. On the eastern and western sides of the city there run two small streams, both of which are nearly dried by the heats of summer and by the channels for artificial irrigation before they reach the sea; that on the east is the Ilissus; that on the west is the Cephissus.

In the midst of this plain rises a flat, oblong rock, the citadel of Athens, inaccessible on all sides except the west, on which it is approached by a steep slope. This is the Acropolis. Its flat summit is 1,000 feet long, east to west, and 500 feet broad, north to south. Here are the remains, multilated, of three temples; the Temple of Victory, the Parthenon, the Erechtheum. Of the Propylea, which was the western entrance or vestibule of the Acropolis, some walls and a few columns are still standing and its magnificent entrance has recently been cleared. Of its Agora, the public place where the citizens met to discuss their public affairs, all that is left is the fragment of a gate. Of the theatre on the south side of the Acropolis, where the plays of Eschylus, Sophocles and Euripides were represented, some stone steps remain, but all attempts to discover the remainder have been unsuccessful. Not a vestige survives of the courts in which Demosthenes pleaded. There is no trace of the Academic porches of Plato, or of the Lyceum of Aristotle. Only a few fragments of the long walls, which ran along the plain and united Athens with her harbors, are yet visible.

The traveller of our day, standing on the site of the ancient Acropolis of Athens and sweeping the horizon, would see something like this : Just outside of the city walls, or what were the ancient city walls, to the northeast, is Mount Lycabettus, the most striking feature in the immediate surroundings of the city. It is to Athens what Vesuvius is to Naples, or Arthur's Seat to Edinburgh, and seems almost to overhang the city, although a mile distant. Over the double-headed Lycabettus, and nine miles to the northeast, is Mount Pentelicus (so famous for its brilliant white marble, better than the Carrara marble of Italy, because entirely free from the metallic stains by which that is sometimes disfigured), its sides sprinkled over with the dwarf oak, the arbutus and the bay, but no large timber.

Three miles beyond Pentelicus is the plain of Marathon, on which was fought that battle which preserved the liberties of Greece, and perhaps of Europe, from the dominion of Persia. Between two marshes, with their backs to the sea and the declining sun of a September day shining full in their faces, 6400 Persians fell before the Athenian forces, with a loss of 192 men, and the famous battle of Marathon was fought and won. Due north from Athens, and at a distance of not more than eleven or twelve miles, is Mount Parnes, part of the chain which separates the Athenian plain from the Valley of Bœotia by a rocky limestone barrier from east to west. As the eye ranges to the west the vision is bounded by a mountain ridge of which the principal summit is Mount Aegaleos, and which stretches southward from Mount Parnes to the bay of Salamis, and then the eye rests on the sea with its islands and the distant mainland of Peloponnesus, and a little to the south of west the narrow peninsula connecting Attica with the Morea ; and just beyond the narrowest point of that peninsula, the towering height of the citadel of Corinth, the Acrocorinthus. To the south is the Saronic Gulf, with Salamis in the near distance, and farther off, and apparently anchored in the blue waves, the beautiful island of Egeria with its Temple of Minerva on the bold headland looking north.

Off to the southeast, and at a distance of twelve miles, is Mount Hymettus, famous for its hives of bees, which have survived all the storms which have swept cities and empires, and which fill the air with their hum of industry as they did 3000 years ago. On the side of this mount is a grotto, a natural cave ; you enter this by a descent of a few stone steps, from which opening the interior is dimly lighted. It is vaulted with fretted stone and the rocky roof is gracefully hung with stalactites. On the rock near the entrance are engraved some ancient inscriptions. One of these says the grotto was sacred to the Nymphs. Another refers to the sylvan Pan and the rural Graces as having a share in the same residence. Coming here from the magnificent fabrics of Athenian worship now lying in ruins in the city of Athens, this grotto, a natural temple on a solitary mountain, dedicated to natural deities, will be an object of profound interest. Here are no ruins. Here time has exerted no power. Sitting alone in the faint light of this cavern and looking on these inscriptions which declare the former sanctity of the place, and on the basins scooped in the rock from which the sacred libations were made, and the limpid well in the cave's recess from which water was supplied for those libations to the rural deities, and with no other objects about us to disturb the impressions which these produce, we might almost imagine that some shepherd of Attica had just left the spot, and that he would return before evening from his neighboring sheepfold on Hymettus with an offering to Pan from his flock, or with spoils of the mountain chase, or with the first flowers of the spring just peeped forth in his rural garden.

The surpassing beauty and clearness of the Athenian atmosphere has been noticed by all travellers ancient and modern. Nothing can exceed the transparent clearness, the brilliant coloring of an Athenian sky, or the flood of fire with which the marble columns, the mountains and the sea, are all bathed and penetrated by the illumination of an Athenian sunset. And yet, to an American who knows what a peculiarly clear, brilliant sky our northwest winds expose, and who looks up on a moonless night and sees the stars almost like sparkling steel, the sky and the atmosphere of Greece have a hazy, dreamy appearance, indescribably soft and delicious, but which the Englishman, so accustomed to fogs and storms and smoke, calls transparent.

An English writer has given us a picture of domestic life among the peasants. "The family consists of the mistress of the house and her two sons, who have now with them some visitors from the village. As we approach the doorway they are sitting down to supper and they invite us to enter. In a few minutes the members of the family have taken their seats on the clay floor around a low, round table, on which is a bowl of porridge to which each guest helps himself by dipping his bread into the bowl. The mistress of the house pours out the wine and hands it to the guests, who acknowledge the attention by complimentary speeches to herself and family, in the same spirit and character as Minerva does in the Odyssey to her hosts, Nestor and his son, on a similar occasion. When supper is over, the youngest son, a boy of twelve years, rises and turns his face to the wall of the cottage, and towards a sacred picture hanging upon it; he then takes off his red skull-cap, and standing before the picture begins to repeat some prayers in Greek, which he follows by a recital of the Creed, and concludes by frequent recitals of the Kyrie Eleison. These are the domestic vespers; a delightful sight, showing that four centuries of cruel bondage under the Turks have not quenched the sacred flame of piety in this much injured land."

"My first visit," says Dr. Robinson, "was to the Areopagus where Paul preached. This is a narrow, naked ridge of limestone rock rising gradually from the northern end, and terminating abruptly on the south over against the west end of the Acropolis, being separated from it by an elevated valley. The southern end is fifty or sixty feet above the valley, though yet much lower than the Acropolis. On its top are still to be seen the seats of the judges hewn in the rock, and towards the southwest is a descent by a flight of steps, also cut in the rock, into the valley below. On the west of the ridge, in the valley between it and the Pnyx, was the ancient market, and on the southeast side the new market. In which of these it was that 'Paul disputed daily' it is of course impossible to tell, but from either it was only a short distance to the foot of Mars Hill, up which Paul was probably conducted by the flight of steps just mentioned."

"The appearance of the Apostle before this august assembly," says another writer, "involved an exhibition of moral courage that has seldom been equalled, and perhaps never surpassed, in the history of our race. He was in the presence of statesmen, philosophers, orators and poets of the most intellectual and refined nation upon earth. He was there to humor no popular sect; to flatter no national vanity; to move upon no springs of ambition or future fame. He was there to unfold, to fortify, and rivet upon the judgment and conscience of his enlightened auditory, doctrines at variance with every previous conviction and present impulse ; doctrines totally subversive of that faith in which they were born, in which their fathers died, and which they wished to bequeath to their offspring.

"He had no splendid and imposing forms of worship or mythological mysteries to aid his arguments or conciliate the pride of his audience. He had no temples, statues, or altars to substitute for those which he would make desolate. He had no divinities peopling each hill and vale and grotto and fount, to take the places of those whom he disclaimed. He had only the pure abstract conception of the one supreme, holy, self-existing God, his universal providence, and man's final accountability. He delivered his message as one raised by his mighty theme above the frown or the commendation of his hearers. He was too clear and discriminating for the subtle sneer ; too earnest and impressive for the skeptical jest, and too cogent and massive in thought for the verbal evasion ; and though no corresponding results were immediately obvious, we cannot doubt that convictions were planted there which struck at length into the very heart of Greece, and which finally enthroned the one only and true God upon the affections and allegiance of the nation."

Many entire volumes and innumerable single discourses have been written to analyze and illustrate this most remarkable sermon of St. Paul. Perhaps an analysis as simple and natural as is needed, especially for our purpose, is the following, the divisions of which, for the sake of convenience, will be stated numerically, as follows :

1. That there is one God.
2. That he dwells not in temples.
3. That the world was not only made but is sustained by him.
4. That all mankind are of one blood.
5. That God has sent his Son Jesus to redeem mankind.

6. That he has raised Jesus from the dead as an earnest of future life.

7. That all men must be judged at the last day.

Before Paul, as he stood on Mars Hill, was the Acropolis, adorned with numerous works of art ; beneath was the magnificent temple of Theseus ; around him were numerous temples, altars, and images of the gods ; facing him, his critical audience. The whole course of the Apostle's oration was regulated by his own peculiar prudence. He was brought into a position where he might easily have been ensnared into the use of words which would have brought down upon him the indignation of all the city. Had he begun by attacking their national gods in the midst of their sanctuaries, and with the Areopagites on the seats near him, he would have been in almost as great danger as Socrates was before him. He not only avoided the snare, but used the very difficulties of his position to make a road to the convictions of those who heard him. He did not say that he was introducing new divinities. He employed the familiar objects of Athenian life to tell them of what was close to them, and yet they knew it not. He had carefully observed the outward appearance of the city. He had seen an altar with an expressive but humiliating inscription ; using this inscription as a text, he spoke the words of Eternal Wisdom— a speech distinguished for clearness, brevity, coherence, and simplicity of representation. We will now consider its statements in detail.

He introduced his subject, not with rude and insulting contempt, but by acknowledging and commending the respect of the Athenians for religion. This was highly conciliatory. There was indeed in his words a very deep and penetrating rebuke, but he did not (like some who profess to be his followers) expect to succeed by affronting his audience. In his opening sentence he declared that he recognized in Athens a very diligent attention to religion. This was un-

doubtedly the character of the place. Josephus says the
Athenians were the most religious of all the Greeks. Paul,
though gracefully stating what is true in this respect, and
thus winning a friendly attention, did not in the least degree
go beyond the truth in any commendation of the quality of
this religion. His aim was to show its hollowness and weakness, and this he did by means of the very illustration he
took of the peculiar religiousness of the Athenians. In
using the word "devotions" he meant to refer to everything
connected with the worship of their gods—rites, ceremonies,
temples, images and altars ; adding, that among these many
altars he had found one with the inscription, "To the Unknown God." One Greek writer says : "It is more discreet
to speak well of all the gods, and especially at Athens, where
are erected altars also to unknown gods." Some light is
thrown upon the origin of these altars by the statement of
Diogenes Laertius, that when Epimenides was brought from
Crete to stay a plague at Athens, he directed white and black
sheep to be driven from the Areopagus, and that where they
first lay down new altars should be built to the appropriate
god, i. e., to the divinity by whom the plague had been in-
flicted, and by appeasing whom, it was to be removed. The
practice thus established or exemplified of trying to propiti-
ate an offended deity, without even knowing who it was,
agrees with the statement of other writers that there were
altars to anonymous or unknown gods.

Some think these altars were so ancient that it was at
length forgotten to whom they were built ; others, that they
express the distinct consciousness by the Athenians, of the
limitations and imperfections of their religious views, and
their consequent desire to avoid the danger of not acknowledging gods who might be unknown to them. But of all the
conjectures on the contested point of the altar "to the Unknown God," the most ingenious and natural is this : There
were very ancient altars, older perhaps than the art of writ-

ing, or from which the inscriptions had been effaced by time ; on these the piety of later ages has engraven the simple words, "To the Unknown God."

"Whom therefore ye ignorantly worship, him declare I unto you," said Paul ; adding, that this God needed no temple made with hands ; pointing, as it were, from the Areopagus to the Acropolis above him, with its Propylea and Parthenon, and the spear and shield of Minerva gleaming in the sun. Thus he refuted the error of Judaism, that the Deity could be confined or unchangeably attached to any earthly residence.

This truth, which he now declared, he had heard and disputed, when, as Saul, he stood among the persecutors of Stephen, "consenting to his death." Now he was ready to declare not that truth only, but God's entire independence of all human care and service as essential to his blessedness and glory. He was not a God to be worshipped "with men's hands." Furthermore, he was the creator of all mankind, notwithstanding their separation into so many nations, and their wide dispersion on the earth. Now the Athenians prided themselves on being distinct from other races, and the offspring of their own soil ; they were not likely to be pleased with this assertion, neither were they ready to believe that in assigning to the nations their respective abodes, God had fixed both the seasons of their prosperity, and the limitations of their territory, i. e., that he had decided when and how long they should flourish, and how far their dominion should extend ; nor that all that power exerted in giving existence to men, controlling their destiny, exalting nations, or casting them down, which they had parcelled out among such an infinity of gods, must be concentrated in a single possessor ; they could not grasp the idea of one infinite creator and ruler. In endeavoring to bring this vast conception before the minds of his hearers, the apostle realized their difficulty in accepting it, and is reminded of the blind who

6

grope in their darkness. He says they should seek this God, "if haply they may feel after him and find him near," adding, "for in him we live and move and have our being, as certain of your own poets* have said." "We also are his offspring." This is a proof of Paul's knowledge of the classics. The celebrated hymn of Cleanthes to Jupiter contains almost the same words.

There is doubtless much mystery here which we shall never be able fully to understand till the whole plan of salvation is brought to its conclusion ; but this at least is evident—in the varied distribution of nations, and in the circumstances under which they have successfully risen and decayed, the experiment has been fully tried as to what man can do in the matter of religion without supernatural help. The result has been universal failure.

The conclusion now drawn by the apostle, and to which he wished his hearers to arrive, is that idolatry is supremely absurd, making that which is destitute of life, motion and intelligence the source of these to others. He softened his rebuke, however, by saying that they had held these views in ignorance ; but having heard the truth they must believe and repent, because God so commanded, and because of the judgment to come. Ignorance of the nature of God and of his just claims during the whole of the preceding ages, or the past history of the Gentile world, was not excusable, but must be repented of. God had "winked at," that is, overlooked, suffered, or endured it, without declaring his disapprobation ; counted not this ignorance itself as a sin, but the abuse of it, by which the heathen sank into deeper degradation. The same argument is found in Romans, first and second chapters. Ignorance is an excuse for sin only so far as it is not blameworthy, and no farther. The civil law in our

---

* Referring to Aratus, a poet of Cilicia, who flourished 270 B. C.

day makes no allowance for ignorance. All people are supposed to be acquainted with the laws.

Paul insisted upon a repentance so broad that it included all men everywhere. It is most interesting to observe how firm and fearless is the ground which he took. He spoke of the call to repentance as a command, and set forth the majesty of Jesus Christ as requiring absolute submission; adding, that proof had been provided for the claims of this announcement in that this Judge and Saviour had been raised from the dead. By him the whole world would be judged, and righteously. Here was a direct appeal to the consciousness of sin and the fear of death. Each individual was reminded of his own responsibility and made aware of his relation to the Unknown God; and the "man" spoken of, by whom personally the just judgment was to be made, was the man Christ Jesus. That his hearers might know beyond doubt to whom he referred, Paul described him as having been raised from the dead.

How much the apostle intended to represent as proved by the resurrection of Christ we do not know exactly; but certainly his divine character and mission, and also the truth of all his claims; markedly, his claim to be a Judge.* When Paul began to speak of the resurrection of the dead he was interrupted by his audience. This belief was not only no part of the Greek creed, either philosophical or popular, but was positively repudiated as a gross absurdity; for the resurrection explicitly declared that another life was to be preferred to the present; another life too, on the threshold of which a judgment was to be encountered. Now to the Athenian the present life was everything.

The closing solemn words of this address were recieved by some with derision, by others with indifference, and by others still, were put off for consideration at a more convenient season.

---

* St. John v. 27, 28, 29.

Having delivered his message with all the force of his convictions and strong nature, he "departed from among them," leaving the assembly, though he does not seem to have been driven away by any tumult or persecution. It is supposed by some that he spent not more than a fortnight in the city.

Notwithstanding the apparent ill success of his labors, they were not without fruit, for "certain men clave unto him and believed." This implies a sacrifice and great effort on their part : as when one clings to a rope or mast in the sea as the only safety, they adhered to him in the face of ridicule and opposition, believing his doctrines and accepting the Christ whom he preached as their Redeemer. Among these converts was Dionyseus, an Areopagite, one of the judges of the court. This is all we know of him certainly, though there are many traditions. He is said to have been the first Bishop of Athens ; also to have suffered martyrdom in that city. Of Damaris we know nothing beyond her name and the fact of her conversion. She was probably a woman of some distinction and the only female convert, therefore mentioned with Dionyseus, the most distinguished male convert.

It is not to be wondered at, that, so long as the apostle preached natural religion, they listened with some degree of patience, wondering possibly what he would be at, what turn he would give to the subject. And we need not be surprised that when he came, in his application, to speak of Jesus and his resurrection from the dead, some ridiculed the whole subject and, mocking him, turned away. To them it was "foolishness," as the apostle says in another place. There were others who said, "We will hear thee again of this matter ;" but whether that was with a sneer or with a desire to hear more we do not know.

We cannot help but regret that Paul should have been interrupted in this sermon. We wonder what he would have said further on such a subject, and to such an audience.

The meaning is somewhat obscured in our version by the use of the addition, "whereof;" the statement, "whereof he hath given assurance unto all men, in that he hath raised him from the dead," being apt to lead the reader to suppose that he means to adduce our Lord's resurrection as affording some evidence that God will, on a certain day, judge the world in righteousness by that Man whom he has appointed. But this does not convey the proper meaning of the apostle's words. What he intends is, that God has furnished to all men sufficient ground for believing in Jesus by having raised him from the dead; in other words, that having raised him from the dead, God has thereby fully accredited him to be all that he claims to be; so that men may, on the most solid grounds, have faith in him as the future Judge of all.

One word in conclusion. If this Jesus is to be our Judge finally, and if our everlasting condition is to be determined by the manner in which we treat him in this life, how infinitely important is it to all of us to be at peace with him now, to love him, to honor him, and to give ourselves to his service.

XV.

THE REVEREND DR. MOSES LAW.

IT is a night in Christmas week. The Library is dressed in green. Festoons of green vines are hanging from the mantle clock, the upper book shelves, the armour, and the chandeliers. The polished green leaves and brilliant red berries of the holly and the white pearls of the mistletoe gleam in the blazing fire-light, and the whole room is filled with the odor of Christmas.

I am sitting in my arm-chair and looking at the fire, which is blazing and roaring up the wide chimney. I am thinking of the Christmas times of my boyhood, in my country home. I seem to see the forms and faces of the loved ones, parents and brothers and sisters, that made my childhood and youth so happy. I recall the lines that I loved so well because they described so truly the life of my early home :

> "Scenes of the good old time—the past,
>   How fast ye lighten on mine eye ;
> As twilight stars come out at last
>   To one who gazes on the sky.
> ·Touch but the light and secret spring
>   That guards those treasures of the soul,
> And back like breezes on the wing
>   The earliest years of memory roll :
> They sweep the spirit's inmost chords,
>   Perhaps for weary years unstrung,
> Awakening thoughts too deep for tears,
>   That make the sad and aged young.
> The Christmas fire ! I seem to gaze
>   Upon its deep and radiant red :

And round the trumpet sounding blaze
  I see the evening circle spread.
Though storms are rushing through the heaven,
  They cannot chill the joyous flow
Of young affections, warmly given
  To hearts, that answer all their glow.
But when the voice of mirth subsides,
  They talk of darkness and its powers,
Of some mysterious form that glides
  In silence through the haunted towers.
And thus with many a fearful tale
  They while away the night,
Till every youthful cheek grows pale,
  With terror and delight."

So I am dreaming, with my eyes wide open—living over again for an hour, the days of my youth—when a card is brought in, on which is the name of Mr. Moses Law, Brainfull, Vermont. Directing the servant to show him in, I will, while my visitor is removing his wraps in the hall, tell you who Dr. Law is. His card is very modest, but he is a Clergyman, a Doctor of Divinity, of distinction, whom I have seen little of for some years, although a good while ago I was quite intimate with him. He is a gentleman of the old school, holding very clear views of religious doctrines, or dogmas, and not at all afraid to express them.

As he enters the room, I step forward and give him a cordial greeting. Approaching the fire and rubbing his hands from the cold, he is the picture of a robust manhood, a muscular Christian. Presently he takes a chair, and we begin to talk. Whether it is the sight of the Christmas greens with which the Library is dressed, or whether it is the evident signs of a joyous season that meet his eyes everywhere, or whether it is that he sees a brass Lectern in the alcove with a very old Church of England folio prayer book on it, I don't know,—but certainly there is an unusual positiveness in his manner and sternness in his voice as he says, somewhat abruptly,

"We pastors who do not observe Christmas and Easter in our churches are naturally and properly asked the reason why?"

"And doubtless," I say, "you are 'naturally and properly' annoyed at the question, and not a little puzzled to give a satisfactory reply."

Without noticing my repetition of his words, he says very promptly and positively,

"We may answer in brief that, festive gatherings and gifts of kindred, that promote filial affection, elevate, sweeten and sanctify home life, are grateful to God and man ; but the stated observance by the church of days not authorized by Scripture, does not receive blessing from God."

"If," I say, "'festive gatherings and gifts of kindred' really 'promote filial affection' and 'elevate, sweeten and sanctify home life,' how are these gracious, kindly influences weakened or hindered by the reading of appropriate Scriptures, and the singing of proper hymns, and the offering of appropriate prayers in the family at Christmas and Easter? You say there is no authority of Scripture for such services. If, however, they are allowable in the family without Scripture authority, what right have you to say that such observances in the church 'do not receive blessing from God?'"

"But," he goes on, "our Puritan and Pilgrim forefathers, observing the unhallowed influence of such institutions, and jealous of any religious worship not instituted by God himself, abolished such unblest days of Papal and Pagan origin."

"Please say when and where 'our Puritan and Pilgrim forefathers observed the unhallowed influence of such institutions' as Christmas and Easter, and abolished them. And if the doings of these worthy men are to be quoted as authority for our doing or not doing certain things now, what do you say of their Sabbath services in their meeting-houses, when conducted without reading the Scriptures, except certain verses in the course of the sermon as illustrating the subject? What do you say of their wooden meeting-houses—their board seats often without backs—their want of carpets—their insufficient warmth—their clear glass windows—their gathering about the door of the meeting-house in summer time and discoursing on secular subjects, going in only after the singing had begun?"

Utterly ignoring my rejoinders, he proceeds:

"Easter, wholly unauthorized by the New Testament, was imported from Paganism, when the church began to be corrupted, in order to please half-hearted Pagan converts."

"Whatever may be said of the 25th day of December," I say, "as the day of the birth of Jesus, it is very certain that he was crucified at the time of the Jewish Passover, and this is about the time that the Christian Church observes with more or less ceremony the Easter season. Does it seem to you," I add, growing earnest, "that putting flowers in the churches and Sunday-schools, and reading the chapters in the New Testament which refer to our Lord's resurrection, and singing appropriate hymns, etc., indicate corruption in the church or a lack of spiritual life?"

But he goes on just as if he were lecturing his own people from the pulpit, or teaching a class where the members were not expected to answer him, and were afraid to ask him questions:

"The Lord's day is the only day to be observed by divine authority, and this celebrates the resurrection of Christ fifty-two times a year."

"Ah, but do the preachers of your church as a rule make any but the slightest possible reference to the great fact of the resurrection fifty-two times in a year? Do they select their scriptural lessons and their hymns, or do they construct their prayers and their sermons 'fifty-two times a year' to keep before their congregations the supreme fact of the resurrection? The answer is 'No;' and there is no force

whatever in your statement.   There is neither novelty nor
fairness in your remark.''

"God's Spirit and providence," he continues, "may lead
to a special series of gospel services with great blessing, but
when the church assumes authority to establish such periods
as Lent or even the Week of Prayer, they are apt to be
characterized by powerless formality, and preceded and
succeeded by evil excesses that overbalance the good in
them.''

" May it not be," I inquire, "that 'God's Spirit and providence' have led the church to have special religious services
at Easter and Christmas ? If not, what was the thought that
suggested these observances?   And if our week of prayer
is right in itself, why not observe it in the season of Lent,
when the hearts of so many Christians are on serious subjects,
rather than about the 1st of January, when business men at
least in cities are so absorbed in their secular duties ?

" Have you good reason, my dear friend," I continue, " for
believing or saying that 'even the week of prayer is apt to
be characterized by powerless formality, and preceded and
succeeded by evil excesses that overbalance the good in
it?'   If this is your experience in Brainfull, alas for that
town !''

Without in the least noticing my rejoinders or my pointed
questions, with the indifference of Poe's "Raven " he goes
on to say :

" The imitation churches, that shun penance, Lent, and
Good Friday, and observe Easter, present to Rome a shrewd
absurdity, and to the world a mere musical entertainment in
which there is no saving or spiritual blessing.''

" What do you mean by ' imitation churches ?' The phrase
is new and requires explanation.   And what is a 'shrewd
absurdity ?'   Can anything that is absurd be shrewd ? And
is ' Rome' a court in Banc to which church observances are
' presented' for approval or condemnation ? Consider, my

good friend, have you a choir in your church that sometimes 'entertains' your congregation with music that has no saving or spiritual blessing? If you have not, you are to be congratulated."

He continues, however, not looking at me, not caring for me, not hearing me indeed, like the river of which Bryant writes—

"Where rolls the Oregon and hears no sound
　　Save his own dashing."

"Christ was not born on December 25th, and the observance of that day with an Advent reference is a fiction like that of Santa Claus."

"If you can prove what you so positively assert, that Christ was not born on December 25th, you will greatly oblige many persons by doing so. Many discussions have been made on this point, many more probably will be, but if you have knowledge for it let me have it, let the world have it, and let one thing at least be settled. If you can't prove your statement, it is your duty to withdraw it, if you have said so elsewhere, and apologize for it."

If I had supposed that my earnest friend, now thoroughly warmed by my good fire, and by his own fiery zeal, will pause a moment to listen to me, after my rather sharp words of advice, I am mistaken, for with the precision and regularity, if not the weight, of a trip-hammer, he goes on to say :

"If God had desired the nativity of his Son to be celebrated, he would have so appointed, or at least informed us of the day of his birth."

"Did our Lord," I say, "desire his disciples to commemorate his death ? If so, why has he not informed us of the day of his death ? Whenever we choose we may commemorate it. The Scotch Church does it once a year, the English Church every day, other churches at their convenience ; who shall find fault with any others who differ ? If you and

I choose the 25th day of December on which to celebrate the birth of our Lord, who has a right to question our judgment or piety?"

My friend has no answer to these questions, or else he is withholding it until he has completed his statements, when he can turn his guns which he has been firing in the air towards me as a target. So I wait a moment, when he breaks out in these extraordinary words :

"The celebration of the birth of Christ by the 'world' that rejected and crucified him, and that will cry out for rocks and mountains to hide them from his face when he comes again, is a solemn mockery."

"Oh, my dear friend, do you really mean what you say? Is it a 'solemn mockery' to close our places of business, our schools, our courts, our legislatures, and gather our families together in reunion, and exchange presents, and remember the poor and the sick, and send them help, because we do so on Christmas day? And may not some heart, that has heretofore been hard and insensible to the love of Christ, be led by the good thoughts that prevail at Christmas time, to reconsider the claims of the Great Redeemer and give itself to his service? Do you consider it solemn mockery for the 'world,' i. e., irreligious people, to pay pew rents in the church, or otherwise support the ministry?"

The fire is burning low, and the room is getting in deep shadows, and there is an increasingly hard and stern expression on his face as he grimly says:

"The persons most devoted to the ecclesiastical observance of this day are not usually most devoted to the person of the Redeemer, and the separated, cross-bearing and consecrated life which he lived."

"Dr. Law, have you really considered this statement? Do you think that members of other branches of the church, who do not observe Christmas and Easter, are 'more devoted to the person of the Redeemer' than the Episcopalians, Moravians and Methodists? What class of religionists is it that labors most effectively in the slums of London and New York? Is it those who care nothing for Christmas and Easter? You must know that it is not. That work, so unattractive to the carnal mind, is done very largely by Episcopalians and Methodists."

I think my friend is inclined to pause and reconsider the sternness with which he is expressing himself, but he is only girding himself for his final charge:

"The general influence of the day," he says, "accords with its Saturnalian origin, in its heart-sickening excesses of drunkenness, debauchery, vice and crime. For this, see the daily papers after Christmas." '

"That is hardly fair," I remark, "for see the daily papers every Monday also! But does this prove that the influence of the Sabbath is bad? If your illustration proves anything, it proves too much."

Now comes his last gun, and he evidently intends it to close ·the conversation, for he loads it with Scripture:

"Let us therefore, of the 'reformed churches,' stand fast in the liberty wherewith Christ hath made us free, and be not entangled again with the yoke of bondage. Gal. v. 1."

"No," I say, thoroughly aroused myself by this time, "No, let those whose hearts are in the condition·of harsh illiberality, of self-righteous assurance, of cold, sneering criticism ; who can see but one side of a subject, and that the narrow side; who are not in sympathy with the infinite tenderness of Him who came to save that which was lost;— let such be ashamed of themselves, and go and repent of their ill nature, their jealousy, their ignorance.of true Christianity. If we are not to observe times and seasons, nor to adopt methods of Christian life and activity and forms of worship, except such as are especially and minutely enjoined in the

Scriptures, we shall find that we lack warrant for many usages, entirely proper, which are so common, that we never think of asking how we came by them.''

My visitor rises at this last rejoinder, and prepares to take his leave. He seems not quite satisfied with the discussion, although he has had full opportunity to say all that he was inclined to say. There may have been something in the tone and manner of my last observation that troubles him. In recalling the words, I am not quite sure that I held myself as much under control as is my habit, more especially as Dr. Law is my guest. But he takes my offered hand at parting, and with a softened and saddened voice expresses the hope that when we meet again we may see things a little more in the same light than we have in this visit; and then he goes out into the darkness.

XVI.

On the Improvement of Church Services.*

I have accepted the invitation to speak to you, with which you have honored me, not without some misgivings, for I have been told that I would be expected, whatever my subject should be, to say something which would provoke discussion. The subject which I have chosen, The Enrichment and Improvement of our Public Services, will, I trust, provoke nothing but kindly discussion, for I shall aim to treat it in a frank and kindly manner, so as not to give offence to any one. In the necessary references which I may make to other branches of the Church, I hope I shall say nothing which would wound or disturb any one outside of our own communion.

I am a Presbyterian, not by birth or education, but from choice ; a choice made fifty years ago, and not regretted. I have never, however, felt it necessary to believe that the polity of the Presbyterian Church is unmistakably outlined in the New Testament, nor do I believe this of any other of the numerous families into which the Church of Christ is divided. There is no special form of Church government which can justly claim to be of divine right. Our Lord did not come to establish an organization.

The Presbyterian Church has a form of government which is venerable and admirable, and more largely in sympathy with the government of our country than that of any other

* An Address before the Presbyterian Social Union, Philadelphia, March 28, 1892.

branch of the Church.   The modifications which have been made in this government are very slight, not affecting the great principles which gave our Church its name, and our people, generally, are content to retain it as it is, although there are some who think it might be improved.

There are, however, many members of our Church, who, while accepting the government and desiring nothing better, are not satisfied with everything else belonging to the Church. Such persons find it difficult, if not impossible, to believe that the statements of doctrine, made some 300 years ago, are such as would be made *now* if the Standards were to be rewritten, nor that certain so-called "proof texts," still printed in our Standards, would be chosen for such purposes under the light of modern scholarship and interpretation.

Some persons of this class go so far as to say that the Scriptures read in the public worship of the Church should be read from the Revised Version, as being the "most approved version" of the Holy Scriptures.   They contend that the company of revisers, who have given the Church at large the best result of their labors, were better qualified to do the work than those who did it in King James' time, and that as there can be no royal authority in this country to impose this version on the churches, the Presbyterian Church in America should adopt it and enjoin its use; or, if this is too much to hope for, that any pastor may have leave to use the Revised Version at his pleasure, without prejudice to his standing with the Presbytery.   He would be accounted a brave or bold pastor who would at this time banish King James' Version from the pulpit and read exclusively from the Revised Version.

Further, there are many persons in our Church who are not satisfied with the forms of worship which prevail among us.   They are aware that certain concessions have been made from the very simple forms used a generation ago, and that no bad effects have followed, and they do not see why other changes may not be adopted, which would not weaken the hold Presbyterianism has now on the Church and the world, but which would add very much to the value and attractiveness of its services.

"The Directory for the Worship of God in the Presbyterian Church in the United States of America," as amended and ratified by the General Assembly in May,.1821, is very explicit in its recommendations. The people are enjoined to take their seats in church decently, gravely, and reverently; during the worship to avoid all whisperings, salutations, sleeping, and smiling. The minister is to read such portions and so much of the Holy Scriptures as he may see proper, and expound any part of what is read. Christians are charged to sing psalms and hymns, and advised to cultivate knowledge of the rules of music. It is suggested as proper to begin the services with a short prayer of adoration, of the expression of humility, of petition for the presence and assistance of the Holy Spirit in the worship, and acceptance through the merits of Christ. Then, after a psalm or hymn, there should be a full and comprehensive prayer of adoration, thanksgiving, confession, supplication, pleading (which may mean importunity), and intercession. After the sermon should be a prayer in relation to the subject which has been treated of in the discourse. After the prayer a psalm, then a collection, and then the Assembly is to be dismissed with the Apostolic benediction.

Such is the Directory for our Public Worship, which the framers suggest gives opportunity for such compass and variety as the officiating pastor may choose to employ. And probably for many generations this form of service was substantially observed in our churches.

In some of our congregations now, the first act in the service on Sunday is the singing of a doxology, followed by the prayer of invocation, and then the reading of sentences from the Scriptures ; then a hymn ; then the Scripture lesson ;

7

another hymn ; a prayer ; reading of notices, like Ezekiel's bones, very many and very dry, often of things which are duly advertised in the daily papers ; another prayer, a hymn, another doxology, the benediction, and then instantly a rush for hats and canes, overcoats having been put on during the singing of the final doxology. How readily we have fallen into these customs !

We no longer stand while we pray, nor sit while we sing, as did our forefathers, nor are we reproached for imitating other churches in these respects.

It seems, therefore, that in many matters connected with our Church, both inwardly and outwardly, we have departed somewhat from the ways of our forefathers, and are apparently none the worse for it.

Shall we stop here? Is it not our duty to make our churches and our church services as attractive as possible, provided we do not give up our polity, our doctrines, and our Scriptural worship? The Presbyterian Church has a splendid history. Her singular devotion to the Scriptures, her jealous care that her ministers should be educated men, her battles in argument, and with the sword in the old times, for the pure Word and for free civil government, the purity of her ministry, the high character of her eldership, her grand contributions to religious literature, the high average of intelligence of her members, her generous benefactions, all these present a magnificent record, and have made impressions deep and enduring on the mind and heart of our wide country. If our Church does not include the larger proportion of the wealthy and fashionable in our great cities, this is not to be regretted, but it is behind no other branch of the Church in the intellectual quality of its adherents. A census of our law courts all over the land, as to their ecclesiastical relations, would probably disclose the fact that more judges come from the Presbyterian than from any other Church.

But is the Presbyterian Church at its best? Is it as aggres-

sive, as efficient, as popular as it can be made? Is it taking
that hold on all classes of society that it might do and ought
to do? Is it making the progress that the Methodist and
Baptist churches are making? In short, is it what it ought
to be?

I venture to say that our church is not at its best, that it is
not doing all that it might do, and that there is nothing, except unwillingness to consider and appreciate the greatness
of the work, and unreasonable prejudice, to hinder a progress
that would otherwise be irresistible. Much might be said
of the development of power among the intelligent laity
outside of the eldership, and our church Sessions could
hardly address themselves to a more important topic for consideration, but my purpose now is to make a few suggestions
concerning the improvement and enrichment of our church
services on Sunday.

1. Let two lessons, one from the Old Testament, one from
the New, not necessarily entire chapters, be read at each
service. Consider how many people there are in all congregations who are deplorably ignorant of the Scriptures.
They will not read at home, and to many of them this is
their only opportunity. Encourage also the placing of Bibles in the pews, for the use of all occupants, resident or
strangers.

2. Let the hymns be selected more generally for their lyrical qualities and for their high poetic character and their expressions of praise, than simply because they suit the subject
of the discourse. The latter quality is not to be disregarded,
but it should not be the first consideration. The greatest
of all hymnists was probably Isaac Watts, but it is by no
means true that all his hymns are lyrics. Much the same
may be said of the hymns of the Wesleys. Some one has
said that there are only about 300 English hymns that are
worth singing, but there are ten times as many that are excellent for reading. Our congregations should have the very

best collections of hymns and tunes that can be made, and
if our present Hymnal does not answer these conditions, it
having been made many years ago, let not the Board continue to publish it because it is pecuniarily profitable, but
let it be put aside and get or make a better one—the best
one.   The value of good hymns and music as a part of public
worship, either as expressive or impressive, is incalculable.
Let the minister refrain from reading the hymns unless he
is an expert as a reader of poetry, and let the organist refrain from playing more than one line of the tune, and have
no interludes, and let the people join heartily, but not too
loudly, in the singing, and, generally, let the hymn be
sung without mutilation, the people always standing.

But our people, especially our young people, now want
more music than the three or four appointed hymns. Something answering to the Anthem of the English Cathedral Service is required. This has led to the introduction of the
"quartette choir," and where the cost is not too great, of a
"double quartette." Of course none but accomplished musicians with superior voices will be accepted for such service.
And it follows surely that such choirs will not be satisfied
with one anthem ; there must be at least two. And the
music selected must be such as to display to the best advantage the admirable voices of the quartette, in solo or duet,
whether it be the most appropriate music for the time and
place or not. I know that I am on delicate ground. I
may be told that I am no musician, that I do not understand
the subject ; but I do know that I have heard much of the
best church music in the world, whether in the English or
the Latin churches. I know that rarely, if ever, in them is
the "ear pained and the soul made sick" by the straining
of voices and the screaming which we have heard at times
from the choirs of Presbyterian churches.

Why cannot we have the Psalms and passages from the
Prophets chanted more frequently, such as the musicians

of the latter part of the last century and the earlier part of the present have embalmed in their heavenly music? Our German music, like our German theology, is not always orthodox. I venture to say that in the English cathedrals, where more study is given to the subject of church music, and more money spent on it than we can possibly give, where the anthems are always announced by name or by the first line, always easily found in the book ; the worshipper is never startled, or disturbed, or distressed by sounds inappropriate in the Lord's house.

This means, however, that the musicians employed to lead us in the devotional part of our Church services ought always to be people of pronounced Christian character, profoundly in sympathy with the service of· song. If church Sessions would take the trouble to inquire, it would be found that in many congregations much harm is done by employing mechanical organists, who are not in sympathy with true church music. We insist that he who leads the devotions of a congregation in *prayer* shall be a godly man. On what principle do church Sessions employ men and women to lead congregations in their hymns of praise, without knowing or caring whether they are even professors of religion, to say nothing of their special fitness for their work ?

3. At some convenient place in the service let a selection from the Psalms be read responsively, not verse and verse about, which is so contrary to the structure and purpose of the Psalms, but "line and line about," according to the parallelisms of the Hebrew original and the usage, in the Temple service. I say *selections* from the Psalms, for all the Psalms are not to be sung or said ; some are better read as lessons. The real characteristics of the Psalms are that they are responsive and antiphonal as well. An effort was made to get our General Assembly at a recent meeting to pronounce against this usage of the Psalms, which has been

adopted in some congregations, but the Assembly declined
to commit that folly.

Can any fair or reasonable objection be urged against the
reading of the Psalms and other devotional Scriptures by the
minister and people responsively? On the contrary, the advantages resulting from such regular and frequent use of
the Psalms, are incalculable. It would be vastly better if we
could chant them, as is so common in the Church of Scotland, but this can be done successfully only after much cultivation. No doubt, however, that we shall attain to it in
time. What we want *now*, and what we can do *now*, is to
read them responsively. But do not allow, as is so common
in Sunday-schools, the reading of undevotional and unpoeti-
cal Scriptures responsively.

"Almost any book might be spared out of the Old Testament Scriptures rather than the Psalms. The Bible as
a religious book would be most incomplete without it, for
in a complete religious book must be not only revelation,
but the response to revelation. And the response is no
whit less inspired and sacred than the revelation is. We
know from whom the inspiration of true worship comes.
The prayer and praise which go up to God from hearts
that worship Him in spirit and in truth, first came down
from Him. And the worship which 'is written in the
book of Psalms,' because it was real worship out of honest
hearts, that meant it when they uttered it; that prayed
because they needed to, and sung because for their religious joy they could not *but* sing; was doubtless prompted
by the presence of the Holiest within them, kindled by the
breath of God, illumined by His light, and quickened by
His life. The Psalms are *real* prayers and *real* praises, most
intensely *real*, and therefore verily inspired. The men who
uttered them and wrote them felt what they said and meant
it heartily. They cried out for help because they must have
help, because if help were not forthcoming they must perish.

They sung praises and gave thanks because their hearts were full, and they could not restrain expression."

Said I not rightly, therefore, that the frequent and regular use of the Psalms would be of incalculable advantage to the Church? This is quite within our reach.

4. Let more attention be given to the matter of public prayer. Can any person give a good reason why so much thought and labor should be given to the preparation of the sermon and so little to the prayers? Let any pastor state frankly how many hours in the week he gives to writing or studying his two sermons for Sunday, and how many to the preparation of his six prayers for the same services, and let him give his reasons for the same. Few pastors, probably, would object to have an accurate stenographic report of their sermons published in Monday's newspapers, but would they read and would their congregations read with the same satisfaction a verbatim report of all the *prayers* they uttered?

We ought not to expect too much from our young pastors in the matter of public prayer. Consider, the prayers should be common prayers, *i. e.*, the confession should be of common sins, the praise should be for common mercies; the adoration should be for considerations which are common to all; and the language employed to express these and other sentiments of worship should be such as can be adopted by all the congregation. The people under some so-called prayers are put in the position of hearers, not worshippers.

Now take a young man just graduated from one of our seminaries, who has a dozen or so sermons ahead. Install him over a congregation in a city or country town in which are a judge or two, a general, a colonel, three or four lawyers, two or three physicians, half a dozen merchants, as many teachers, in short, a congregation with one or two score of educated, thoughtful people, who read the best literature, and who form cultivated society, and require him to preach two sermons and extemporize six prayers every Sunday, and to vary them all, so that no two of these services shall be exactly alike, are you not imposing an intolerable burden upon him?

For a time, and while their sympathies are moved towards their young brother, the people will bear patiently with his crude discussions of religious truth, being written, but will they as patiently listen to his more crude, because unwritten and unstudied, prayers? For they *must listen;* they can hardly make such prayers their own, because of their incoherence; their perpetual repetitions of the name of God; their didactic and sermonizing character; their unconnected and inappropriate quotations of Scripture; their want of solemnity, beauty, and devotion; their too common violations of syntax; and for other qualities which are in no way devotional.*

"Consider how rare is a really finished master of speech,

---

* This is the " prayer " offered by the chaplain of one of our Legislatures when the cable announced the death of the eldest son of the Prince of Wales and the death of Cardinal Manning.

"Oh, adorable God, the heavy news comes from across the sea that the heir presumptive of the British crown is dead, and that the homes of an empire on which the sun never sets are shrouded in mourning. Hear our devout and earnest prayer for that most illustrious and gracious lady, the sovereign Queen Victoria, whose reign has been a benediction to the world; the pillars of whose throne are the faithful hearts of her subjects; whose name and person are dear and sacred in this land as well as in her own.

"Again and again has she been called upon to drain the cup of tears. Uphold her with Thy mighty hand, assuage her grief at the death of her grandson, and grant her Thy peace, which passeth all understanding. Comfort the Prince and Princess of Wales, and all the royal family in their great sorrow, and grant that they may find that great consolation that palaces and hovels alike may find in Thy love and promises. Especially do we commend to Thy fatherly comfort the mother who mourns the death of her firstborn, and the young affianced bride whose husband has been snatched from her by the Lord of death. As America stands with England uncovered at this new-made grave, may a brotherly sympathy and tenderness of feeling throughout our vast country bind together the two countries, the fountain of whose blood, speech, conscience and faith is one.

" Nor do we forget the death of that eminent prelate, scholar, churchman, one who can on all occasions express himself with accuracy and propriety, with elegance and force, who is always found ready to say on the spur of the moment what ought to be said, and *as* it ought. This is confessedly as rare, as it is assuredly an admirable gift. . . . Why, then, should we expect that extemporary prayer should be the common gift of every minister, when the faculty of extemporary speech on other subjects is confessedly exceptional ? "

What is the remedy ? To read the six prayers from a book ? Not of necessity, but at least there should be as careful a preparation of prayers as of sermons. And how ? Let the young, the inexperienced pastor write his prayers, after studying approved models, and if he cannot commit them to memory (an unnecessary drudgery), let him lay the manuscript, as he does his sermon, on his open Bible and read it in a reverent, devotional tone, as he utters his extempore prayers, making no concealment of his preparation, as if afraid of having the people know that he reads. He will not need to write as many prayers as sermons, for very shortly he will have accumulated a store which will bear repetition more frequently than his sermons. The late Professor Hart, while superintendent of the Sunday-school of the Tenth Church, uniformly wrote and read his Sunday-school prayers. Do not let the young pastor be afraid that some eye, that ought to be closed in devotion, will see him as he reads his prayer and report him. How much it would add to the dignity and comfort of public worship if ministers had the courage sometimes to write and read their prayers !

Cardinal-Prince of his Church, whose whole life has been a supreme dedication of himself, his vast power and accomplishments to the cause of our common Lord and Master, and of his fellow-men ; especially the poor. Embalm him in the memory of the millions of his brethren. May his noble example stir up all Christian people to a completer consecration of themselves to Him who gave Himself as a ransom for us, and who opened the gates of living love alike to priest, cardinal and beggar."

"In all cases of public worship, we must never forget that the speaker supplies a form of words for those who join with him in the service, whether he extemporize, or repeat what he has prepared, or read from a manuscript or a book, in all these cases alike, the spoken prayer *is a form* to the congregation. This is evident. The question is whether the generality of ministers, or rather ministers universally, should be considered competent to produce, without writing them, without preparation, or if they so please, without one moment's previous study or consideration, a whole public service for hundreds or thousands of people, and that from week to week and from year to year? Whether the stupidest, rawest, least learned and accomplished stripling, whom any Presbytery may have licensed to preach, or on whose head they may have laid their hands, shall be esteemed qualified to produce six public prayers every Sunday out of his own mind on the spur of the moment, and also to extemporize, as the occasions occur, services for baptism, for marriage, and for the celebration of the most solemn rite of the Christian Church, the Lord's Supper? Those who expect that such services, produced in this way, should be what they ought, must at least have conceived a very low idea of what is required."

It is to be said, also, that if these services, as they are often performed, are not a great strain upon the intellectual forces of clergymen, they are a great and unnecessary strain upon the endurance of the congregation.

The masterly discourse, better though it be and generally is than can be heard in other churches than ours, is not in itself worship, is not the prime object of the church service, as has been asserted. The grand object of the church service is prayer and praise, and the Presbyterian Church will never accomplish her glorious mission until, along with her well-equipped pastors, she carries a people who express their devotions in well-ordered prayer and praise.

Must, then, the prayers of the sanctuary be all extemporaneous, or all in inflexible forms? Is there no alternative? Cannot a liturgy be constructed of forms of prayer so general as to suit all congregations, and with a place in every service for special or extemporaneous prayer to suit any occasion? And can there be any objection to a pastor in his study, with his freshly written sermon before him, with his emotions all aflame and the condition of his people weighing on his heart—can there be objection to his writing his prayers and reading them, instead of reciting or declaiming them?

For the assembled people are not a dumb crowd, to be spoken *for* or spoken *to*, but living members of Christ, each of whom is privileged to say for himself:

> "O Lord, open Thou my lips,
> *And my mouth shall show forth Thy praise.*"

Hear what the Rev. Dr. Henry A. Boardman, so long pastor of our Tenth Presbyterian Church, said :

"An *imposed liturgy*, minute and inflexible, which is by many devout Christians held to be only less precious than the Bible, would be to me as much a yoke of bondage as would have been the Levitical ceremonial to the early disciples. But carefully composed forms of prayer were much in use among the reformers, and are to be found among the writings of most of those illustrious men whose names adorn the annals of the Presbyterian churches of Europe. The weak point in our services is the devotional offices ; the preaching is better than the praying. The *gift* of prayer is but scantily bestowed upon some who are not lacking in the *grace* of prayer. And ministers who are liberally endowed in this respect are not always able to command the sacred faculty. Every pastor knows what it is to go to his pulpit with an aching head, with nerves all ajar from a sleepless night, burdened with some sorrow, harassed with some vexing care, or otherwise unfitted to lead his people to the mercy-seat and speak with and for them to our Father in heaven.

What a relief it would be to pastors in circumstances like these to have at hand some suitable form of prayer, and how much it would contribute to the edification of believers. Why should not our General Assembly provide a few such forms, not to be imposed upon the ministry, but to be used by them at their discretion?

"Again, if our methods could be revised, I should insist upon the concert of pastor and people in the audible offering of the Lord's Prayer and the reciting of the Apostles' Creed once every Sabbath, together with the responsive Amen at the end of every prayer. In respect to the Creed, there are probably many Presbyterians who are ignorant that it is the common heritage of the churches, that it has always been included in our Confession of Faith. As the superintendents of our Sunday and mission schools have judiciously introduced these two exercises into their stated services, the way, it is hoped, may be opened for copying the example in our ordinary Sabbath worship."

I am perplexed by the unwillingness that persons have to written prayers, and I have tried to analyze it, for it is undoubtedly true that most Presbyterians object to prayers read from a book. The strange thing about it is that the same people do not object to written prayers read from a book, if they are in *verse*. In such cases we *sing* our prayers devoutly and most profitably. We all do this. Now why object to reading the same sentiments, the same prayers in *prose?* Very largely, I think, from prejudice, and for no better reason.

There is, however, an impression, more or less prevalent, that a prayer read from a book is not as devotional as a spoken extempore prayer. Is this so? How is a blind person to know whether the person uttering the prayer is reading or speaking unprepared language? How would any congregation know, if their eyes were closed, as they ought to be, whether the minister was reading a prayer from a book, or reciting it from memory, or extemporizing it?

I think it probable that the fact is this.. The effort to offer prayer in unprepared or extempore language arouses an intellectual glow which the speaker mistakes for devotional fervor, and under this mistaken view he naturally supposes that the congregation shares with him this aroused emotion, while the truth often is that the congregation is not moved at all. I think this will account for much of the unwillingness of the minister to read his own written prayers, and you see how little force there is in that objection. Of one thing I am sure, that if ministers would write one-fourth as many prayers as they do sermons, whether they use them or not, their spoken prayers would be immeasurably improved in phraseology and spirituality. We all *read prayers* and use prepared *forms* of prayer when we read the *Psalms*.

If it should be said that any Presbyterian church, that chooses to do so, may worship according to liturgical forms, and therefore there is no need of pressing this subject upon the consideration of the people, let me say that while any church may have the right, public opinion at present is such, that to do so would be likely to provoke most unfavorable criticism. A man has the right to go to a funeral in full evening dress if he chooses, or to go to a wedding in a suit of mourning, but no man in his right mind would choose to do so. What we desire is, to create a public opinion which will not be startled at such a change in our forms of worship.

Let any one examine the programme of the Christmas festivals, the "anniversaries," the Easter services, even the form of introductory service in many of our Sunday-schools, and ask himself what is likely to be the effect of such education. It is doubted whether the elders of the Church are consulted in the preparation of these responsive or antiphonal services, but can any one doubt what will be the effect of this training? Will these young people, who are accustomed to alternate reading of the Psalms in the Sunday-school, be content when they become men and women, to sit passive and dumb in a church service where the pastor does all the praying and the choir does all the singing?

At the end of the benediction, let the congregation pause for unspoken prayer at least one-quarter of a minute, in deep silence and stillness, before they leave their places, and let there be no "playing the congregation out" by the organist, as if for troops returning from a military funeral. If the organist desires to play, let it be an appropriate selection from one of the old masters, chosen with knowledge of the sermon, and then, if he is a real organist, the people will be in no hurry to go out.

Again, let the Lord's Prayer, as recorded in St. Matthew, be recited once in every service by pastor and people in unison (this *is* common prayer), and occasionally, say at the communion at least, let the Apostles' Creed be recited in unison. And once a month, or oftener, let the Ten Commandments be read.

I believe the time will come when the General Assembly will prepare a liturgy, not composed of ecclesiastical, but of Scriptural prayers (there is a wide difference between the two); a liturgy, not compulsory, but optional, or, at least, as Dr. Boardman pleads, prayers that may used as the pastor chooses.

The General Assembly now provides prayers to be sung in *verse* for church services, why not provide prayers in *prose* to be said also?

I would have our services such that our people would look forward to the Sabbath and the going to church, not merely to hear the sermon, but to take part in and enjoy the services, the prayers, the Scripture readings of the congregation. We have a right to the best preaching, the best prayers, the best music that can be obtained. Nothing is too good for the service of the Lord's house. Let us not forget that our offering is to God and not merely to please ourselves.

There is an unmistakable tendency towards ritualism in all churches. We cannot shut our eyes to it, we cannot prevent it. Let us meet it and provide for it and control it by the enrichment of our own services, such as will give our people some part in them and so deepen the interest of the young, and keep them from wandering to other places and more attractive worship.

Now what may be looked for, from such consideration as we are giving to the subject of improvement in our public worship? What we want is improvement in the dignity, the comfort, the spirituality of the devotional part of our public services.

May it not be hoped that some clergymen who have been accustomed to spend hours and even whole days in the preparation of the language of their sermons to the people, may see the advantage of putting their prayers, which are addresses to the Most High, in language at least as carefully prepared ; and that such clergymen as are deficient in the grace and gift of public prayer may not be ashamed to read their own prayers in public worship when they feel so inclined?

Let us hear also what dear old George Herbert said in his quaint verse. I am sure Dr. Boardman would not object to the association of his name with that of the English churchman. For they both loved and served the same Master here, and they are both before His throne now :

> "They that in private by themselves alone
> Do pray, may take
> What liberty they please
> In choosing of the ways
> Wherein to make
> Their souls' most intimate affection known
> To Him that sees in secret, when
> They are most concealed from other men.

"But he that unto others leads the way
　　In public prayer,
　　Should choose to do it so
　　That all that hear may know
　　　They need not fear
To tune their hearts unto his tongue, and say
　Amen ; nor doubt they were betrayed
　To blaspheme when they should have prayed."

There are four great events that I think may well be observed by the Church in all its branches. They are the
Nativity of Christ, the Crucifixion of Christ, the Resurrection of Christ, the Ascension of Christ : or, as we say in
home language, Christmas Day, Good Friday, Easter, and
Ascension Day. Why not gather our families, especially
our children, in church on Christmas Day, and have appropriate services? To say that we do not know that Christ
was really born on the 25th of December is a mere evasion,
for, whether true or not, all the Christian world keeps that
day.

Why not on Good Friday go to our churches and have a
service in remembrance of the death of Christ on the Cross?
There can be no doubt of this day.

We have been practically forced to a partial observance of
Easter, for we cannot well keep out of "the stream of tendency" in that direction.

Let us add one more day, and that the Ascension; and
have appropriate church services and let the people know
how much the Ascension means, for they do not know now.

Shall it be said there is no warrant for the religious observance of these days in the Bible? Admitting this to be
true, shall we apply this test to other observances? Where
is the Scripture warrant for the modern Sunday-school with
women for teachers, or for the written sermon, or for the
quartette choir, or for the costly organ? But no one doubts
the propriety and value of all these things.

These questions might be still further extended. It is fair

to say that anything that will increase the efficiency of the Church, and deepen and promote its edification and spirituality, ought to be adopted, whether we can find chapter and verse for it or not.

We lose much, I think, of reverence and respect for our Church by the way in which we speak of it, and permit others to speak of it without protest in our hearing. We ought never to speak of any branch of the Church as a *denomination*. The word is almost as much a commercial as an ecclesiastical term. There is but one Church, made up of the whole company of believers, and the various branches of this Church, as long as they hold to the divinity of Christ and His sacrifice on the Cross, are the true Church. There are two words, Church and sect, words each of one syllable, which may be better used than the word denomination, a word of five syllables.

Sometimes we hear ourselves spoken of as a "religious body." We ought always to resent this when it is intended to be a qualification or evasion of the use of the word church, and insist on being called a Church.

The one great hindrance, the greatest of all hindrances to the spread of Christianity throughout the world, is the want of Christian unity. All the persecution which the Church suffered in the earliest days ; all the opposition, however manifested, of later times ; all the arguments of later times ; all the falling away of the professors of the faith, are as nothing when compared with the want of hearty unity among the people of God. The world, as opposed to Christ, presents a vast army, all under one flag, with unbroken front, rank behind rank, of men fully equipped, fighting for life, while the Church stands, with scattered army corps, with broken front and various banners, quarrelling as to the rank of the different commanders, disputing as to who shall have the right or the left or the centre of the advancing columns, questioning as to this regiment, whether it is of the regular army, or as to

8

that, whether volunteer troops have any right to go to the front. I have said that this condition of things does more to hinder and delay the triumph of the religion of Christ than all the hostility of the world. But I know, and I thank God for it, that the responsibility for this does not rest with the Presbyterian Church. *We* raise no barriers against any other branch of the Church of Christ. *We* make no conditions except loyalty to Him. Our skirts are clear, for our Church is ready to meet the foe on any field. We are ready to stand shoulder to shoulder with any Christian soldiers, without asking or caring whether they are regulars or volunteers ; all we want to know is, Are they true to the cause, *will they fight?*

Time does not permit me to speak of the sacraments of baptism and the Lord's Supper, these most important parts of the services of the church, nor of the burial service, but it is most devoutly to be wished that the General Assembly would authorize and adopt Scriptural forms (you see we cannot escape from forms) for the proper and uniform observance of these rites and ceremonies. I trust that in the near future people of our Church who go from one part of the country to another, will not be so disturbed by the wide differences they observe in the administration of the sacraments and in the burial of the dead.

I have now tried, most inadequately, to show what is within the reach of the Presbyterian Church, what she can do for the world if she will. I cannot think that the views I present, if adopted, would weaken the hold the Church now has on her children or on the world, or would lead to the giving up of anything really valuable. If I thought so, I would almost be inclined to say, in the words of that hymn which is sometimes sung with so little sense of its fearful meaning :

> "This hand let useful skill forsake,
> This voice in silence die."

XVII.

How to Deal with the Wednesday Evening Meeting.

THE subject for our meditation to-night is "How to make the Wednesday evening meeting effective;" and it is in order to consider at the beginning, the question, What is the object of the meeting?

1. It is spiritual refreshment. We live in a busy time. It is a time of "doing" rather than "being." It seems to be easier to float with the current than to withdraw and think—easier to go to church than to secure the advantage of church going. It is well, therefore, to turn aside in the middle of the week, and think of what we are doing—and how we are living.

2. We need to grow in grace. The Divine life in the human soul must be cultivated, like plants, which need constant care and attention. Spirituality does not naturally increase in the heart—the trend is in the opposite direction; it must be nursed and trained and developed by judicious culture and activity. The mid-week evening service, when properly conducted, is a great help to growth in spirituality; but it is not absolutely essential to that growth. The many instances of high spiritual life, in persons whose days are spent in the country, away from towns and villages, as well as in many invalids who cannot go to church at all, show that growth in grace is the result of close communion with God wherever the Christian is.

3. The familiar instruction is of great advantage. There is apt to be a stateliness and dignity, and sometimes a formalism in the Sunday sermons, which are out of place in a

week-day evening. We get closer together ; and the subjects of remark are more simple and more practical than those
of the Sunday discourse.

4. There is opportunity here also for the cultivation of the
gifts of speech and prayer which we do not have elsewhere.
Possibly the Society for Christian Endeavor is a better place
for these ; but, indirectly and incidentally, much improvement may be accomplished in this meeting also.

5. There is fine opportunity here for becoming acquainted
with our fellow-Christians. The seats are all free ; we sit
where we choose ; we meet our friends (whom we get close
to only once a week) ; we exchange greetings and inquiries
for each other's families ; we grow more social, more like
Christians ought to be with each other.

Such are some of the advantages which may be looked for
by those who attend the Wednesday evening meeting.

Now how shall the meeting be made effective? There is
space to give only a few outlines or hints.

1. Large numbers are not necessary. It is not denied that
there is a sort of inspiration in numbers, but many of us can
recall meetings where very few were present, but where we
seemed to get very near to the Lord ; and we must not forget
the very cheering promise that he made to a company so
small that it counted only "two or three."

2. Much learning and great talents are not necessary,
either in the leader of the meeting or in those who take
part ; nor are these always within reach ; but such conditions as aptness, earnestness, directness, in the leader,
and teachableness and willingness on the part of the people,
a clear view of the subject under consideration and of the
Scriptures bearing on it, are necessary ; and one or more of
these can always be within reach.

3. It is not necessary to read long chapters from the
Scriptures, but it is very desirable that the Scriptures which

are read shall have the clearest and closest application to the subject.

4. Long speeches and long prayers are not necessary. If the pastor or leader makes remarks and offers prayer at an early stage of the meeting, none of the remarks or prayers from others which follow, need be more than four or five minutes in length.

It is important, however, that the subject chosen should be very practical. Meetings sometimes fail of their purpose, for want of practicalness. Any subject is appropriate that has reference to Christian thought, Christian life, Christian experience, Christian duty—what we ought to do and especially what we ought to be ; and the more direct and personal we make it the better. While it is desirable that the attention shall be held to the subject announced, it is not absolutely necessary. If the meeting drags because none can or will speak to the appointed subject, let the people be encouraged to speak on any subject which is not inappropriate. Some one may have read a book or tract with profit, and would like to speak of it if he felt free to do so ; he has been helped ; others may be.

On Sunday there should always be an announcement of the subject for Wednesday evening, and it is desirable that certain passages of Scriptures bearing on the subject and illustrating it should be mentioned.

If the meeting is to accomplish its best purpose, there must be careful preparation by the leader. Not that he may make a long discourse, but that he may condense his thoughts ; not that he must say much, but that what he does say must be just what ought to be said. "Out of the abundance of the heart the mouth speaketh ;" but it does not necessarily say much.

It is well that those who are expected to take part in the meeting should be advised beforehand. Things that are said "off-hand," except when they are the utterances of well-

furnished and well-trained minds, are not, as a rule, con-
ducive to instruction or spirituality. Let Mr. A. be asked
to speak on the subject of Scriptures assigned ; and let
him provide a substitute if he cannot be present, or an
alternate to take up the subject if there should be a break
down ; though the latter contingency is remote. Let the
same notice be given to those who are expected to offer
prayer. If the persons so designated choose to write and
commit to memory, or even read prayers, let them feel that
they can do so without prejudice. It is quite the custom
nowadays for people to "read papers" on given subjects—
why not on the all important subjects of religious discourse
or prayer? And let persons who take part in these meetings
speak or pray so that they can be heard all over the room.
Many persons do so in low tones of voice, which are very
proper in family worship, but entirely unsuited to a large
room.

Why should not women participate in these exercises ?
They outnumber us probably five to one—they are more devotional—more emotional. Why not have the advantage in
spoken words, of their spirituality? Should they desire to do
so, why not encourage them to speak or offer prayer? Or
if this is too great a change from existing methods, let them
write brief observations and send them to the desk to be read,
with or without the name of the writer. Women speak in
Sunday-school teachers' meetings—asking questions—why
not in the weekly meeting of the church for prayer?

Very much depends on a judicious selection and use of
hymns. And hymns should not be mutilated. The writer
of a hymn never contemplated the breaking of it up into
parts. If a hymn is very long, let a few verses be sung
at one time and the rest of the hymn afterwards, and to
the same tune always. Where the music is in the books,
it is not necessary for the organist to play the tune
before singing, nor for the leader to read more than one

stanza. It takes too much time. In no case should hymns be used in whole or in part to break supposed monotony or to fill up the time. A prayer-meeting of twenty minutes, with half a dozen or more scraps of hymns interspersed, is almost an abuse of the hymn. Singing is just as much a part of true worship as prayer, and almost if not quite as essential to the effectiveness of a prayer-meeting as any other feature. Some hymns are for the worship and praise of God —some are appeals to other people to worship and praise him—some are for personal reading and never intended to be sung. Many of the latter class are found in our Hymn books, and unfortunately are sometimes used in singing. They are simply didactic theological statements and not always expressed in true poetry.

If the subject of the evening or the appointed Scripture is disposed of within the hour, it is not necessary to wait until the clock strikes. Better close the meeting in three-quarters of an hour than to let the last quarter drag. Better go away hungry than overfed. If there is unusual interest, extend the time beyond the hour occasionally.

Let there be no long pauses. There will be none if the foregoing hints are observed. More than one person will be so full that he will be glad to speak.

The great danger is from formality. Break it up. Let this be a time when all formalism is excluded. We are all one family.

Occasionally it might be well to reverse the usual order, viz.: Let the members do their part first and the leader close by summing up. This will give variety to the order of the meeting.

These hints or suggestions may not all be practicable, may not all be within our reach ; but if only one should be thought worthy of consideration, and should lead to the edification of only one disciple, these words are not spoken in vain.

XVIII.

How to Promote a Revival of Religion.*

SOME winters ago the clergy of the Established Church, in London, held what they called a "Mission." They set apart a period of ten days before the beginning of Lent as a season of special preparation for that solemn season. The Bishop of London and the Bishops of Winchester and Rochester, whose dioceses now encroach upon the widening borders of that great city, were in hearty accord on the subject. They invited some of the ablest, the most popular, and the most evangelical clergymen in England to come to London and help them. The first day they met in St. Paul's Cathedral, and held three public services, which were thronged by clergymen and laymen. These services occupied almost the whole of the short winter day. The clergy had selected for this purpose churches in all quarters of the city, but more especially such as were located in the lowest and most degraded parts, and were nearest to the theatres and places of resort for the classes usually considered farthest away from the influences of the Gospel. Having chosen these locations, they sent a request to the pew holders that for a period of ten days they would vacate their pews, or at least claim no exclusive privileges there.

Then bands of church members, men and women, were organized, whose duty it was to canvass thoroughly those parts of the city where the services were to be held ; and distribute tracts, handbills and printed invitations to the people to go to church.

---

* A Wednesday evening talk.

All these preparations having been made, the introductory services were held at St. Paul's. The preaching was very earnest and searching, and the prayers, although read or sung from their liturgy, were offered with feeling and faith. The next day the preaching services were held simultaneously in all the appointed churches, morning, afternoon and night. The preachers were all first-class men, the lay workers were thoroughly in sympathy with them, the churches were crowded, and those near the theatres and other places of resort held services late at night, so as to catch the pleasure-seekers before they went to their homes. Thus for ten days and nights these services were sustained with most extraordinary success, and at the close the church passed into the season of Lent, with its peculiar, protracted and solemn services; and for forty days longer the attention of the people of God in that communion was held to the consideration of the great doctrines of the Cross.

There are no means of estimating the results of this "Mission." I do not believe that any effort was made to count up the numbers whose "confirmation," which means publicly professing Christ, could be traced to these efforts. It is quite possible, however, that part of the success which the American evangelists achieved in that great city some time after, especially the favor with which they were regarded by some of the clergy of the establishment, was due to these extraordinary services.

And the Church of England, we must remember, is extremely conservative, not ordinarily counting anything necessary for the propagation of religion, the evangelization of the masses, beyond its own calm and quiet daily service.

I do not speak of this because I suppose such a course would be the best thing in our city, but only to show how thoroughly a community may be moved when the church sets to work in real earnest.

The question then is, Shall there be among us a revival of religion?

And I venture to put this question with earnestness, for the field is large, and white already to the harvest. There is a large number of people (most of them young) who seem to be waiting for some influence to come and move them. I believe, too, there is a class, and a very large class, of Christian people, more or less well furnished for the work, who are waiting for some voice to say "here is your work, do it." I believe if religion should be thoroughly revived and all these dormant energies aroused and set in action, and under wise supervision, that not only this room, but this church, would be crowded every Wednesday evening, and so a great many people, especially the young, would be brought into the church by a public profession of religion.

Some one has said that the great awakening in the days of President Edwards, 150 years ago, was largely owing to preaching and the peculiar character of that preaching; and that the revival which swept over our land in 1857 was very much in connection with public prayer-meetings, some of which were continued without intermission for years. If there should come another great revival, does it not seem that it may be largely owing (humanly speaking) to Bible study—certainly never so general or so conscientious as at this time?

How, then, can we promote it?

Do not let us depend on any man or any number of men : great helps are they ; but let us all understand that a revival that is to do us any good must be first in our own hearts and then in the church.

A revival means that the people of God are stirred thoroughly, and that with quickened spiritual perceptions and increased faith they are to work for the conversion of other people. And the best results of this may be expected to come from the Sunday-school.

The soil has been prepared in the weeks and months that are past, the seed has been sown, the harvest is to be gathered here and soon. And the workers in connection with the Pastor are not only the Elders—his constitutional and spiritual advisers—but you Sunday-school teachers, you Christians, you who gave yourselves to the Lord in the work of the church when first you professed your faith in Christ; you are to help in this work, each one in his own sphere.

What methods can we adopt? What can we do to promote these good ends?

I mention four things, some one of which is within the reach of every man and woman, every boy or girl in this room.

1. Personal conversation. And this is the best of all. If there is any person whom you love or care for, whether relation or friend, who you have reason to believe is not a Christian, and whom you earnestly desire to see on the Lord's side and in the church, determine to go to that person, and with all the courage and earnestness which you can summon, and with the love of Christ in your heart, have the fullest, the freest talk with that person. At first it will not be pleasant to either of you, and it will be well if you fortify yourself with earnest prayer for wisdom and grace to say the best things in the best way. But in almost every instance, after the first few words, the work will be easier, the way plainer, and your success more assured. Do not, however, look for success immediately; it may require many a visit, much conversation, and many a prayer, before you gain your prize; but think what it is—the salvation of a soul—a soul, it may be, very near and dear to you, that but for your effort might never find the way of life. I say this is the best of all, for when you come face to face with one whom you wish to move to the most important of all acts,

your own soul will gleam in your face, and your friend will
be more likely to be won in this way than by any other.

2. But if you are timid and inexperienced, if you are con-
fident that you cannot go and speak directly to your friend,
then write a letter. Here you will have more freedom ;
you can choose your thoughts and your language delib-
erately ; you will not be discouraged by any flashes of
indignation at the liberty you are taking on this most personal of all subjects ; you will go straight on putting your
case in the strongest light you can ; and behind your statements will be the strength of your own personality. You
can say many things in a letter that you may not have the
courage to say directly and personally, and what you do say
remains. Words are uttered and often forgotten, but that
which is written is more likely to be remembered ; it can be
read again and again, and, best of all, it may lead to a personal interview, and if this should be the result of your letter
you have almost surely won your case.

3. If you have not courage to write a letter, or no skill
in writing, or little or no facility of expression, then send
a book. There are many books especially adapted for
this purpose. If you do not happen to know of any book
that will suit the particular case you have in mind, your
Pastor or some of the Elders will doubtless point you to just
the book you want, the book which will exactly suit that
case. When you get the book, read it yourself, or at least
make yourself well enough acquainted with its contents to
know how to talk with your friend about it, and especially
that you may pray over it before you send it and after your
friend has received it.

4. If you do not know of any book yourself, or if you are
not pointed to one by others, or if you are afraid to send the
book when you have found it, one thing yet remains—you
can pray for your friend. There is no hindrance here, no
want of skill or experience, no need of courage, no embar-

rassment of any kind. You can pray earnestly, persistently, frequently. You know that God hears you ; you know that he is on your side ; you know he has promised his blessing in answer to just such prayers ; and you can pray in faith, believing that your prayers will be answered soon or later. Besides, you can get others to pray with you ; you can always do that ; you can agree on.times and places, even if you cannot meet for the purpose, and you can have the additional promises to the prayers of two or three. And, better still, it may be that this persistent, faithful, united prayer will be answered in giving you the true Christian courage to send the book, or write the letter, or go in person to your friend and save him.

XIX.

The Place of the Hymn in Social Worship.

WHAT is a hymn? Webster says "it is a short poem composed for religious service, or a song of joy and praise to God." There is much religious poetry found in hymn-books which is not lyric, and which, even if intended by the authors for public or social worship, cannot properly be so used. There are descriptive, narrative, didactic, hortatory hymns that are very well, as religious poems for private meditation, but which have no place in public worship.

It was the custom formerly to have one hymn-book for the Sunday services, and another and smaller collection for the weekly lecture and prayer-meeting, and still another for the Sunday-school. It is still the custom generally to have a special book for Sunday-schools—which would not be necessary if the church book were compiled with more liberal reference to children. But, taking our hymn-books as we find them, how shall we use them?

No religious service is well ordered and complete without appropriate hymns. In many congregations the hymns are selected by the pastor from a classified table of contents, without much reference to the poetical quality of the composition, and sung by a quartette choir, with little participation by the congregation. In such instances the chief office of the hymn is to prepare the people for the sermon, or to deepen the impression of it. And under such conditions it is just as likely that the hymn shall be sung to the congregation as to God. When this purpose is not in the mind of

(126)

the person who makes the selection, the hymn is apt to become a mere means of varying what might otherwise become monotonous services, where the people sit and listen to the reading of the Scriptures, to the singing of the choir, and to the discourse from the pulpit.

When we come to consider the social meeting on a week-day evening the subject assumes additional interest. In some congregations, instead of a stately, formal lecture, differing from the Sunday sermon chiefly in that it is spoken and not so long, which prevailed in the old times, with a supplementary prayer-meeting later in the week, where there was freer prayer and from more persons, we now have a compromise between these two, or a combination of both. It is quite usual now to find churches with one weekly service—held, say, on Wednesday evening—to which the more spiritual members of the church resort. Not infrequently, also, after remarks from the leader of the meeting on some passage of Scripture, the meeting is "thrown open" to any who may be disposed to make addresses or prayers. If the church is in a lively condition its best material will be gathered here, and the services most probably will be interesting and edifying. But if otherwise, which, alas! is often the case, the meeting drags. Now comes in the hymn. The meeting would be, but for this most useful factor, an utter failure. The leader calls upon two brethren to pray, one following the other immediately, with no interval. Then what? There is nothing to do but to call upon the hymn. So used, it is intended to break the monotony of the service, or to act as a stimulating influence on the minds of the sluggish congregation. May the suggestion be ventured that this is not the true intent of a hymn? It is, or should be, praise to God, an address to God, not too often prayer to God, and not an address to men, or even to angels. Many a devout and penitent soul, not able to express devotional thought in spoken prayer, or debarred from the privilege because of sex, has been hurt and distressed by the misuse or abuse of so-called hymns.

Will not our pastors and leaders of meetings consider this subject and treat our hymns more kindly, and not give out a single verse or two verses to fill a gap in a meeting? The true intent of the hymn is praise to God, therefore just as much worship as prayer. Its purpose is to excite the emotions, elevate the affections, quicken the spiritual perceptions, and so lift the soul nearer to God.

If this is so, why should organists pause between the stanzas and play what is called an "interlude," while the congregation is standing? and why, especially, should they do so when the structure of the poetry forbids a pause? Is it to "breathe" his choir, or to exhibit his skill with his grand instrument, or to permit the worshippers to inspect each other's dresses, or to allow the pastor to run his eye over the assembly to see who are absent? Think of all this in the act of worship to Almighty God!

XX.

THE HOLY COMMUNION.*

As we approach the Communion Season, many of us begin to consider whether there is anything within our reach to help us to observe it properly, so as to get the most good from it.

We turn to the four gospels and we see that although St. John gives the fullest details of the incidents that occurred at the Passover Supper, he gives no account of the institution of the Supper itself. The other gospels give the account with more or less particularity. Then we turn to the First Epistle to the Corinthians and read the earliest, the fullest, the most satisfactory account of all—and yet this is from the pen of one who was not present. He had better authority, however, than even his memory, if he had been present, for this account was given to him by our Lord by direct revelation to his servant Paul. These accounts, with occasional references in the same epistle, give us all we know from the sacred records of the institution of the Lord's Supper, and the purpose for which it was established.

We look about among the literature of this subject and we find books and books in many languages, by many authors living in different centuries, in different parts of the world, and belonging to different branches of the church. These books treat the subject in every variety of method.

Some regard the bread and the cup as really, tangibly, visibly, the body and blood of our Lord ; and they say that

---

* A Saturday evening meditation.

in no other view can the taking of the sacrament be of the
slightest possible good to any communicant. The "real
presence" with them means that by a miracle, after the
prayer of consecration offered by a priest episcopally ordained, the bread and the wine have been converted into
actual flesh and blood. Their authority is the Saviour's
words, "This is my body ; this is my blood."

Others who do not go so far as this, lest perhaps they
should worship these elements, say that substantially, though
not actually, the body and blood of Christ are present on the
table after the prayer of consecration, but that they can be
apprehended only by the faith of the participant.

There are those who regard the bread and the wine only
as bread and wine, and not to be made by any prayer of consecration anything more than these. They believe that our
Saviour took some of the passover bread that was left of the
passover supper, and some of the simple red wine in such
common use then as now in that country, and made these the
symbols of his body and blood in the institution of the last
supper; and they contend that the nature of these elements is
not changed by any consecrating prayer, but that they are to
be received by faith in the Son of God as the Saviour of sinners, and that without faith in the heart of the recipient the
sacrament cannot do him any good.

These probably are the three principal views which, with
many modifications, are held of the bread and the cup. And
around this solemn ceremony have clustered the most devout, the holiest thoughts of the disciples of Christ in all
ages since his death. Books, almost without number, have
been written to sustain these several views and to give com-
municants comfort in the celebration of the supper.

But what good shall we get from the supper or sacrament
to-morrow? What do we expect from it? How shall we
approach the table? The circumstances about the original
institution have disappeared. The upper room—the preced-

ing meal—the Master with his twelve disciples (unless indeed Judas had gone out)—the evening hour—the absence of women—all these have been changed to our present necessary or more convenient surroundings. But the great fact remains. What shall we do with it?

Certainly it should be the most helpful, the most important of all the services of the church. So important, do some Christians hold it that they find comfort in the celebration every Sunday, or even every day,—while in some congregations it is celebrated only once a year, and then preceded by many meetings of preparation and much fasting and prayer. Others again celebrate it once in three months, with two preparatory services.

There is danger that it may be thought to be only an occasion of receiving new members into the church; while this is indeed only an incident, for we should have the Lord's Supper if no new members were added to the church.

The purpose (we have the highest authority for saying so) is to "show the Lord's death till he come." But how can I do this? How can any young and feeble disciple do this? If there was an expectation at that day that the Lord would come speedily, the words "till he come" had a more vivid meaning than now ;—but we too can show the Lord's death till he come by "doing this in remembrance of him." And whether he come or not in our time, he will at least come to each one of us at death.

But is this all? No—surely more than this. To us as a congregation, as individuals, it means something besides this. We enter the church to-morrow. The table is spread and covered with a linen cloth. Under that cloth are the sacred vessels containing the bread and the wine, the symbols of the body and blood of our Lord. In many churches of the Protestant faith there would be above the table a crucifix with the figure of our Lord in the agonies of death. We do not need this—for our desire is to think of the Saviour, not as enduring mortal agony, but as establishing a ceremony of remembrance and love which shall continue through all time and "till he come." The table is for his disciples, and all are welcome, but no others have any place there. This thought, however, must not keep church members from the table, who have fear and trembling lest they should eat and drink unworthily. No one who is sorry for his sins and who intends to abandon them, and who believes in Christ as his Saviour, need be afraid to come to his table, even if he cannot be absolutely sure that he is a Christian. Even an apostle said that he feared even after preaching to others he might be a castaway ; and many a disciple, many a minister since, has had the same fear ; but this ought not keep any one from the communion table ; it certainly would not have kept the apostle Paul from it.

It is not necessary that any disciple should perfectly understand why it was necessary for our Lord to die that cruel and lingering death upon the cross that we might be saved ; it is only necessary for us to believe that he did die for sinners ; and that through that death, if we believe in him and follow him, we shall be saved.

Some things seem, however, to be necessary on our part before we can fairly expect much good to come to us from the communion.

1. If we have enmity in our hearts towards any human being, it ought to be put away before we go to the table. No feelings of hatred, such as would lead us to do harm by word or deed to any person whatever, can be indulged by any disciple of Christ, and if any of us have such feelings they must be put away. This is entirely within our control.

2. No conscious sin can be entertained at that table. We are all sinners else we should not need a Saviour, and that table is for sinners; but it is for penitent sinners, who intend by God's grace to lead a new life, and not for those who

are consciously indulging any sin. This also is entirely within our control.

3. It must be a season of personal and continual prayer, and renewed consecration to God. If there is ever a time when the disciple should, more than at any other time, feel in the immediate presence of his Lord and Master, it is when sitting at his table. Now is the time to make a new and unconditional surrender of everything one has and is to the service of Christ. Let nothing be held back ; let the soul lie at the feet of Christ willing to be anything or do anything for his service.

4. It ought not be a season of gloom. It is not a funeral : it is a feast—a glad though solemn feast. He who sits at the head of that table has no pleasure in looking on sad and sorrowing faces or hearts. There is peace and true joy even in deep penitence; and he gives peace, such as the world cannot give.

When our Lord sat down or reclined to eat his last passover with his disciples, he said, "With desire I have desired to eat this passover with you before I suffer."

We, his disciples, also should have a deep and sincere desire to meet the Lord at his table.

A Protestant bishop once said to his people that unless they took Christ in their heart they would not meet him at his table. I would not press that thought, for the Lord sometimes reveals himself to his disciples in the breaking of the bread, and sometimes to the doubting ones by showing them his hands and his feet.

We should not be content by doing this one thing in remembrance of him. He has given other commands : we may not choose which we shall obey—we must obey them all.

So if we go to the table to-morrow with some such feelings as I have so briefly suggested, we shall turn from it after partaking with glad and thankful hearts—our weak souls having been nourished and fed with spiritual food, even as our fainting bodies are made strong with substantial material food ; and we shall have the grand old sentiment in our hearts even if we do not express it in song, that sentiment which the ancient church always associated with her communion seasons, the fine Tresagion : "Therefore with angels and archangels and with all the company of heaven we laud and magnify thy glorious name; evermore praising thee and saying, Holy, holy, holy, Lord God of Hosts : heaven and earth are full of thy glory : glory be to thee, O Lord Most High.   Amen."

Ye who· do truly and earnestly repent you of your sins and are in love and charity with your neighbors, and intend to lead a new life, following the commandments of God, and walking from henceforth in his holy ways, draw near with faith and take this holy sacrament to your comfort, and make your humble confession to Almighty God.

Almighty God, Father of our Lord Jesus Christ, Maker of all things, Judge of all men, we acknowledge and bewail our manifold sins and wickedness, which we from time to time have most grievously committed, in thought, word and deed, against thy divine majesty, provoking, most justly, thy wrath and indignation against us ; we do earnestly repent, and are heartily sorry for these our misdoings.   The remembrance of them is grievous unto us ; the burden of them is intolerable.   Have mercy upon us, have mercy upon us, Most Merciful Father, for thy Son, our Lord Jesus Christ's sake ; forgive us all that is past, and grant that we may ever hereafter serve and please thee in newness of life, to the honor and glory of thy name, through Jesus Christ our Lord. Amen.

XXI.

The Crucifixion.*

O FOOLISH GALATIANS, WHO HATH BEWITCHED YOU, THAT YE SHOULD NOT OBEY THE TRUTH, BEFORE WHOSE EYES JESUS CHRIST HATH BEEN EVIDENTLY SET FORTH, CRUCIFIED AMONG YOU?—*Galatians* 3:1.

WHEN you take up the Epistle to the Galatians several questions arise which seem to claim immediate attention, whether answers are readily found or not. Such questions are not as to the authorship, for the first word in the epistle gives the name of the writer, and almost every verse reflects his life and character, but as to the region called Galatia ; in what part of Asia Minor it was located (and in the uncertainty of boundary lines of the geography of the first century it is not easy to answer this question), and as to the people themselves : who were they? where did they come from? how long had they inhabited this region? and what were their mental and social characteristics? Then as to the churches of Galatia, whether we are to understand by them Christian congregations gathered by the Apostle Paul in cities, the names of which we do not know ; or, whether the Galatian churches were gathered in the cities of the Pisidian Antioch, Iconium, Lystra, and Derbe. Then as to the date of the epistle, and where the Apostle was when it was written, and especially why he wrote it ; what are its character and contents? Some of these questions are readily

---

*This lecture was given as an introduction to a course of lessons to a Bible-class on the life and writings of the Apostle Paul.

answered, and some will forever remain in obscurity.   Nor
is it my purpose in the remarks which follow to answer
them, though possibly a solution to some of them may be incidentally alluded to.   My purpose is to make what the book-
men call an "explication" of the verse which I have read.

The language, you observe, is highly figurative and pictorial.   It may help us a little to the meaning, if I take a
few moments to explain the words and further illustrate the
metaphors.

The remonstrance so fervently urged in this verse follows
naturally the strain of remark in the preceding chapter.
The apostle had been detailing his experience some time
before with the Judaizing teachers, who came down from
Jerusalem to Antioch and hindered him in his ministry
there.   He dwells at some length upon that sad experience
with Peter, who, with that unsteadiness which marked the
early years of his Christian life, shrunk from the plain duty
of admitting Gentile converts to the full fellowship of Christian brethren.   Defining his own position at that time, and
narrating the rebuke he administered to Peter, Paul passes
on to show that it is too late to look for justification by the
law,—for that he who lives to God must be *dead* to the *law*.
And then, in passionate words, he exclaims, "I am crucified
with Christ : nevertheless I live ; yet not I, but Christ
liveth in me : and the life which I now live in the flesh I
live by the faith of the Son of God."   Any other view
would be a practical denial of the efficacy of Christ's death.
And under the influence of these feelings he turns upon
them, saying, "O foolish Galatians, who hath bewitched you,
that ye should not obey the truth, before whose eyes Jesus
Christ hath been evidently set forth, crucified among you?"

The word "bewitched," which recalls the superstitions of
youth and the stories of the "evil eye," so common among
an uncultivated people, might, with equal accuracy, have
been rendered "fascinated," and if so, there is a sort of

parallel with the words farther on in the verse—*"before whose eyes* Jesus Christ has been evidently set forth "—as if the fascinating influence had passed from the eye of the be-witcher to the eye of the recipient ; that being the most direct channel of communication and impression. The word *foolish*, or *senseless*, may have a possible reference to the fickleness of their nature, as he says, in the 6th verse of the 1st chapter, " I marvel that ye are *so soon removed* from him that called you into the grace of Christ unto another gospel." The words "*that ye should not obey the truth*" are said by scholars not to be in the earliest and best manuscripts, and have been added by some unknown hand to show the *effect* of the bewitching or fascinating influence,—viz., a turning away from or not obeying the truth. The sense, you may observe, is complete if these words are dropped.

The word rendered by the English equivalent "*set forth*" may be translated, "*placarded*," and is the word commonly used to describe all public notices or proclamations. It is further explained and intensified by the use of the word *evi-dently,—i. e., plainly, openly, unmistakably.* " Before whose eyes" (bringing out the idea of *confronting*, as when one's eyes rest on a huge placard),—before whose eyes Christ crucified was set, as in a picture ; and this brings to our minds similar pictorial language used by the same writer in one of his Corinthian epistles (2 Cor. 3 : 18), " But we all, with open face *beholding as in a glass* the glory of the Lord, are changed into the same image from glory to glory, even as by the Spirit of the Lord."

The words "*hath been evidently set forth* " refer to a time previous to the writing of this epistle when Paul had preached Christ among them, in a vivid and almost startling manner, reaching their *hearts* as if through their *eyes ;* in-dicating not only the plainness of his preaching, but the interest and liveliness with which they received the image —beholding, as in a picture, the sufferings of Christ. " Who could have betwitched you" by his gaze, when you had only to fix your eyes on Christ, evidently set forth crucified among you, to escape the fascination?

It would be of the very highest interest if we could conceive of the personal appearance and the manner of the Apostle Paul as he preached to the Galatians. "If we may picture him to ourselves as he appeared to them—a friendless outcast, writhing under the tortures of a painful malady, yet instant in season and out of season ; by turns denouncing and entreating ; appealing to the agonies of a crucified Saviour ; perhaps also, as at Lystra, enforcing this appeal by some striking miracle—we shall be at no loss to conceive how the fervid temperament of the Galatian might have been aroused."*

It would be very interesting also to examine his recorded discourses and his epistles ; to learn his style of address, whether written or spoken ; to notice the peculiarities in his mode of thought and expression ; the striking similarity in his style, even though quite distant in time, and under quite different circumstances. For he has a style of his own, whether in the didactic and argumentative chapters of his epistle to the Romans ; the reasoning, chiding earnestness of his epistle to the Galatians ; the long parentheses of his epistle to the Ephesians ; or the tender, manly, human counsels to Philemon and Timothy. So striking and identical are these peculiarities that there is only one of the books of the New Testament generally ascribed to him of which there is any doubt whatever as to his authorship ; I mean the epistle to the Hebrews.

One thing, however, we do know, that he preached *Christ and him crucified.* And I think the language of the text justifies the belief that when he wished to call men to repentance he dwelt much on the sufferings of Christ on the cross.

---

* Bishop Lightfoot.

It is my belief also that he dwelt in much detail on these sufferings ; that his references were not merely to that death in general terms as an expiation for sins, but that the agony of the cross as endured even unto. death, in all its thrilling and harrowing details, he was accustomed to describe with the utmost vividness and particularity. How else shall we understand the words, "*Jesus Christ hath been evidently set forth crucified among you ?*" Paul had not witnessed the crucifixion scene himself, but it was a not uncommon mode of punishment. He may have seen other victims suffer thus. He knew what it was to suffer, for he had been present at the death of Stephen, and he had been stoned almost to death himself at Lystra.

And if this epistle was written, as may be believed, from Ephesus, there is a peculiar significance in the "sentence at the close of it, where, after speaking of his own sufferings (as he rarely did however), he sums up with these words, ' From henceforth let no man trouble me, for I bear in *my body the marks of the Lord Jesus.*' " *

It has been sought in all ages of the Christian Church to reproduce the scenes of the crucifixion. Sacred drama in scenic representations, sculpture, painting, sacred poetry, sacred music, sacred rhetoric—all have lent their highest conceptions, to make impressions through the senses on the emotional nature of man, by depicting the last hours and sufferings of our Lord upon the cross.

Perhaps the most remarkable scenic representation of sacred subjects ever produced is that which is made every ten years in the village of Ober Ammergau, in the highlands of Bavaria. And the most interesting and instructive accounts that I have seen of this most extraordinary spectacle are those given by the Baroness Tautphoeus in her novel "Quits," by Dean Stanley, and by Mr. George C. Thomas.

---

* Bishop Lightfoot.

The representation is very comprehensive, and includes
many of the most interesting incidents in all Bible history—
those from the Old and New Testament mingled in their
order, so as to relieve and vary by tableaux and chorus the
otherwise monotony of chronological regularity.   But I refer
to it for the purpose of dwelling, at no great length, however,
on the crucifixion scene.

    " The curtain falls (says Mr. Thomas) on the tableaux
immediately preceding the crucifixion,—and there is an
interval of breathless suspense ; then the sound of many
voices is heard, and presently a horseman emerges at
the head of an excited procession from one of the gates
of Jerusalem.   As the procession winds its way slowly
into view, the mother of Christ and Mary Magdalen, with
other women and St. John, appear some way off, coming in
an opposite direction.   They are greatly agitated, and as
they scan the advancing throng, they see turning the corner
of Annas' house the Man of Sorrows, blood-stained and bent
beneath the weight of his heavy cross, which he evidently
cannot bear much farther.   Some of the soldiers, observing
this, seize hold of Simon of Cyrene, who meets them acci-
dentally, and compel him to bear the cross.   At this point
Veronica, accompanied by two other women, comes out and
fulfills the part assigned her in the legend—the only incident
of the play not directly founded on Scripture.   As he ap-
proaches Calvary, Christ addresses the daughters of Jerusalem in the well-known words, and in a short time he passes
out of sight.   After the procession had departed the chorus
came on the stage, in black mantles, and sang a mournful
song.   Through the melody of the song you hear the sound
of the hammer.   When the chorus have finished and the
curtain rises you see two crosses erected, each bearing its
victim ; between these, a taller cross with a sad, pale figure
nailed to it.   It is slowly raised, fixed into its socket, and
there, hanging before you, seems to be the crucified one

himself. The body is covered with a tight-fitting, flesh-colored garment; a crown of thorns is upon the brow; you see the nail marks, and apparently the blood dripping from the wounds; and over his head the inscription written by Pilate."

"A sceptic (I quote from the novel referred to, 'Quits') might perhaps have followed the representation with criticising curiosity, a less imaginative mind with calm self-possession. Nora forgot herself, time, place, spectators, everything, and saw, heard, felt, with a vividness that at length completely overwhelmed her. As the crucifixion was finished, a shudder of horror passed through her whole frame; a sensation of extreme cold seemed to thrill her blood; and after some ineffectual efforts to control, at least outwardly, her emotions, she bent down her head and covered her face with her hands, remaining motionless, until a voice whispered, 'Madam, allow me to advise you to leave the theatre now; another scene might weaken an impression well worth preserving in all its strength.'"

While none of those who have witnessed and described the scenes at the Ammergau mystery have failed to be interested and affected in the highest degree, none are of the opinion that it would be proper to produce it elsewhere. "All that is most peculiar in the performance there would die in any other situation. Its whole merit and character lie in the circumstance that it is a product of that locality, nearly as peculiar to it as the rocks and fruits of the natural soil. The theatre is in the open air, surrounded by a rough wooden enclosure or stockade, capable of containing five or six thousand people. The green meadow and the circle of the hills form the background. Its illumination is the light of the sun, poured down through the long hours of the day, and the effects of light and shade are the natural changes of the rising and declining sun and of the passing clouds. The stage decorations and scenery are painted in the coarsest and

simplest style, and the dresses of the actors are the work
of the villagers.   The actors themselves, in all about five
hundred, include most of the population of the village.
They look upon their calling as actually a religious service ;
they begin the day with divine service in their church, and
the scenes are represented apparently as if the actors were
unconscious of the presence of an audience.   The spectators
sit in almost breathless attention during the long hours of
the summer day, and nothing disturbs the solemnity of the
scene.   Even Luther is reported to have said, ' Such spec-
tacles often do more good and produce more impressions
than sermons.'   In England they were performed in the
time of the first Stuarts, and Milton's first sketch of the
Paradise Lost was a sacred drama, of which the opening
speech was Satan's address to the sun." *

The Roman Catholic Church has ever been fond of representing in sculpture and painting the passion of our Lord.
Beginning with very low forms of art, she advanced in cultivation, borrowing largely from the Greek models, until, in
painting at least, she has left little to be desired.   The
Eastern Church cared not to cultivate this taste.

From the rude and sometimes most repulsive figures that
confront the traveller in the wayside chapels and shrines of
Catholic Europe, to the divinest conceptions of the great
masters of sculpture and of painting which adorn the
churches and the museums of the great cities, the contrast
is immeasurably wide, but the purpose is the same ; and the
peasant who lifts his hat and crosses himself as he passes, or
the country girl who leaves her bouquet of simple wild
flowers as she kneels and says her short prayer, receives the
same impressions probably as the devotee of the upper
classes, who kneels and worships before the glorious pictures
of Rubens or Van Dyck.

---

* Dean Stanley.

Figures of Christ have been cut from every conceivable substance. Gold, silver, bronze, and all the baser metals; ivory, common bone; the finest marbles, and the coarsest sandstone; wood, plaster and clay, have all been employed with greater or less effect to depict the sufferings of Christ. Depending largely on the senses for the inculcation of truth, the Roman Catholics have exhausted high art in their efforts to produce impression. Every household has one or more crucifixes. No individual member is complete in his panoply of devotion without one. No church would *be* a church without a high altar and the figure of the Saviour stretched upon the cross. In some of the village churches in Switzerland these figures are formed sometimes so coarse and repulsive as to be positively hideous; but the people who worship before such shrines, or through such images, are in a very low scale of Christian civilization, and susceptible to the most vulgar appeals.

But the highest success of a church which depends less upon the intellect than the senses, in teaching religion, is found in painting rather than sculpture. Almost everywhere in Europe her sanctuaries possess the works of the old masters. There was an age when the brightest, the divinest genius, was consecrated to the work of adorning the churches with representations of Scripture scenes, and especially of the passion of our Lord. They were very rude in their beginnings, but sacred art reached its highest success in the days of Leonardo da Vinci, Raphael, Michael Angelo, Guido, Rubens, Van Dyck.

There is a picture in the museum at Antwerp, by Van Dyck, representing Christ on the cross. It is the only figure on the canvas. The background is black as night, except in the upper part of the picture, where the sun is seen just passing under a total eclipse. The artist has seized the moment apparently when the Saviour, with his eyes turned towards heaven, is saying, " My God, my God, why hast thou forsaken me!" The body, nailed to the rough uplifted cross, with no covering except about the loins, seems to stand out from the canvas as a real human form in the agony of death. The tension of the arms, the nailed wrists, the writhing body, the trickling blood, cause the spectator to shudder and involuntarily turn away, but he returns again and again, as if fascinated by the thrilling spectacle.

Another, and in the same collection, but by Rubens, is after the death of Christ, but while his body is still suspended. The Roman soldier is piercing his side with his long spear, to hasten his death, but *he is dead already*, and the death stroke is not needed. Here there are three crosses —and the writhing, struggling forms on the other two, as they shrink from the crushing blows of the executioners, show that with them life is not yet extinct—they did not "give up the ghost." At the foot of the cross of Christ, leaning her face almost against the sacred feet, and with her hands stretched out imploringly towards the soldier with the spear, as if she felt its keen point in her own bosom, her hair streaked with his blood, her face swollen with grief, her eyes and mouth expressing most piteously her great sorrow, is Mary Magdalene, who has struggled through the crowd and the soldiers to be near her Master in his last agony. Other figures are there, but we care not to notice them. The eye that for one moment takes in the whole scene, rests on one figure, on one face, and that is the central one—the figure, the face of Christ. The darkness, the gloom seem to be relieved by a supernatural light that shines upon the body and discloses the pallor of death. The head with its crown of thorns hangs heavily on the chest, for the life is gone. The eyes are closed, the muscles, lately quivering with agony, are relaxed, and the whole body hangs helplessly from the pierced hands.

Another picture in the same city, by the same artist,

Rubens, but in the famous Cathedral, is "The Descent from the Cross." The great master seems to have exhausted himself on this wonderful picture. The grouping, the attitudes, the coloring, all make up a picture which of its kind has no superior in all the world. There is but one cross, and the background throws out the scene as if the figure were real. Ladders have been raised, and his disciples are detaching the body from the cruel tree. The flesh is livid as in death ; they have loosened one arm from its fastening, while the other is still held, and the head hangs on the drooping shoulder. The body is not yet rigid in death ; the muscles are limp and relaxed, and blood has flowed in streaks down the limbs. It is quite in keeping with the whole scene, and very surprising, too, to observe with what delicate hands the disciples touch the sacred form and release it from the iron grasp of the nails. One assistant on the ladder, and bending over the upper part of the cross, is holding the white cloth in his teeth, his eyes streaming with tears, while others carefully wreathe the white cloth round the lifeless form. No woman's touch could be more gentle and delicate than the hands of the disciples who slowly lower the limp and lifeless body to the embrace of his mother, and Mary Magdalene, and the other Mary, who wait to receive it at the foot of the cross. No better criticism of the marvellous power of this painting could be adduced than the story of two friends who stood before it entranced and spell-bound. At length one of them, less imaginative, or less devotional, perhaps, than the other, said, "Let us go." "Wait," said his companion ; "wait till they get him down."

It is this picture which has been made the model for the scene in the Ammergau drama, "and it is related that some Munich painters, in their artistic pride, were endeavoring to persuade the village priest who superintends the play, that it would be much more effective if the virgin mother of Christ swooned at the foot of the cross, instead of stand-

10

ing, as she does in Rubens' picture, with clasped hands, her eyes fixed upon him. 'Gentlemen,' said the curé, 'the Scripture says she *stood* at the foot of the cross. That is enough.'"

The oldest Christian *Hymn* is undoubtedly Mary's song of thanksgiving in response to Elizabeth's salutation. "My soul doth magnify the Lord, and my spirit hath rejoiced in God my Saviour." Certainly, from that day to this the Magnificat, as it is called, sometimes set to the rudest music, and sometimes to the grandest and sweetest strains, has thrilled many a devout Christian heart, and will do so till the end of time.

It does not fall in the way of these remarks to notice that sweet hymn, "The Celestial Country," written by the monk of Cluny in 1145, so quaint, so beautiful ; nor that most awful of all death-songs, the "Dies Iræ, Dies Illa," especially when sung to Mozart's music, written one hundred years later by a Franciscan monk ; one of the best translations of which is by our own General Dix, ex-Governor of New York ; but I may refer to that hymn which, though not the grandest, has been called the most pathetic of hymns, which the Latin church, for six hundred years, has identified and embalmed in her service for Good Friday, *The Stabat Mater!* Of the various English translations of this hymn perhaps the best is the following :

> By the cross, sad vigil keeping,
> Stood the mournful mother weeping,
>   While on it the Saviour hung ;
> In that hour of deep distress,
> Pierced the sword of bitterness
>   Thro' her heart with sorrow wrung.
>
> Oh, how sad—how woe-begone,
> Was that ever blessed one,
>   Mother of the Son of God !
> Oh, what bitter tears she shed,

Whilst before her Jesus bled,
　　'Neath the Father's penal rod !

Who's the man could view unmoved
Christ's sweet mother, whom he loved
　　In such dire extremity?
Who his pitying tears withhold,
Christ's sweet mother to behold,
　　Sharing in his agony?

Ever with thee, at thy side,
'Neath the Christ, the crucified,
　　Mournful mother, let me be !
By the cross, sad vigil keeping,
Ever watchful, ever weeping,
　　Thy companion constantly.

　　　　　　　　　—*Lord Lindsay.*

The following hymn was written by the French monk St.
Bernard, who lived in the early part of the twelfth century,
whom Luther called the best monk that ever lived. "He
it was who persuaded the King of France to undertake the
Crusade of 1146."

O sacred head surrounded
　By crown of piercing thorn,
O bleeding head so wounded,
　Reviled and put to scorn ;
Death's pallid hue comes o'er thee,
　The glow of life decays,
Yet angel-hosts adore thee,
　And tremble as they gaze.

I see thy strength and vigor
　All fading in the strife,
And death, with cruel rigor,
　Bereaving thee of life ;
O agony and dying,
　O love to sinners free,
Jesus, all grace supplying,
　O turn thy face on me.

The following hymn, by Dr. Faber, a clergyman of the
Church of England, who at the age of thirty-one joined the

Church of Rome, may have been written as Sodoma painted his famous head of Christ, weeping and praying as he worked. Whether written before or after his perversion, it seems to bring one to the foot of the cross as the Divine Sufferer is bleeding and dying.

O come and mourn with me a while,
  O come ye to the Saviour's side ;
O come, together let us mourn ;
  Jesus, our Lord, is crucified.

Have we no tears to shed for him,
  While soldiers scoff and Jews deride ?
Ah ! look how patiently he hangs ;
  Jesus, our Lord, is crucified.

How fast his feet and hands are nailed ;
  His throat with parching thirst is dried ;
His failing eyes are dimmed with blood ;
  Jesus, our Lord, is crucified.

Come, let us stand beneath the cross ;
  So may the blood from out his side
Fall gently on us, drop by drop ;
  Jesus, our Lord, is crucified.

A broken heart, a fount of tears
  Ask, and they will not be denied ;
Lord Jesus, may we love and weep,
  Since thou for us art crucified.

The next illustration I give is that well-known and much loved hymn from the pen of the poet Cowper. It must have been in one of the few brighter or at least more hopeful intervals of that malady which brooded over his soul and threw a dark cloud over his life, that he sung those strains which the church so loves to sing when she comes round the table of the Lord.

There is a fountain filled with blood
  Drawn from Immanuel's veins,

And sinners plunged beneath that flood
  Lose all their guilty stains.

The dying thief rejoiced to see
  That fountain in his day,
And there *have** I, as vile as he,
  Washed all my sins away.

E'er since by faith I saw the stream
  Thy flowing wounds supply,
Redeeming love has been my theme,
  And shall be till I die.

A writer of one of the "Oxford Essays" calls the following Watts' finest hymn. I read but two stanzas :

When I survey the wondrous cross,
  On which the Prince of Glory died,
My richest gain I count but loss,
  And pour contempt on all my pride.

See! from his head, his hands, his feet,
  Sorrow and love flow mingled down :
Did e'er such love and sorrow meet ?
  Or thorns compose so rich a crown ?

And the two stanzas which I now read, written by a
Scotch baronet, Sir Robert Grant (if prayers may properly
be turned into hymns), may be accepted as one of the best
hymns of that class, and if read or sung with a true devotion,
will bring the soul to the foot of the cross, with eyes uplifted to the sufferer there :

By thine hour of dark despair,
By thine agony of prayer,
By thy purple robes of scorn,
By thy wounds, thy crown of thorn,
By thy cross, thy pangs and cries,
By thy perfect sacrifice ;
Jesus, look with pitying eye ;
Hear our solemn litany.

---

* Not *may* I, nor *would* I.

By thy deep expiring groan,
By the seal'd sepulchral stone,
By thy triumph o'er the grave,
By thy power from death to save ;
Mighty God, ascended Lord,
To thy throne in heaven restored,
Prince and Saviour, hear our cry,
Hear our solemn litany.

Another hymn, and the last that I shall quote, and in a very different strain from the last two, is one, the authorship of which has been claimed by two persons, or rather by the friends of two persons ; although to us, who are living a century later and in another hemisphere, it matters little from whose heart and mind it did spring. It is said to have come originally and roughly from James Allen, who was born in Yorkshire, England, and settled as a minister in a chapel which he built on his own estate ; and afterwards to have been found as a rough diamond by the Hon. and Rev. Walter Shirley, who polished it to the precious gem as we now have it.

Sweet the moments, rich in blessing,
  Which before the cross I spend ;
Life, and health, and peace possessing,
  From the sinner's dying Friend.

Here I'll sit, forever viewing
  Mercy streaming in his blood ;
Precious drops ! my soul bedewing,
  Plead and claim my peace with God.

Truly blessed is this station,
  Low before his cross to lie ;
While I see divine compassion
  Floating in his languid eye.

Here it is I find my heaven,
  While upon the cross I gaze ;
Love I much ? I've much forgiven,
  I'm a miracle of grace.

> Love and grief my heart dividing,
> With my tears his feet I'll bathe ;
> Constant still in faith abiding,
> Life deriving from his death.

Whoever wrote it, we know that we love to sing it ; and that there are times in Christian experience when it furnishes expression for certain emotions which no other hymn supplies.

But it is not merely sacred poetry which has lent her divine muse to illustrate the passion of our Lord. Sacred Music also, in strains which seem almost borrowed from celestial harps, has moved and thrilled and melted the soul.

Such strains cannot be reproduced in language, and I can, therefore, do no more than refer you to the famous Passion Music of Sebastian Bach, and the almost heavenly compositions of Mozart, Mendelssohn, Rossini and Handel, especially in the Messiah. I dare not even specify particular passages of these wonderful composers of sacred song—it is not within my range. I cannot describe, I can only enjoy. I know, as all of you know, what it is to be swayed by the power of music, whether by a delicate and effective solo, or by the volume of a vast chorus. I know, as all of you know, that the simplest strains, when they embody depth of feeling and are appropriately rendered, lift the soul on the wings of love and faith, or plunge it into the depths of despair. The Roman Catholics understand this power, and they have seized on some of the finest compositions and incorporated them in their most solemn and impressive Masses. Our Methodist brethren understand this, and with great skill they have wedded the best hymns of their own Wesleys —hymns fairly saturated with the tenderest and deepest feeling—to the simplest and most touching music, whether sacred or secular. Hence the unusually large proportion of the members of that church who sing, and hence the successful use they make of sacred song in their most devotional services.

I borrow for a further and final illustration of this part of my subject the following from a well-known American writer : *

"At nightfall I urge my way into the Sistine Chapel and look upon the gaunt figures of Angelo's ' Last Judgment.' The choir chants the Miserere. The twelve candles by the altar are put out one by one, as the service continues. The sun has gone down, and only the red glow of twilight steals through the dusky windows. There is a pause, and a brief reading from a red-cloaked cardinal, and all kneel down, and the sweet, mournful voice of the Miserere begins again, growing in force and depth till the whole chapel rings and the balcony of the choir trembles ; then it subsides again into the low, soft wail of a single voice—so prolonged, so tremulous, and so real, that the heart aches and the tears start, for *Christ is dead!* Lingering yet, the wail dies not wholly, but just as it seems expiring, it is caught up by another and stronger voice that carries it on, plaintive as ever ; nor does it stop with this, for just as you looked for silence, three voices more begin the lament—sweet, touching, mournful voices—and bear it up to a full cry, when the whole choir catch its burden and make the lament change into the wailing of a multitude, wild, shrill, hoarse, with swift chants intervening, as if agony had given force to anguish. Then, sweetly, slowly, voice by voice, note by note, the wailings sink into the low, tender moan of a single singer, faltering, tremulous, as if tears checked the utterance, and swelling out as if despair sustained it."

There is not time to speak at length on the power of *Eloquence* when enlisted on the side of sacred truth. Rich as our English language is in sermons on the death of Christ,

---

* Donald G. Mitchell.

other languages of Europe have also their mines of wealth in the same direction. Without attempting even a glance at such literature in the far-off ages, it is enough for my purpose to mention the names of Claude, Bossuet, Bourdaloue, Fénelon, Massillon, in the French church of the past century, or of the brothers Monod and Pressensé in the present, or of the Italian Gavazzi, whose thrilling eloquence is still ringing in our ears, and others of less fame but of great power.

Some of you may be familiar with the account which William Wirt gives of the blind preacher :

"It was an old ruinous wooden church in Virginia. It was a day of the administration of the Lord's Supper, and the sermon was, of course, on the Passion of our Lord. The preacher was a tall and very spare old man ; his head, which was covered with a white linen cap, his shrivelled hands and his voice, were all shaking under the influence of palsy ; and a few moments ascertained to me that he was perfectly blind. As he descended from the pulpit to distribute the mystic symbols, there was a peculiar, a more than human solemnity, in his air and manner, which made my blood run cold and my whole frame shiver. He then drew a picture of the sufferings of our Saviour—his trial before Pilate, his ascent up Calvary, his crucifixion, and his death. I knew the whole history ; but never until then had I heard the circumstances so selected, so arranged, so colored. It was all new, and I seemed to have heard it for the first time in my life. His enunciation was so deliberate that his voice trembled on every syllable, and every heart in the assembly trembled in unison. His peculiar phrases had that force of description that the original scene appeared at that moment acting before our eyes. We saw the very faces of the Jews —the staring, frightful distortions of malice and rage. We saw the buffet ; my soul kindled with a flame of indignation, and my hands were involuntarily and convulsively clenched. . . . But when he came to touch on the patience, the forgiving meekness of our Saviour; when he drew to the life his blessed eyes streaming in tears to heaven, his voice breathing to God a soft and gentle prayer of pardon on his enemies, 'Father, forgive them, for they know not what they do,' the voice of the preacher, which had all along faltered, grew fainter and fainter, until, his utterance being entirely obstructed by the force of his feelings, he raised his handkerchief to his eyes and burst into a loud and irrepressible flood of grief. The effect is inconceivable. The whole house resounded with the mingled groans and sobs and shrieks of the congregation."

"I wonder not," says the eloquent Bascom, "if one may for a moment personate the divine sufferer, I wonder not that in the garden my disciples, who thought themselves so brave, at the first appearance of the soldiers should have forsaken me and fled ; they are unused to scenes of strife. I wonder not at the cruel buffetings, the spittings, the mockery, the scorn—human malice finds satisfaction in such expressions. I wonder not that the soldiers should look on my dying agonies with indifference—their trade is blood. I wonder not that the sun should hide his face from this awful scene and refuse to gaze on it—his office is to illuminate and warm and cheer. I wonder not that the very earth should shrink and quake, and the rocks should rend asunder, as if nature herself could not bear the sight—*but, my God, my God, why hast thou forsaken me?*"

One of the traditions of the early church is that St. Luke was a painter, and there are not wanting those who believe that some rough scenes on canvas or in fresco, now shown to the curious in Rome, came from the hand of the good physician. But the Apostle Paul held no painter's brush. His presentations of truth, though highly pictorial, were word pictures, with every variety of expression, and in metaphors drawn from architecture, from the army, from agriculture, and from social life.

But that which more than anything else made him a successful preacher, and which, as a writer (aside from inspiration), has caused his letters not only to be preserved through these eighteen centuries, but to maintain a growing, a constantly increasing influence on the mind and in the heart of the church, is his impersonation of the character, or rather of the sufferings, of his Lord. "*1 am crucified with Christ,*" he says in this same epistle to the Galatians. Remarkable language! It is as if he had taken the place of the penitent thief who hung on the cross at the side of Jesus, and suffered with him the agonies of crucifixion.

While Peter and John, on being let go from the council, could speak in prayer and praise of the "holy child Jesus," Paul preached Christ *crucified*.

Such are some of the methods by which sacred art and sacred music and poetry and sacred eloquence have lent their aid to set forth the great cardinal truth of Christianity, "Jesus Christ and him crucified." And in all the ages with more or less effect have these means been employed to soften and mould human character.

We Protestants do not need high altars and paintings and statuary in our churches, nor oratories and crucifixes in our houses. We depend more on the intellect and the reason, and less on the sensuous and emotional, in our worship. We depend more on the Word of God as revealed in the Holy Scriptures, and on the exposition of that word by his ministers, and on the communications of his grace in answer to prayer, than we do on the traditions of the fathers or the gorgeous ceremonies of a brilliant and imposing ritual. But we ought not to forget that all minds are not alike ; that birth, and education, and culture, and taste create wide differences between those who are of the same spirit ; and we ought not to frown upon real piety wherever we see it, nor deny to other Christians any helps which draw them nearer the infinite Father, through Jesus Christ his Son. "And

John answered and said, Master, we saw one casting out devils in thy name, and he followeth not us; and we forbade him because he followeth not us. And Jesus said unto him, Forbid him not, for he that is not against us is for us."

But this subject will be quite incomplete if I leave it thus. I want to come a little closer to you. I want, in the fewest words, to bring it home to the hearts and consciences of all present.

To you who are Christians I can say nothing new. You have heard this story a thousand times before, and you know what effect it had on you when the Spirit of all goodness and truth first opened your eyes to see your helpless, lost condition, and the means of escape through the death of Christ. You may not, you probably did not, understand "the philosophy of the plan of salvation;" why it was necessary for the Infinite Father to send his Son into the world to lead a life of suffering, and finally to die a cruel and lingering death on the cross. You may never, in this world, understand it, but you believed it then, you believe it now, and you are glad to rest your hopes of heaven on that death and sacrifice. Do not forget the price that was paid. Do not forget the sad scenes of Gethsemane, the judgment hall and Calvary. Do not allow the world to draw you off from your devotion to Christ; do not wait to be reminded, by the table covered with a white linen cloth and spread with the emblems of the body and blood of Jesus, of the infinite obligations you are under to the divine Redeemer, but live, as in his presence, a life of purity and godliness, and never be ashamed to confess him before men.

If there be any here who are not Christians, who have lived through the years of childhood and youth to this hour, who are now living without gratitude, without love to this Redeemer, whose hearts are unmoved when Jesus Christ is set forth evidently crucified, let me say, with all plainness and sincerity, yet in all tenderness, that so far as can be learned from the Holy Scriptures and from human experience, there is no other hope of eternal life ; and that if you yield not to the influences of the Holy Spirit as he takes of the things of Christ and shows them to you, there remaineth no more sacrifice for sins, but a certain fearful looking for of judgment.

XXII.

An Easter Talk.*

THIS is Easter Sunday, a great church festival, the observance of which, until recently, we have been content to leave largely to the Roman Catholic and Protestant Episcopal churches.

To get a fuller view of its importance and glory, it will be well to contrast it with the two or three days which preceded it.

On Thursday evening last, as we sat down to supper, some of us thought that at the same season of the year, on the evening of the same day of the week, and at the same hour of the day, about eighteen hundred and sixty years ago, our Lord, with his twelve disciples, sat down to eat the Passover Supper. It was the last time they were all together (one of the disciples was soon to desert them), and it was, in a certain sense, the last Passover that was ever celebrated. After the supper, our Lord instituted what we call the Lord's Supper (which, forever after, was to take the place of the Passover), by taking some of the bread and wine that was left from the Passover, and so consecrating them for a memorial, gave them to his disciples, directing them forever after to do the same thing in remembrance of him. Then follows the wonderful discourse recorded in the fourteenth, fifteenth and sixteenth chapters of St. John ; then the prayer in the seventeenth chapter. Then they all left the upper room, went

---

* An address to the Sunday-school of the Woodland Presbyterian Church, Philadelphia, Easter, 1892.

(158)

out into the street, out of the City gate, down the hill, across
the valley and the stream to the garden of Gethsemane.
Then follow the agony in the garden, and the bloody sweat,
the weary hours, the betrayal, the arrest, the desertion of the
disciples, the two mock trials, the sending to and fro between
Pilate and Herod, the condemnation (there was no conviction), the delivery to the soldiers and the Jews, the procession to Calvary, the crucifixion at nine o'clock (I cannot dwell
upon that), the agony from nine to twelve o'clock, intensified
by the taunts and jeers and mockery of those who looked on,
as well as by the inflammation and fever from the wounds,
then the total darkness and silence from twelve to three
o'clock ; ah ! who does not know how darkness aggravates
suffering ! As our Lord hung there, in that appalling darkness, what immeasurable depths of suffering he must have
endured, ended at last by that cry, piercing the gloom, the
full meaning of which we shall never in this life know :
" My God ! my God ! why hast thou forsaken me ? "

There is one glimpse of light, and only one, in this horror
of great darkness. There came from the lips of the Divine
Sufferer the words, " I thirst ; " feeble they must have been,
perhaps not much more than a wail, but distinctly heard in
•that awful silence, " I thirst." And one of them—a soldier
possibly, we do not know his name ; whoever he was, God
bless him—one of them took a sponge and dipped it in vin-
egar, their light, sour wine, and with a reed pressed it to the
lips of Jesus. It was not refused this time.

Then came the taking down from the cross, done by tender
and loving hands we may believe, the burial in Joseph's
new tomb, and all is over on the FIRST Good Friday.

Saturday morning comes; a guard is set over the tomb; the
stone was sealed. The long hours of Saturday pass ; all is
still ; the night comes and goes.

Very early Sunday morning, certain women went to the
grave with spices to embalm the body of Jesus. They found

the stone rolled away ; they looked in ; the body of the Lord was gone ; the grave was empty ; the grave-clothes were there ; even the napkin which had been used, then as now, to compose the features of the dead, even the napkin was folded and laid by itself, but the body was gone. They expected to find Jesus there. There were angels, one or two, at one time visible, at another not, who anticipate their question—"He is not here! He is risen!"

(How slow they were to believe!)

Then follows the appearance of our Lord to Mary. She was weeping at the tomb—weeping because she could not find the Lord.

Suddenly the words were spoken : "Woman, why weepest thou—whom seekest thou?" She turned to the speaker, and, either in the dim light of the early morning or because her eyes were blinded with tears, supposing him to be the gardener, said : "Sir, if thou have borne him hence, tell me where thou hast laid him, and I will take him away." But when he said, "Mary," she answered, "Rabboni! Master!"

(Let me say to you girls, especially, that the first person to whom our Lord made himself known after his resurrection was a woman.)

In the afternoon of that day, and probably just about this hour, two men in earnest conversation were walking along a country road. Suddenly there appeared at their side a stranger, who asked them what they were talking about so earnestly, looking so sad. They expressed great surprise that he, apparently just coming from Jerusalem, did not know of the great events that had just happened there. Then they told this stranger the story of the crucifixion, the darkness, the earthquake, and all the horrors of that awful Friday, and ended by telling him of the death of Jesus, who, they added, "we thought would have redeemed Israel." Then the stranger began to talk—"O foolish ones, O slow to believe," he said, "ought not Christ to suffer these things and to enter into his glory?" And beginning at Moses and the prophets, he expounded to them the things concerning himself.

Then they came near to the village where the two men were going, and the stranger would have passed on, but so charmed were they with his conversation (O that we knew all that he said!) that they insisted he should go in with them—"Abide with us, for the day is far spent." Then all went in, the table was spread, they sat down; the stranger, in the most natural way, becomes the head of the house, the entertainer; he breaks the bread. Ah! what is this? Is it the manner of his breaking the bread, or do they see in the uplifted hands, as he asks the blessing, the prints of the nails? "It is the Lord! the crucified one!" Their eyes are opened. He vanishes.

Ah! they know him now! Why did they not know him before? why did they not feel his presence as they walked and talked in that country road? No supper for them now. He had disappeared. They rise, they go back again to Jerusalem, they seek the disciples, they tell the glad tidings—"The Lord is risen. We have seen the Lord,"—and suddenly, the doors being shut, he comes in and reveals himself to them, saying, "Peace be unto you."

So ends the first Easter. Easter is the greatest of all the festivals of the church. Even in those branches of the church which make the most of great days, Easter is the highest, the best. In nature it is the time of revival. The long, cold winter is gone; spring is come again; the birds have come back—where from? How did they know the way? They look like the same birds that left us when the winter came. The trees are beginning to put out pale, green shoots, the grass is green again, the flowers are here—how beautiful! Look at them—who brought them here? Why are they brought here?

They are the evidences of a new life. The dead things

11

are no longer dead ; they are alive. Jesus Christ was dead ; he is alive again. He rose from the tomb. Death could not hold him ; nor can death hold us. Because he lives we shall live also.

It is a time of gladness. Flowers make people glad. Many a sick-room is brightened this Easter Sunday by flowers, especially lilies sent by loving Christian hearts to poor sick sufferers. Many a dull eye is brightened to-day by the gift of Easter flowers. Why do we bring them to church? To make the Lord's House beautiful ; nothing is too good to offer him. Then we shall send them before the bloom is gone to the sick, who cannot come to church or to Sunday-school.

Easter is the gladdest day in the year. It is children's day. Last Sunday—Palm Sunday—might have been children's day, when the children met our Lord on the way to Jerusalem shouting, "Hosannah to the Son of David !" but to-day is better. Then he was going to his death ; *now he is alive.*

What a blessed thought it is that Christian people all over the world to-day—the Roman Catholic Church, the Greek Church, which so far outnumber us, and all the many other sects and fragments into which the body of Christ is unhappily divided—that all of us to-day are keeping, with more or less uniformity, this splendid Easter service ! Is not this a most hopeful sign that the friends of Christ are coming more and more close together, and that in the near future we shall be seeing each other in a better light, as workers in a common cause and all devoted to a common Saviour?

It was at Westminster Abbey, in the afternoon of Easter. There was a great crowd, so that I could not get near enough to the preacher to hear him. But I went really for the music, and in this I was not disappointed. A boy with a soprano voice sang, with great expression, "I know that my Redeemer liveth," to the end without faltering, and at the end the whole choir followed with the "Hallelujah Chorus."

And there I sat in the Poets' corner almost under the mural tablet erected to Handel, the author of this heavenly music ; and looking at his white marble effigy holding in his hand a scroll with the words, "I know that my Redeemer liveth," it seemed almost as if he were listening to it and joining in the music. And while the boy was singing the sweet strains, "I know that my Redeemer liveth," I thought of another boy who some years ago used to touch and soften our hearts at home by his sweet singing of the same divine music ; and when the "Hallelujah Chorus" came in, I could not doubt that he was joining in the heavenly chorus, "King of kings and Lord of lords ! King of kings and Lord of lords !" for those two pieces of Handel's Messiah are always associated in my mind with my dear son.

Why is Easter so important? Because it is the anniversary of the resurrection of Christ from the grave. If Christ did not rise from the dead, there is no truth in Christianity. He said he should rise ; the disciples did not understand, did not believe. They could hardly believe he had risen. Some people who call themselves disciples don't believe it now.

But if Christ did not rise, then there *is no* resurrection, and we must drop from the Creed those magnificent words, "I believe in the resurrection of the body and the life everlasting." And if Christ did not rise from the dead, how can we hope to see again those whom we have loved and lost a while ?

> Saint after saint on earth
> Has lived and loved and died ;
> And as they left us one by one,
> We laid them side by side.
> We laid them down to sleep ;
> But not in hope forlorn ;
> We laid them but to slumber there,
> Till the last glorious morn.

Some of us know what these lines mean. We have all parted from those we love ; they have gone from us into the eternal world. We bade them good-bye ; we even sent messages of love by them to those who had gone before. Does this mean nothing ? Why, we expect to meet them, to see them again. Surely a time will come—

> " When with the morn those angel faces smile,
>   Which we have loved long since and lost a while."

Lost a while ; not forever, as it would be if Christ is not risen.

"If a man die, shall he live again ?" said Job ; and the answer comes from the lips of our Lord himself : "I am the resurrection and the life. He that believeth in me, though he were dead yet shall he live ; and whosoever liveth and believeth in me shall never die."

"O blessed day of the Resurrection, which of old was called the Queen of Festivals, and which raised among Christians an anxious, nay contentious, diligence duly to honor it ; blessed day, once only passed in sorrow, when the Lord actually rose and the disciples believed not, but ever since a day of joy to the faith and love of the Church ! In ancient times Christians all over the world began it with a morning salutation. Each one said to his neighbor, 'The Lord is risen ;' and his neighbor answered, 'Christ is risen indeed, and hath appeared to Simon.' Even to Simon, the coward disciple who denied him thrice, is Christ risen ; even to us, who long ago vowed to obey him and have yet so often denied him before men, so often taken part with sin and followed the world when Christ called us another way, even to us is Christ risen."*

---

* *Newman.*

XXIII.

The Sunday-school Teacher's Work,

What it is—How to do it.*

I come to speak to you on the Sunday-school teacher's work.

I hardly suppose I can say anything new. Very likely everything I may say has been already said by others. I have no new theories to present.

You will all admit, however, that the Sunday-school work is a great work. It is not a small thing to teach small children. I have no fear that it will be overestimated. The church generally does not appreciate its importance. If we could realize that the boys and girls that gather round us in classes will, in five or ten years or so, occupy our places, we should have a higher estimate of the importance of the work.

The family is a divine institution, and is the first in the order of time and importance of all the appointments of God. God made man and woman in Eden and gave them children, and wherever the knowledge of God has come, the family and the church continue.

The church has continued, in various forms—once the state, as in the Hebrew theocracy; sometimes allied to and established by the state, as in England, in Russia, and other countries; and sometimes entirely independent of the state, as with us. But who is bold enough to say that the diverse

---

*Superintendents' Association of the Presbyterian Church.
Germantown, May 19, 1884.

forms and organizations in which the church now exists are all of divine appointment?

Next to the family and the church I think, comes the Sunday-school. We do not claim for it a divine appointment. But it is justly claimed that the Sunday-school is the natural and proper outgrowth and development of religion through the family and the church.

The grandest occupation on earth is teaching. Nothing can be more important than to give instruction, especially in such knowledge as is essential to happiness.

The Sunday-school teacher's authority to teach comes from the same divine source as does that of the ordained clergyman to preach the gospel—"Go ye into all the world, and preach the gospel to every creature." The command is so broad that it includes all efforts everywhere and by whomsoever made, to make known the religion of Christ to those who are ignorant of it. The call is from God, and it comes to every one who has himself accepted the overtures of grace and professed his faith in Jesus Christ.

The call does not come to all disciples with the same application. Some accept it in its most literal signification, and they go to heathen lands as missionaries; some accept it in the light of a call to preach the gospel as ordained clergymen at home, and they at once set about a careful and laborious preparation for the great work; others take it as a call to labor with the pen in the presentation of Bible truth in the printed page of a book, paper, or magazine; others in the daily life of business or manual labor; others again in the patient training of children in the family circle; but very many disciples accept the call as a commission to labor as teachers in the Sunday-school,—for this is on many accounts, outside the family, the simplest and the cheapest of the means of propagating the Christian religion.

It is well known that in the beginning of the Sunday-school work the primary object was to collect ignorant and destitute children and give them the rudiments of an English education. This was all, and the first teachers were paid for their work. Then, as the schools were held on Sunday because poor children could better attend on that day, and as the teachers were Christian people, naturally religious instruction largely entered into the plans of the teachers. As this instruction advanced to higher methods and attracted more cultivated teachers, the character of the teaching became so much more systematic and thorough and practical that the children of the middle and upper ranks of society could not afford to be excluded, and in time the Sunday-school grew to be what it is now—an institution embracing among its teachers some of the best and most cultivated minds of the church, and among its pupils the children of all classes of society, from the highest to the lowest.

A Sunday-school may be said to be in good condition when it contains as many pupils as can be accommodated within its walls ; when there is a sufficient number of teachers, who are regular and punctual in their attendance, and whose constant aim is to impart spiritual instruction clearly and thoroughly and affectionately ; when its officers are experienced in the best modes of managing its machinery, and are intelligent and spiritual and zealous and persevering, and when the Spirit of God is present, quickening and converting.

The great object of the teacher is undoubtedly to bring the children and youth committed to his care to the Saviour. But how is this to be done ? What means shall the teacher employ to secure this end ?

It is easier to ask these questions than to answer them. Yet there must be an answer, if we can find it, and a satisfactory answer.

The instrument to be employed in the work is the interpretation and application of the sacred Scriptures. I wish I could say these words so that they might reach the minds and hearts of all who are engaged in this work. I repeat them.

The object of Sunday-school teaching is to lead children and youth to the Saviour.

The means to be employed are the interpretation and application of the sacred Scriptures.

You see at once that this is real hard work. It cannot be taken up as a pastime, pursued for a time with little study, and laid aside at pleasure, with any hope of success. It will tax the powers of the greatest intellect and the profoundest scholarship, to do the work in the very best way, and yet the helps to do it well, are within the reach of all who with good common sense and a common English education, and a sincere love for the young, will earnestly address themselves to the work.

The Scriptures cannot be satisfactorily explained without patient study. This preparation cannot be made in one hour or two hours. Every lesson properly studied will require more time than this. I fear you will not agree with me. Your mind goes back to your own methods. You recall the fact that you often meet your class when you have found the lesson so plain and simple that a half hour or an hour was all that was needed to prepare you to teach it.

Ah, no, you are wrong ! If you have the genius of Paul and the eloquence of Apollos you may meet your class weekly with a half hour's study or with no study, but not otherwise. The best man to prepare Sunday-school lessons that I have ever known was accustomed to spend two or three hours on a single lesson, and he was a man of disciplined mind and large information and great aptness to teach, and thoroughly at home in the Scriptures.

Notwithstanding the aid afforded by the several writers on the series of " International Lessons " so generally in use, it is very important to have a meeting of the teachers for the study of the lesson. While I am not prepared to say that no school can prosper without such a meeting, I do say that few can afford to do without it.   There are many teachers who have not the time, nor the habits of study, nor the helps within reach to prepare lessons by themselves ; if such could have the advantage of a meeting once a week for this purpose, where the best informed of the teachers compare the results of their study, and talk over points not always noticed by stately writers on the passage, it would be of immense advantage to the school.

Such a meeting would be especially useful for the younger and less experienced teachers, and would be well worth all the time and pains it would cost.   But almost everything depends on the knowledge and skill of him who conducts such an exercise, to see that time is not wasted on unimportant passages, and to secure the advantages of the best scholarship within reach, and to prevent the meeting from becoming common-place and protracted.

I am thinking of the teacher as he meets his class.   The opening exercises, whether brief or protracted, appropriate or inappropriate, are over, and the class settles around the teacher.   Whatever the preparation may have been, whether elaborate or insufficient, the time is now come for work.

How much depends upon the character of the first question asked, and upon the tones of the voice which utters it !   The pupils see at once whether the teacher is master of the subject, and whether his heart is in the work.   If they see in the teacher's eye an intelligent interest, if they observe ' in the tones of his voice that he is in earnest, their own eyes brighten, their own interest is quickened, for young people love to be taught, they are curious, they are inquiring, and they will not be satisfied by dullness or commonplaces.

You need not tell them that you have not given the subject as much attention as it deserved—they knew that before ! You ought not to apologize too often for want of preparation ;

their good nature will not excuse always. They are quick
to discern and appreciate, and you must not think you can
deceive them.

Every word and phrase and sentence of the lesson ought to
be explained. Who was the writer? In what language did
he write? Was that the language of the country? What
was he trying to teach or explain by this passage? What is
the relation of this verse or sentiment to that which preceded
it, and to that which follows, or to the subject in hand?
What is the general scope of the subject? Who or what are
the characters on the scene? What are the surrounding incidents? Then, if the nature of the subject will permit,
illustrate it by contemporary history and biography, by
geography, government, literature, language, science, architecture, military life, agricultural and social life. There are
many parts of Scripture, especially of the New Testament,
which will admit of this comprehensive method of treatment.
In all our language there is no finer example of this kind of
illustration than in Conybeare and Howson's Life and Epistles of St. Paul.

Then faithfully apply the teachings, the thought of the
passage to the hearts and consciences of your pupils. Do
not hesitate about this. Do not be afraid of giving offence.
You cannot be too plain if you are kind, and if your pupils
see that you mean what you say; but if this is done from a
sense of duty and with a sort of professional air, you would
better leave it unsaid.

Avoid, if you are at all inclined that way, the habit of
lecturing or preaching to your pupils. It is easy for a teacher
who has free command of language to dwell upon prominent
topics in the lesson, and to deliver very excellent and edifying lectures upon them, but this is not the best method.
That form of instruction where question and answer follow
in quick succession, eliciting remarks and questions from
the pupils in return, arousing and stimulating thought

and expression, has always seemed to me the more pleasant and profitable method.

It was formerly thought that none but clergymen could explain the Scriptures. A knowledge of the Hebrew and Greek languages was considered indispensable. But this is not so now. Common sense, and a heart glowing with love to God and to the souls of men, are better than all the learning of the universities without these.

Commentaries explanatory, textual, expository, homiletical, are multiplied now and published so cheaply as to be within the reach of all teachers ; and the most learned of all the writers on Scripture in our language, Alexander, Hackett, Owen, Bush, Barnes, of the United States ; Alford, Trench, Stanley, Ellicott, Jowett, Lightfoot, Westcott, Davies, Wordsworth, Vaughan, in England, and the various writers in Lange's great and voluminous work, have all labored in the highest regions of sacred criticism to bring the result of the profoundest research to the comprehension of the plainest English scholar. This has never been so before, and therefore the present time—the time in which we live—is better than any other time for the interpretation and application of Scripture truth. Take the comfort of this thought home to your hearts, and let it help you in your studies and stimulate you to faithfulness, that the present is the best time the world has ever seen for Sunday-school instruction.

Do not forget, as you take your seat in your class, that you are the pastor of that little flock. · To many of the scholars in our Sunday-schools this is true in a very important sense, for they have no religious instruction at home, and the modern plan of holding the Sunday-school in the afternoon, with the second church service in the evening, excludes practically a large proportion of Sunday-school pupils from the house of God, and gives them up to Sunday-school teachers. And if any of the children from non-church-going families stray into the sanctuary morning or evening, the sermons which they hear will probably go over their heads, having been prepared for adults and cultivated persons. If the time should come when the Sunday-school service is immediately followed by an appropriate church service attractive to children, it will be a bright day for Sunday-schools and for the Church.

Do not forget then, I repeat, that you are the pastor of that little flock. Of some of them it may be said that all they ever learn of religion and of religious truth they will learn from you. You have some advantages over the pastor. He deals with adult minds, many of them hardened and dulled by long familiarity with the most solemn truths, and fixed in habits of indifference. You have before you, minds in the freshness of youth, with character and habits unformed and immature. He speaks from the pulpit to an audience so large and so far removed from him that he loses in some degree the magnetic contact so important in moving and swaying the mind and heart; while you sit face to face with your audience, so close that you can see the tear in the eye and put your hand upon the shoulder. Do not forget that you are the pastor, and that it is your duty to bring your pupils to the Saviour. The work then is very great. The time is very short; all you see of your class is for an hour and a half or less in a week.

How much you have to do! If you have any control over the lessons, make them short, for the instruction must be thorough, and while the lesson is the great thing, the primary object, indeed, of the school, it is too apt to be made subordinate to the opening and closing exercises.

Maintain perfect order in your class; let there be no trifling, no insubordination, no unmanliness; respect yourself, and your pupils will also respect you. And remember you have other things to teach besides the lesson—things which you must teach incidentally.

The proper use of the library must not be overlooked;

what books to read, how to take care of books ; sometimes a
review of a book which has been read ; the lending of an
appropriate book of your own, not in the school library ;
hints about other literature. You must also guard your
pupils from the influence of others in the school and out of it.
You must tell them to be careful what they read ; what company they keep ; what they do on Sundays ; how to behave
in church, at home, in the street and in public places, at
school, in their daily business ; in short, you must, next to
their parents and family, be their best friend.

You must tell them what true manliness is : that it consists not in imitating the vices or the foolish habits of men ;
not in gay dressing ; not in chewing and smoking tobacco
(I do not say that the use of tobacco is not consistent with
true manliness, but I do say that true manliness does not
consist in these things); not in drinking beer or wine or
whiskey ; not in the use of profane or obscene language ; but
that true manliness consists in straightforward, upright truthfulness, consideration for others, kindness, forbearance, un-
selfishness !

But no matter how earnest and faithful and persevering
we may be in all these respects, what can we hope to accomplish without prayer ?   Not the opening and closing prayers
of the schools merely, not an occasional meeting for prayer,
not the prayer of the closet merely, nor the prayer of the
pulpit ; but the united prayers of the teachers and scholars
together.

I do not mean the setting aside of the school lesson to hold
a Sunday-school prayer-meeting, sometimes a very dull affair ; but suppose, where the Sunday-school session is not
followed by the church service, the superintendent and such
of the teachers as can make it convenient should linger in
the school-room, inviting the larger and more thoughtful of
the scholars to join them, and should spend fifteen or twenty
minutes in united prayer, *not in much singing*, for the bless-

ing of God on the labors, the teachings of the day. What do you think would be the effect of such a meeting? I have no doubt, from observation and experience, that the influence would be most happy, and that ere long the hearts of the teachers would be gladdened by the conversion of very many of their pupils.

A successful Sunday-school is the best adjunct to a church. Most of the activity of the church's life is here. The pastor looks to his teachers as his most efficient fellow-workers.

What would the church be without the Sunday-school? Observe those who at the stated seasons come from the world to profess their faith in Christ, and see how many come from the Sunday-school. How few, indeed, come from elsewhere! Very rarely do heads of families join on profession, nor do they add much to the strength of the church unless they are in early life. Examine carefully any church and analyze its elements, and you will invariably see that most of its life and force come from the Sunday-school.

You see, then, how important it is that the work of Sunday-school teaching should not be left too much to quite young teachers. Admitting that we need here as elsewhere all the freshness and vigor of youth, we must not forget that the work is to lead souls to Christ through the *interpretation and application of the sacred Scriptures*, and this is or ought to be the work of mature minds.

The subject is a large one, and if time permitted I would like to say more on some of the points that I have barely touched.

For I do not think that the Sunday-school has done as much as might fairly have been expected of it.

When we consider how simple and cheap is the machinery, that the children are all about us, that they are easily attracted to the schools, that their attendance does not interfere with the secular schools, nor with their necessary occupation ; that it is easy to find a place to hold a Sunday-school, in the church, in a public school-house, in a kitchen, out of doors ; when we consider how good and cheap and popular a literature is provided especially for such schools, how readily teachers can be found who are willing to work without pay ; I say, when we consider how favorable the conditions are, have we not a *right* to look for larger and better results than we find? Great advance has been made in the knowledge of the Holy Scriptures, and innumerable conversions have been made among the children, but what shall be said of the behavior of Sunday-school boys and girls in the streets, in street cars and in other public places? It is becoming the reproach of our times that the young are so indifferent to their behavior in public. Many of these young persons are from families where there is little or no attention paid to decorum. The secular schools dare not, or *do* not, except in the most superficial manner, touch upon this subject. The Sunday-school teacher can, and must, or it will not be done. A little book under the title of "Don't" has been published lately that deals with kindred subjects, a book that I have had introduced into a large secular school with which I have something to do in the hope that the manners of the pupils may be improved.

When we see a Sunday-school dismissed and the children rushing out into the street, shouting, throwing stones, etc., making the air hideous and the highway dangerous ; when we hear loud talking and laughing and see rude behavior in street cars and other places, and know that the boys and girls who behave so are Sunday-school scholars, and some of them from families where no word of advice is ever given on the subject of behavior, we cannot help asking whether the Sunday-school work has been thoroughly done.

The truth is that the *discipline* of the Sunday-school is not what it ought to be. We are so anxious to have very *large Sunday-schools* that we are afraid to control them as day-schools are controlled. Do you suppose that a teacher of a secular school would permit the wish or fancy of a pupil to hinder his transfer from one class to another? Yet are not Sunday-school superintendents thwarted in their wishes sometimes by the threat that if a pupil cannot go in a certain class he will leave the school?

Dr. Arnold said: "It is not necessary that there shall be five hundred boys at Rugby, but it is necessary that those who are at Rugby school shall be gentlemen."

When I say that the Sunday-school has not done all that might fairly have been expected of it you will ask me, "Why?" One reason is, it has attempted too much. It tries to conduct a Sunday-school and a church service at the same time, and within the compass of an hour and a half. The reason given for this is that as the children will not go to church, the church must be brought to them in the Sunday-school hour. This requires time and machinery, the use of which must be deducted from the time for teaching. The two things are *not identical*. The church service ought to follow the Sunday-school service, and the pupils should be *required to attend*, and the service should be brief and appropriate. This was in my mind when I said just now that the church does not appreciate the Sunday-school. If something in the line of what I have suggested could be adopted, you would soon see a marked change.

The other reason I give why the Sunday-school has not done all that it could have done is that the teachers are not fully equipped and qualified for their work.

I ask any superintendent to look over the roll of his teachers and ask himself the question, How many of these most excellent men and women (or boys and girls, as the case may be, for often very young people are so employed), how many of these unquestionably good people are *really teaching?* They are all Christians, no doubt, and are anxious or very desirous at least to have their scholars saved, but what do they know about *teaching?* How many of them would pass a very easy examination on the theory and practice of teaching? How many are students of the Holy Scriptures except of that portion assigned for the weekly lesson? How many would pass such an examination as would entitle them to a teacher's certificate to teach in our public schools? How many of them have much or any literary taste or are readers of books?

I know this is not an assuring view to take of the situation. I know the standard suggested is high and not easily reached ; I know that people who work for no pecuniary reward are in one sense beyond criticism—nevertheless, I think this is the truth I am speaking, and it seems to me somebody ought to say it.

Why do I say such plain things? I thought that one who has been engaged in this blessed work as many years as I have, and who loves it so well, ought to be able from the stores of his experience to say some things which might help some of the less experienced of teachers. Some of you have long been workers in this field, and some for a much shorter period. Some have had a varied experience, and some have had hardly any experience at all. Some of you love the work most heartily, while some do it from a sense of duty only. Success has crowned the efforts of some, while others have labored apparently almost in vain. And so I have ventured to trespass on your forbearance.

What good will come of it? As you look forward, what are your views of duty? Who can say that he has been as faithful as he might have been? Who can say he has been as watchful, as industrious, as earnest, as he might have been? What are your purposes for the future? What resolutions have you made, and when will you begin to perform them? Oh, teachers, the highest interests on earth are committed to you! If you are faithful, prayerful, devoted, if you turn many to righteousness, you shall shine as the stars

12

for ever and ever !   But if you neglect these interests, if you
are cold and careless in your work, if you have little prayer
and less zeal, and if you allow your children to grow up careless, unimpressed, unconverted, you will be called to a strict
account.   The blood of souls may be found in your skirts,
and how shall you go up to your Father's house and these
children and youth not go with you ?

XXIV.

The Girard College.*

"I was glad when they said unto me, Let us go into the house of the Lord."—*Psalm* 122 : 1.

THIS psalm was intended to be sung by the people, as they climbed up the rocky steeps to the walls of Jerusalem ; or as they passed through the streets to the temple to offer worship to the great God ; or it was intended to express the delight which filled the heart of the pious Jew when he started from his distant home to go to the Holy City on one of the three great annual feasts.

Whatever may have been the occasion of its production, it is now a most expressive instruction to us of the feelings with which we should regard the worship of God in his house and on his day. And I have chosen the passage for the purpose of speaking to you about the services in this Chapel, to which you are called every day, and every Sunday.

Although Mr. Girard enjoined that no ecclesiastic, missionary, or minister of any sect whatsoever, should ever hold or exercise any station or duty whatever in the College, nor ever be admitted for any purpose, or even as a visitor, within the premises appropriated to the purposes of the College, he is careful to say that he does not intend to cast any reflection on any sect or person whatever ; only intending to keep the

---

* An Address delivered in the Chapel of the Girard College, on the occasion of the introduction of the New Manual, July 22, 1883.

minds of his pupils free from sectarian controversy until
their matured reason should enable them to adopt such
religious tenets as they may prefer.

When the College was opened there were many persons
living who were better able to determine the meaning of this
clause of Mr. Girard's will than some of the critics of our
day ; and the first directors without hesitation provided for
religious services in a place set apart for the purpose.

So, for many years, and as long as the number of pupils
did not exceed five hundred and fifty, the room in the southwest corner of the main building was appropriated for the
purposes of a chapel ; and Judge Jones, the first President
of the College (except one who served for a very short period),
delivered a course of lectures (afterwards published) on the
life of Joseph. When the population of the College was
increased above five hundred and fifty, some years ago, this
Chapel was built for the purposes of daily and Sunday
worship, as well as for other purposes, when all the schools
are assembled in one place.

We are sure then that it is quite within the purpose of
Mr. Girard that the principles of our common Christianity
should be taught to his pupils. We believe, indeed, that
we should be wanting most seriously in our duty to you if we
did not provide appropriate religious instruction. So this
Chapel was erected, and here we meet every day and every
Sunday to worship God. Although not permitted to have the
assistance of men who are devoted to the sacred ministry,
we believe that acceptable worship can be offered to Almighty
God in any place and by any persons.

Long ago, in patriarchal times, a man who was fleeing as
a fugitive from the vengeance of his brother, whom he had
deeply wronged, found himself at nightfall in a wild and
rocky place, and, gathering some stones for a pillow, lay
down to sleep. He was alone. There was no house near
him, he had no tent to cover him, and he lay down under

the clear starlit sky to rest.   It was no common sleep, for he
had a most wonderful dream.   The last things that his eyes
rested on before they closed were the deep vault of heaven
and the bright stars, nowhere more brilliant than in that
country.   And in his dream he saw a ladder with the lower
end on the ground near his rocky pillow, while its top
reached up to the stars, and bright angels were ascending
and descending on that ladder, and God stood at the top and
talked with the sleeper.   And when Jacob awoke from his
sleep he said, "Surely the Lord is in this place . . . This
is none other but the house of God ; . . . this is the gate
of heaven."

So the next morning early he took one of the stones on
which his head had rested in the night, and set it up for a
memorial of his vision, an altar to God, and poured a little
oil upon it as a sort of sacrifice, and called the place about
there Beth-el, which means "the house of God," because
there he met God and communed with him and worshipped
him. . . .

About eighteen hundred years after this, in the early spring,
and not very far from the same place, a young man, weary,
hungry and thirsty, sat down by the side of a well.   He was
alone.   Looking down a hundred feet or more into its depths,
he saw the clear, cold water, but could not reach it.   He
had nothing to draw with.   It was midday, and the hot sun
poured down its scorching beams on his unprotected head.
While he sat there, waiting for the return of his companions,
who had left him a little while since, a woman came from
the near village to draw water from the well.   As she came
up he asked her to give him a drink.   She looked at him,
surprised that he should ask so unusual a favor.   And why
unusual?   Because there was something in his dress or his
accent which showed her that he belonged to another people,
and a people who generally would hold no intercourse at all
with her countrymen.   This surprise she expressed not only

in her looks, but in the question which immediately followed :
"How is it that thou, being a Jew, askest drink of me, a
Samaritan woman ?"

Then followed that conversation between Jesus and the
woman of Samaria—one of the most remarkable that ever
occurred.

"If you knew," said he, "who it is that talks with you,
you would ask me, and I would give you living water."

"How could you give me water?" said she, mistaking
his meaning. "The well is deep; you have nothing to
draw with."

The conversation goes on. I do not give the literal
Scripture. He explains that he is not speaking of the water
in the well, but of the *water of life;* but she is very slow to
learn or very unwilling to learn, until presently he says
something about herself which startles her, for she supposes
it impossible that a stranger could know. It was something
which she was unwilling to talk about, for it was of the im-
proper life she was living. So she tried to change the subject
—it was becoming too close, too personal—and, with the ex-
clamation that he must be a prophet, she tries to lead him
into a theological discussion by saying, "Our fathers worshipped in this mountain," pointing up to Mount Gerizim,
where the Samaritans at that day offered their sacrifices, and
where even down to our own time they slay and eat the
lamb at the passover. "Our fathers," said she, "worshipped
in this mountain, but ye say that in Jerusalem is the place
where men ought to worship."

Then came those grand words which have been so often
read, so often quoted, and so little understood, which ought
to have had so much influence in the world and which have
had so little.

"Woman," said he, "there cometh an hour, it is even
now come, when ye shall not only in this mountain nor in
Jerusalem worship the Father. True worshippers must

worship the Father in spirit and in truth, for God is a spirit."
As if he had said, "Heretofore public worship has been
limited to sacred places, but now and hereafter worship, if
spiritual, may be offered in any place."

"The true Christian ideal is this : a holy season extending
all the year round, a temple confined only by the limits of
the habitable world, a priesthood coextensive with the
human race." * In other words, all spiritual worship is
acceptable to God, no matter *when*, *where*, or *by whom*
offered. Such is the worship which we offer in this house.

In accordance with this grand principle we are assembled
to-day, in this Chapel, for the worship of God.

How shall this worship be offered ? What is expected of
you as to your part in the service? what is expected of us
who conduct or direct these services ?

What is expected of *you ?*

1. *Strict attention.* The services will not be long—hardly
ever more than an hour in length. So careful are we to
protect you from speakers who forget that many of you are
very young, and some of whom are apt to speak longer than
you can be expected to listen patiently, that a card has been
prepared and placed upon the desk with these words—"As
so large a proportion of this congregation is composed of
very young children, it is particularly requested that the
address shall not exceed twenty minutes in delivery."

When you come into Chapel there should be no conversation whatever. Unless you watch yourselves carefully you
will forget this. It is entirely unnecessary, and cannot be
permitted. Neither should there be any effort on the part
of any boy to attract the attention of another. There must
be no shuffling of feet, no coughing, nothing that will disturb
him who sits next you, or anybody else. In short, there
should be no necessity for supervision by an officer or teacher.

---

* Bishop Lightfoot, Durham.

I believe it is quite possible for this large congregation to sit as quietly and behave as well as any other congregation. And I believe the time will come when you can be trusted to behave yourselves without the oversight which now seems to be necessary.

2. *Active participation in the services* is also expected of you.

The Board having authorized the preparation of a new Manual, it is in your hands to-day. There is a selection from the Psalms, or from some other part of the Sacred Scriptures, for the morning and afternoon services of thirty-one days. This will give great variety in the readings. The Psalter will not become tiresome from frequent repetition. Indeed this could hardly be so, even if you read it every day in the week.

The advantages of the reading of the Psalter are very great. You will become familiar with the most poetical and the most devotional part of the Scriptures by this frequent reading. And you cannot estimate the value of this knowledge of the Holy Scriptures. You will observe that the selections are not printed in the usual prose form, but in shorter lines. To the eye it resembles blank verse. Hebrew poetry did not rhyme as our English poetry often does, nor has it the rhythm which marks our poetry. Its chief characteristic is parallelism of meaning. That is, instead of being measured by syllables, or flowing in natural easy measures, or ending in rhymes, it repeats itself in parallel meanings.

This may not always be apparent, but it is generally so if the lines are properly divided.

Now this will give you something to do ; for I think it very important that you should have a part, and an important part, in this Chapel service. The Psalter is to be read by yourselves. The lines are very short, your attention must be held to the page, the type is large and clear, and after a few services it will become very easy and agreeable to you.

When I said the Psalter is to be read by yourselves, I meant that he who conducts the service is not expected to read with you.* It is to be desired that the teachers and officers who have charge of you in Chapel will take part in the reading of the Psalter. It will add much to the precision and spirit of the service. Some day it is hoped it may be possible to sing the Psalter. It was so intended by the holy men who wrote these parts of the Scriptures, and they were undoubtedly sung in the daily temple service in the old times. For I look for great improvement in the vocal music here. Much has been done, but much more is to be done, and *you* are to do it.

When the Scriptures are read, remember that they are the truth of God. *He* is speaking to *you*. In the far-off ages of the past he spake from Mount Sinai, with thick darkness on the mountain, the earthquake, the thunder and the lightning; now he speaks through the Sacred Scriptures and by his Spirit.

Listen earnestly, patiently, to the speaker. No matter how dull he may be, there is something in the address that will do you good if you are on the lookout for it. That must be a very poor speaker indeed that has not one good thought for you. We who come to speak to you are not clergymen—we are business men—but we claim to be students of the Holy Scriptures. We love to explain them, and we love you. We are not paid for coming. We may not know as much as we ought to know, nor as much as we desire to know, but we know that you are our young brothers—that we are travelling on the same journey of life. We know that we have the start of you by many years, that we know the road better than you do, and we want to help you in the journey. We do not come to teach new truths. Our purpose is to explain and illustrate the Bible, and apply

---

* You are to read the lines antiphonally.

its plain teachings as closely and personally as we can.   You may not know, from anything we say, to what branch of the Church we belong, though all of us do belong to some branch of the Church.

We do not come to persuade you to join the church— there is no church here to join—but we do ask you to believe in the Lord Jesus Christ and be saved.   Then, at a proper time, we hope that you will seek some church that is most convenient to you, or most in accordance with your tastes or the religious views of your kindred, and join it.   For we are so dependent on each other for counsel and sympathy, and are so helped by Christian fellowship, that your Christian life is not likely to be well rounded or very efficient unless you join yourselves to some one company of Christian disciples and live and labor with them.

I did not take my text as a mere motto for this discourse. I chose it because it is the fitting expression of the feelings which we should have as we think of the house of God.   We should be glad when we think of going to Chapel.   The services here ought to be such that we should look forward to them with eagerness and pleasure.   I hope that in the cultivation of vocal music you will take great pleasure.   To many persons there is nothing so sweet as the voices of young boys cultivated in sacred song.   There is a quality of excellence in boys' voices which does not belong to the voices of girls.   I am not musician enough to explain this, but it is so ; and the fact that the finest music in the great cathedrals is made largely by boys' voices proves what I say. Why should not we here give such attention to this most beautiful accomplishment as to reach a high success?   I assure you this is quite worth your while, not only for the present orderly service of the Chapel, but when you acquire a knowledge of sacred music and leave here to make your way in the world, you will learn that it is no mean acquisition ; but, on the contrary, such is the attention given now to this subject in the churches, that a boy who has cultivated his voice in childhood and understands music and has a good voice will find that he can add to his income very handsomely by an engagement in a church choir.

The speakers here are laymen of different branches of the Church, but they will not teach any other truths than those in which all Christians agree. I hope these truths will be made so plain that you cannot misunderstand them, and I hope and pray that the Holy Spirit will impress them upon your hearts.

But is God really here? You look around. God is everywhere. We cannot see his form nor hear his voice, for he is a spirit. He is here, however, just as really as if we could see him and hear him and touch him.

Come, then, and worship God to-day. He is present by his Spirit. It is difficult to have any distinct idea of God, but you can easily think of Jesus Christ the Saviour. He was once as young as you are. He grew up through the helpless years of infancy as other children ; dependent on his blessed mother, as you were on your mother. He grew to be a man, as you are growing to be men. He was tempted to do wrong, as you all are, but he did not sin ; he was pure, he was holy. But as he was, and as he is, of our nature, he knows how to sympathize with us who are tempted. And he will help us when we are tempted. He, and he only, can help you to keep your good resolutions ; he, and he only, can change your hearts.

Do not forget, then, that worship—true Christian worship of Almighty God—will be just as acceptable to him when offered here as if this were the grandest temple in the world.

The time will come when these seats will be filled by other boys, who will gather here every Sunday for instruction and worship. You who are now here are passing through your school-life, and will soon be gone, but others will take your places ; we who are here as teachers and

friends will pass away and be forgotten ; this house itself, if
not consumed with fire, will one day crumble into dust ;
but the words that shall be spoken from this desk, if only they
be right and true words, will never die.   And the souls that
shall be gathered here for worship and instruction, the hundreds—aye, the thousands—of boys who shall sit on these
seats will live forever.

Oh, that this house may be to all these souls the house of
God, the very gate of heaven !

XXV

THE BIBLE: WHAT IT IS—HOW TO STUDY IT.*

THE world is full of books. If the author of Ecclesiastes could say nearly 3000 years ago, "Of making many books there is no end," however we may understand that passage, what could he say in our day with the accumulations of these centuries? More than 700,000 volumes are said to have been burned in the Alexandrian library, but our regret at such wholesale destruction of literature is lessened when we reflect that much of it must have been worthless. The press in our day, however, turns out every year more than the contents of that vast library.

The multiplication of books within the last half-century is almost marvellous. Before this there were few books in our country except in the libraries of colleges and other public libraries. The American Sunday-School Union was the first institution to prepare a wholesome and cheap literature for the young. All the books that were accessible to children and sought by them before this, might be counted on your fingers, and were certainly not of the highest character. Now many kindred societies and firms are engaged in publishing books that are so attractive and so cheap that they are in the hands of almost all the young. I wish it could be added that all these volumes are sound and practical and safe.

Fifty years ago few families, except the wealthy, had any

---

* A Bible-class study, 1870.

books besides the Bible and a few books of devotion. Now
almost every household has its book-shelf with a few or more
volumes.

It is less than 500 years since printing from types was
invented in Europe, though the Chinese are said to have
printed books from blocks a thousand years before. But the
making of books does not depend upon printing. Men began to write very early. Probably the earliest method of
communicating thoughts, other than by speech, was by a
rude sketch. Thus, if a savage wished to convey the idea of
a battle, a horse, a fish, or anything, he would doubtless
make a rude picture of it on the sand, on the bark of a tree,
or anything else convenient, and this picture would be more
or less perfect, according to the state of art among such
people.

This led to engraving, which in the time of Moses must
have been more or less known. I believe it is not possible
to determine how early in the history of the world an alpha-
bet or written language of letters and words was used. Some
have thought that when Abraham bought his burying-place
from the sons of Heth, the minute details (in the twenty-
second chapter of Genesis) imply that he received a deed, or
bill of sale. We learn that God with his own hand wrote
the ten commandments on two tables of stone, and in letters
and words which Moses and the children of Israel could read
and understand. But after men in those far-off ages had
written with various implements on the bark and the leaves
of trees, on bone, ivory, on metallic and wooden tables,
a higher culture led to the use of the skins of animals,
dressed for the purpose, and characters, letters and words
traced thereon in ink. These were but poorly prepared until
about two thousand years before Christ, when the art was
carried to a great perfection at Pergamos, from which circumstance they were called pergamena, and from this comes
our word parchment. The ink which they used in the

earliest ages was made of charcoal, pulverized, dissolved in water with the addition of a little gum.

The Bible is the best book in the world. Why is it so? It is the book of God. I mean by this, it is God's book. He is the author. It is his revealed will. It teaches the way of salvation.

The fact that God is its author, even if its contents did not concern us, would give it transcendent importance. If a book should now be discovered whose authorship could absolutely be traced to some great writer of a past age, whose works it had been supposed were all collected years before, how would the world rush after it ! A few years ago thousands of persons read a novel of English life and manners, not because it was considered particularly brilliant, or that it contained information that was new or important—not because of the interest of the story, or of any grace or elegance of style, but because it was written by a prime-minister of England. Curiosity was excited to know what such a man thought of events which were occurring at that time. Had the book been published anonymously, it had perhaps hardly been reprinted in this country. But the author was a man who, earlier in life, had been distinguished in literature, and in later years had held the highest place in the government of Great Britain, and the public wanted to know what sort of a book he would now write.

When we take the Bible in our hands we know it is no human production. We have evidence the most conclusive, external and internal, that it came from God. You cannot believe in the existence of a God, supreme and infinite, governing the world, without supposing that there must be some means by which he makes known his will to his intelligent creatures. When Adam and Eve were created and placed in the garden of Eden, and were sinless, God talked with them, face to face, as a man talketh with his friend. He made known his will by his spoken words.

Farther on, and in the days of the patriarchs, he com-
municated with men by means of visions and dreams.
Sometimes he appeared in an assumed form, either of an angel
(at least under that name) or in the form of a man. Not
until the days of Moses was the will of God made known
through the medium of writing, and in his case he wrote
precisely what he was directed to write. After Moses other
historians, Joshua, Ezra and some others, continued the history through the succeeding centuries, and one prophet after
another took up the strain until the Captivity, and even to
the return of the Jews from Babylon, when prophecy ceased,
and for some five hundred years the voice of inspiration was
hushed.

During this period other historians arose who wrote as
men write history now. But their narratives have not been
included in our canon, though we sometimes print them in
our Bibles under the name of "The Apocrypha."

The Bible teaches the way of salvation. The doctrines of
vicarious suffering, of expiatory sacrifices, may be found
among people where the Bible is not known, although there
is little doubt that these doctrines have been handed down
by tradition from Scripture sources. But nowhere except
in the Bible and books drawn from it, do we find the
great truth of salvation from sin by the death of the Son
of God.

The Bible not only reveals this great doctrine, but it de-
scribes the means by which it is made available. It is true
that Jesus Christ died to save men, that he came to save that
which was lost. The terms of salvation, which can be
learned nowhere else, are plainly declared in the Bible.
"Repentance toward God and faith toward our Lord Jesus
Christ." "Go ye into all the world and preach the gospel
to every creature." "He that believeth and is baptized
shall be saved; but he that believeth not shall be damned."
"Thy faith hath saved thee, go in peace."

The obligations of the world to the Bible are immeasurable, almost infinite. If any one doubts this, let him contrast the condition of the nations of the world that are without the Bible, with Great Britain and the United States. Look at the civilization, the government, the domestic life of such nations and then look at ours. Look at the lands where Christianity is disseminated and developed, not in connection with the printed Bible, scattered everywhere as with us, but where its propagation depends upon a gorgeous ritual and blazing altars, and where music and painting and sculpture and incense and architecture and robed priests all appeal to the senses. What makes Spain and Italy and France, and indeed almost all continental Europe, differ so widely in their government, the education of the common people, their literature, their domestic life, from the United States but the fact that here the Bible is scattered everywhere, read in our churches, taught in our Sunday-schools and found in so many of our families, while in most of those countries the Holy Scriptures are not within reach of the common people, and not considered necessary to the development of a healthy civilization.

" Whether, then, we look at legislative science, the principles of which are found in the writings of Moses, the Hebrew lawgiver, or to civil liberty, most free in our own country, but destined to pervade the world, or to religious liberty and the rights of conscience, to secure and maintain which have cost oceans of blood, or to public or private morality, or to the abolition of human slavery, or to the Sabbath, or to true religion, or to human happiness generally in its highest sense, we cannot but feel that the Bible alone has brought us all that is good, and relieved us of what is bad." *

The Bible is at once the easiest and the hardest of books.

---

* Dr. Spring.

It is the easiest because all that is necessary to learn from it as to the way of salvation may be learned by the plainest and most uncultivated mind.

No learning, beyond the simple ability to read, is necessary to enable one to understand the ten commandments, the Lord's prayer, and the sermon on the mount. The parables of the Saviour, though volumes have been written to unfold their meaning, are so plain in their application at least, that he that runs may read. The poor black man in his log-cabin with only one of the gospels, which he spells out by the light of his pine-torch, the rough sailor in his forecastle berth by the light of his swinging lamp, with the Bible in his hands, may understand enough to point them both to the Lamb of God that taketh away the sin of the world; and so, says the poet Cowper, speaking of Voltaire, in contrast with

> " Yon cottager who weaves at her own door
> Pillow and bobbin, all her little store,
> Content though mean,"

can and does know more of the blessed Bible than the gay and brilliant Frenchman ever knew.

The apostle Paul in writing his Second Epistle to Timothy reminds him that from a child he had known the Holy Scriptures.

It is evident from this not only that it is our duty to teach the Scriptures to children, but that they are able to learn them. And this, I take it, means not only committing the verses of Scripture to memory, a custom somewhat out of fashion in these days, not merely telling the beautiful stories of the Bible, but explaining it to those who are quite young. Dr. Alexander modestly entitles some of his commentaries, explanations, thus: " The Gospel According to Matthew Explained;" " The Acts of the Apostles Explained," as if his ideal of a Scripture commentary was simply an explanation. Here is encouragement and warrant for Sunday-school teachers ; for if it is right to teach these great truths to the children of our own households, how important is it to gather in the neglected ones who have no "Mother Eunice" nor "Grandmother Lois," as Timothy had, to teach them the Scriptures at home.

The Bible is also the hardest of books. In its very structure it is to a great extent fragmentary. It is not a distinct treatise, but a collection of sixty-six books. Its historical narratives, simple and natural and beautiful as they are, are not always consecutive, and are sometimes quite difficult to harmonize. Its authors are many, and although they spoke and wrote as they were moved by the Spirit of God, they were men of varied ability, attainments and tastes. Their writings are in different languages, not now spoken as then, and the Hebrew having little contemporary literature to illustrate it. The books themselves were written by their different authors stretching over a period of more than fifteen hundred years. Some of these books are simple narratives ; some are poetry—the very laws of which are not easy to understand, but wholly unlike our poetry. Some of this poetry is lyrical, some declamatory ; some of the books are mixed prose and poetry ; some are allegories, abounding in oriental metaphors, the clue to some of which is lost. Some are prophecies fulfilled and unfulfilled ; some are the relations of eye-witnesses ; some the records of accounts given by others. Some are essays and arguments on the foundations of Christian truth, so profound that the ablest minds have been unable clearly to unfold them. Some are the ecstatic utterances of those who were caught up into the third heaven—all are expressed in glowing, figurative language, some of the traces of which, in their common life, we have lost.

Then the chronological arrangement as we find it in our English Bibles is very imperfect ; whether we consider the history itself or the time when it was written. Some have thought that the book of Job should be placed somewhere in the book of Genesis. With this exception, if this be an exception, the five books of Moses (the Pentateuch) are in proper order. So are the books of Joshua and Judges. But after this, all the books of the Old Testament are in irregular order as to time. The Psalms, which are collected in one book, were written at periods ranging as far back probably as Moses in the Jewish history and as far down as the latest Old Testament prophet.

The Gospels were not written in the order in which they occur in the New Testament, and the Epistles are grouped without reference to any natural laws.

Then, too, the Bible in its separate books is broken up into chapters and verses, and while this is very convenient for purposes of reference, it is often very violently and arbitrarily done and greatly hinders the meaning. You all know that the division into chapters and verses is a merely human arrangement, and is not pretended to be inspired.

The New Testament, which you can buy for a few cents, is a volume made of paper, printed from types with black ink, the sheets of paper folded and stitched and bound with pasteboard and covered with muslin or leather. All this is the work of men's hands, just as other books are made by tens of thousands every day. It is not, however, a dissertation, an essay, a connected narrative or history, with an introduction and divided into sections, chapters and paragraphs, the work of one author, but is made up of twenty-seven books, of which four are biographies of our Lord, more or less complete, one is a history, "The Acts," twenty-one are Epistles or letters, and one is a prophecy or series of prophecies—"The Revelation."

Of the Epistles, fourteen were written by Paul, if we may count that to the Hebrews as his, three by John, two by Peter, one by James, and one by Jude. Besides his three Epistles, John wrote the Gospel which bears his name and the Revelation. Besides his Gospel, Luke wrote the "Acts of the Apostles," which is a continuation of his Gospel ; Matthew wrote the Gospel which bears his name, and Mark probably that which bears his.

Matthew and John, disciples of Jesus, wrote describing what they saw and heard ; Luke and Mark, who were not followers, wrote from the testimony of others. Mark it is supposed wrote at the dictation of Peter, or related the events as Peter, from time to time, described them to him, so that in this sense his Gospel may almost be said to be that of an eye-witness.

As to the language in which the books were written, if we must except the Gospel of Matthew, as some think, all the others were written in the Greek language. The language of the Old Testament is nearly all Hebrew.

Three hundred years before Christ, Alexander the Great had carried the Greek language all over the Eastern world, as far at least as his conquests reached. "It was the most widely spread language in the then civilized world, and was therefore best adapted for the instruction of all. It was most readily understood by the greatest number of persons. When Christ appeared it was current in Palestine ; it was the language of literature and of the courts. It differed by some strong contrasts from the flowing style of the pure classic Greek and was full of the figures and coloring of the ancient Hebrew."

It is supposed that few of the books of the New Testament were written by their authors' own hands ; even had it been so, they would all have been lost before our day. The writers who lived very near to the time of the evangelists and apostles make no reference to the originals. The materials on which they were written were perishable and were soon lost. Probably most were written by dictation,—there being an educated class at that day whose business it was to commit to writing the thoughts of others. "In the case of

Paul," says the eloquent Stanley, "we seem to see an old man bearing in the pallor and feebleness of his frame traces of his constant hardships, his eyes at times streaming with tears of grief and indignation, the scribe catching the words from his lips and recording them on the scroll of parchment or papyrus which lay before him, sometimes writing a part himself, and at others seizing the pen from the hand of amanuensis and writing as a conclusion, ' You can see how large a letter I have written unto you with mine own hand,' or, 'look you in what large letters I write with mine own hand.' "

It is supposed that the original text of the New Testament was written continuously, with no division of words and sentences and paragraphs. The fac-similes of some of the oldest MSS. favor this supposition. But this was very inconvenient, and then copies were made in lines containing about as many words as could be read uninterruptedly and resembling somewhat in appearance an inscription on a monument. It was hundreds of years before the laws of punctuation were understood and applied, and not until printing was discovered were the Scriptures accurately punctuated. If you wish to see how important this is to a proper understanding of the New Testament, just obliterate the punctuation marks and see how difficult it is to read it. Then if you drop the artificial division of chapters, paragraphs, verses, words, capital letters and marks of punctuation, and just print the text, one letter after another and from the beginning to the end of a book, you will see that it is almost impossible to read the text at all.

The whole of the New Testament, then, has been handed down from the days of the apostles to our own times by these successive copies. This must have been a work of the greatest, the most conscientious care. See how extremely careful the Jews were in making their rolls or sacred books for Synagogue use.

The parchment must consist of the hides of clean animals, prepared by a Jew especially for this purpose, and joined together with thongs of the same material. Every skin must have a certain number of columns which are equal throughout the whole. The roll must be ruled ; must be written with black ink of the purest kind ; the transcriber must follow an authentic manuscript, writing nothing, not even the smallest letter, from memory. Words must not be divided at the end of lines ; a certain space must be left between each word and section ; some books may close in the middle of a line, but the fifth book of Moses must close exactly with the end of a line. The scribe must sit in his full Jewish dress and as often as he writes the name of God must purify himself and wash his whole body. There is an almost endless detail of other directions which I will not weary you by relating, and the failure to comply with these requirements might destroy the value of the whole book.

If there was anything like this care in bringing down to the time of printing our New Testament Scriptures, you have some idea of the cost. Indeed, much of the time of the monks in the middle ages was occupied in multiplying copies. of the Bible and books of devotion.

You can see, too, how, notwithstanding all this care, it is quite possible for omissions of words and sentences to have occurred in the copies, and how errors in copying letters and words may have crept in. Therefore the great object of modern scholars and critics has been to reach the oldest and most authentic and most complete manuscripts and make the most exact and literal translation.

There are three manuscript copies of the Bible which by scholars are valued more highly than all others (and there are a great many). I mention them in the order in which they were discovered.

1. The Codex Vaticanus, so called because it is in the library of the Vatican at Rome ; when it was placed there, is not

known. But the first catalogue of that library, dating 1475, contains it. The text is written three columns to a page. There are certain features of arrangement of the text, the handwriting and the character of the text itself, which apparently fixed its date at about the middle of the fourth century.

2. The second is the Codex Alexandrinus, now in the British Museum, sent as a present to Charles First of England from a man named Cyril Lucar, who had once been patriarch of Alexandria, hence its name. It has two columns to a page and is supposed to be as old as the middle of the fifth century.

3. The Codex Sinaiticus, discovered in the Convent of St. Catherine on Mount Sinai in 1859 by Tischendorf. This is the most complete of all the old manuscripts, at least as far as the New Testament is concerned, for that is entire. Tischendorf had spent about thirty years in exploring the libraries of Europe, as well as the monasteries in the Asiatic and African regions where Christianity had been planted, in search of the most ancient copies of the Bible. He was travelling in 1859 under the patronage of the Emperor of Russia, to whom, under a lively sense of gratitude, he transmitted this copy, and it is now in St. Petersburg. All three of these manuscripts were written on pages in the book form, instead of on rolls in the map form, and fac-similes have been made of them all. The date of the Sinai manuscript is supposed to be about the middle of the fourth century, or the same as that at the Vatican, and is considered by Tischendorf to be the best.

Valuable as these are, however, they are not the oldest copies of the Bible. Two or three hundred years before the date of these, the New Testament had been written, read in the churches, and scattered all over the Christian world. There are translations of the New Testament into the Syrian,

Egyptian, Ethiopic and other languages as early as the latter part of the second century.

Then there are many Christian writers from the first century to the fifth whose works we have, who constantly quote the New Testament as it was in their time, and of course the quotations of the first three centuries are earlier authority for the original text than any of the (three) manuscripts named.

But let us pass from the old Greek copies and contemporary writers.

More than six hundred years elapsed before any part of the Bible was translated into Anglo-Saxon or English. The first parts so translated were the account of the creation, the exodus, and the life and death of our Lord. This did not pretend to be an accurate translation, but was rather a paraphrase. A few years later a version of the Psalms was made by the first Saxon, a monk named Gurthlake. In the year 706 Aldhelm, Bishop of Sherborne, translated the Psalter. He praises certain nuns for their daily study of the Holy Scriptures, which seems to indicate that they had copies of the Bible in Anglo-Saxon.

Twenty-six years after the death of Aldhelm, the venerable Bede translated another portion of the Scriptures into his native language (English). At that period there stood on the south bank of the Tyne a monastery called Jarrow. The surrounding country was then thinly peopled. The river flowed silently through wooded banks and long reaches of moorland, past the towers of the Roman wall and the cliffs of Tynemouth. On the evening of the 26th of May, 735 (Ascension day), an unusual stillness pervaded the sacred retreat. The monks spoke in anxious whispers. On a low bed in one of the cells lay an aged priest. His wasted frame and sunken eye told that death was near. His breathing was slow and labored. Near him sat a young scribe, with an open scroll and a pen in his hand. Looking with affec-

tionate benevolence in the face of the dying man, he said :
"Now, dearest master, there remains only one chapter, but
the exertion is too great for you." "It is easy, my son ; it
is easy," he replied. "Take your pen and write quickly ;
I know not how soon my Master will take me." Sentence
after sentence was uttered in feeble accents and written by
the scribe. Again there was a long pause. Nature seemed
exhausted. Again the boy spoke. "Dear master, only one
sentence is wanting." It, too, was pronounced painfully
and slowly. "It is finished," said the scribe ; "It is finished," repeated the dying saint, and then added : "lift up
my head ; place me in the spot where I have been accustomed
to pray." With tender care he was placed as he desired.
Then clasping his hands and lifting his eyes heavenward, he
exclaimed : "Glory be to the Father, and to the Son, and to
the Holy Ghost," and with the last word his spirit passed
away. Thus died the venerable Bede, and thus was completed the first Anglo-Saxon translation of the Gospel According to St. John.

We must pass over the numerous translations, in whole
or in part, that succeeded, barely mentioning only a few.
There was Wyckliffe's, a noble work, which prepared the
way for, and gave a distinctive character to, the Reformation
in England. But this version was not fitted to occupy a
permanent place. The style is rugged and homely ; in fact,
English was yet in its infancy and Wyckliffe did not translate from the originals.

A hundred and fifty years after the publication of Wyckliffe's Bible, a small party assembled one evening in spring
in the dining-room of Sudbury Hall near Bristol. It con-
sisted of Sir John Walsh, the lord of the manor, his Lady,
several children and two priests. One of the priests was a
man of distinguished appearance. He was in the prime of
life, grave and thoughtful, but of extraordinary and brilliant
powers of conversation. He occupied the humble place of

tutor in the knight's family. The other priest was a man of high social position and much scholastic learning. During dinner the conversation turned on those theological questions which were then moving England and Germany. The conflicting views of the speakers soon became apparent. After some sharp passages the strange priest exclaimed : "Better be without God's law than the Pope's." The tutor, suddenly turning upon him with a look of great dignity and determination, exclaimed : "In the name of God, I defy the Pope and all his laws. If God spare my life, ere many years, I will cause the boy that drives the plough to know more of God's law than either you or the Pope." That tutor was William Tyndale.

Nothing could be more interesting than a history of Tyndale and his labors in translating and publishing the manuscript. I barely touch it. He was driven from England ; found an asylum in Hamburg, then in Cologne, at that time (1524) famous for its printing establishments. Here his translation of the New Testament from the Greek, entirely his own work, was put to press ; but before it was printed the authorities were informed of it by a priest, and Tyndale and his assistant had to escape up the Rhine to Worms, where the first complete copy of the New Testament in English was printed, and not at Antwerp, as is generally supposed.

The Roman Catholic Church condemned the book, and burned all the copies they could find, in the presence of Cardinal Wolsey, in front of St. Paul's Cathedral, London, on Sunday, February 11, 1526. But the vengeance of the church did not stop here. While in Antwerp Tyndale was betrayed by a spy, sent by the King of England for the purpose, and he was dragged to the castle of Vilvoord, near Brussels, where, after an imprisonment of two years, he was executed. His last words were worthy of the cause for which he lived and for which he died. Standing beside the stake

where he was burned, he lifted up his hands and prayed :
"Lord Jesus, open the eyes of the King of England." His
prayer was answered, for in less than a year from his martyrdom, a complete English version of the Bible was freely dis-
tributed in England by royal authority.

Tyndale's translation is the basis of our English Bible.
Then came Coverdale's,—then revisions of these by various
hands ; and then the "Great Bible," as it was called, published under the authority of Cranmer, which was the first
authorized version. From this the Psalter, in the "Book
of Common Prayer," is taken, word for word, and the ten
commandments and some other parts of the Episcopal
Church service.

Then came what was called the Bishop's Bible, because it
was prepared or revised by a number of bishops in the year
1568, while Elizabeth was on the throne.

The next in point of time is that which we now call the
authorized version, our common English Bible. It was
translated afresh from the Hebrew and Greek originals and
is not a revision of previous translations. It was begun by
Royal Commission in the reign of James First, in 1604, and
finished in 1611. Three years were occupied in preliminary
arrangements and individual investigations on the part of the
fifty-four scholars nominated to do the work, and numerous
others whom they consulted. They were divided into six
classes, and they divided the Bible into numerous sections.

They met in classes in London, Cambridge and Oxford.
Each member of each class translated all the books entrusted
to the class ; then the whole class met, and, after calm and
thorough revision, adopted a common text ; then that text
was transmitted in succession to each of the other classes for
revision; then a text, approved by the entire six classes, was
submitted to the final revision of six selected delegates,
with six consulting assistants, and their approved manuscript was finally placed in the skilful hands of Dr. Smith,

Bishop of Gloucester, who wrote the preface, to examine and prepare for the press. Immense labor and care were taken to bring out the exact sense of the originals. Every clause, and indeed every word, was anxiously weighed, and no point was considered too minute for the keen, critical eyes of the laborious and conscientious translators. Sometimes when they could not agree upon the proper English equivalent, by which to render the Hebrew or Greek word, where it was a choice between two, they wrote one in the text and one in the margin. Sometimes when the exact literal translation would sound very strange in English they put it in the margin—thus, "A word fitly spoken" * reads in margin, "A word spoken on wheels ; " and whenever it was necessary to supply a word, or more than one, to complete the sense, the words so supplied are always printed in italics.

The grammatical knowledge of the Greek language is much more thorough now than it was in the sixteenth and seventeenth centuries, and the apparatus for critical study is far more complete. By these means we are now able to de-, tect grammatical inaccuracies in our version which mar its beauty and obscure its sense. The finer shades of meaning, especially in the Epistles·of Paul, are occasionally lost by a failure on the part of our translators to perceive, or at least to express, the precise force and bearing of a tense or a case or a particle. Within this century some of the ablest minds in England and Germany and in our own country have been devoted to the critical unfolding of the New Testament. Such men as Archbishop Trench and Bishops Ellicott and Wordsworth and Canon Lightfoot and Dean Alford and Professor Davies and Dean Stanley and Professor Jowett and Dean Plumtre, in England ; and many kindred spirits in Germany (unhappily not all as orthodox), and Moses Stuart

---

* Proverbs xxv. 11.

and Addison Alexander and Professor Hackett and Albert
Barnes, and many others in our own country, have laid the
church and the world under immense obligations for their
contributions to sacred exposition.   Dean Alford especially,
in his New Testament for English Readers (a book which I
wish could be placed in the hands of every student of the
sacred Scriptures), has labored to put the English reader,
who is ignorant of Greek, in possession of some of the principal results of the labors of critics and scholars on the sacred
text.

The best Greek text of the New Testament is that which
Tischendorf prepared or edited, and on which he spent the
last years of his most useful life.   It is undoubtedly nearer
the exact words spoken and written by our Lord and his
apostles than any other whatever.   But the language is read
by so few that its usefulness is necessarily limited to scholars,
and Tischendorf wished it to be read by all English-speak-
ing people.   He therefore asked his friend, Dr. Davidson,
than whom no one was better qualified, to translate it into
English.

Dr. Davidson performed that task, and some years ago the
book was published in English.   I am sure there must be
many who will desire to have a most accurate translation of
the purest Greek of the New Testament.

But I have left myself little time to give hints as to how to
study the Bible.

So much of it is devotional—prayers and praises, the expression of devout minds and hearts—that all that is necessary to a very high enjoyment of it, is to be in a devout frame
of mind.   So that if you have nothing but a simple copy of
the Bible, without note or comment, or marginal references
to parallel passages, you may sit at the feet of Jesus, as Mary
did, and drink in his words of heavenly wisdom, words that
have not lost their power though handed down these eighteen
hundred years and expressed in a different language from

that in which he uttered them, and without the tones of that voice which spake as never man spake.

Some familiarity with the book is necessary to ascertain its true excellence.

In one of the galleries of the Vatican in Rome is the statue of the Apollo Belvidere, probably the most perfect piece of sculpture in the world. The Abbé Winkleman, a classical writer upon the fine arts, after descanting with great zeal upon the perfection of sculpture as exhibited in this statue, says to young artists : "Go and study it, and if you see no great beauty in it to captivate you, go again, and if you still discover none, go again and again. Go until you feel it; for be assured it is there."

So I say of the Bible. You may not, you cannot discover its worth at a single reading. Its great truths are plain and easy to be understood, but it requires mental exertion and continuous, regular reading to comprehend and feel the power of so vast a book. "Search the Scriptures," search them daily, search them not from curiosity merely, though curiosity and learning are amply repaid by the search, but from a deep and personal interest in their instructions.

So much has been done by modern travellers in the East in the observation and description of the manners and customs of Bible lands, which are so essential to the illustration of the Scriptures, that it is quite necessary to read these researches. It is worth knowing that among the best books in the English language on this subject are the volumes written by our own Professor Edward Robinson, late of the Union Theological Seminary, New York, and also "The Land and the Book," by Dr. Thompson, an American missionary.

Next to commentaries, however, special and general, and in some important respects superior to them, is the "Dictionary of the Bible," by Dr. Wm. Smith. It is in four large volumes, which, unfortunately, cost so much that they

cannot be owned by everybody. It is made up of contributions of many of the ablest writers of our day, and is undoubtedly the best book of the kind ever made. The best
edition of this work is that edited by Dr. Hackett.

One of the best ways to get at the meaning of Scripture,
whether it be one or more verses, is to make questions upon
it. Take a paper and pencil, with your Bible, and select a
portion and ask yourself all the questions you can think of
and write them down. Do not limit yourself to such questions as you are able to answer, but ask yourself every question that occurs to you to bring out the meaning. You may
not be able to answer one-half of them, and there will be
many probably that nobody within your reach and no books
in your possession can answer for you, but there is an answer, probably, for them all, and you will dig deeper and
deeper at every such experiment you make in this direction.

It is a fact, I suppose, and none the less true because
lamentable, that very few Christians study the Scriptures.
With the exception of clergymen and theological students
and Sunday-school teachers, there are few Christians who
systematically study the Bible. The loss to the church in
its vitality and its aggressive force and influence on the
world is, of course, immeasurable, and the dwarfing and
freezing of individual souls and the barrenness of Christian
experience are deplorable. What can be done to remedy it?
What can be done to rouse the church to its solemn duty and
its high privilege in this respect?

Have you not observed that few persons have Bibles in
their pews now-a-days, and when the Scriptures are read
from the pulpit very few follow the reading, Bible in hand?
We lose greatly our interest in and our love for the Holy
Scriptures because we make so little use of them either at
home or in the church.

There is not time to speak of the arguments for the authen-
ticity of the Scriptures, or of the authority for believing

that the books of the Bible as we now have them are those only that properly belong there ; or of the meaning of inspiration, the "inspiration of the Scriptures," or of the principles of interpretation :—these are subjects any one of which is more than enough for an entire lecture.

No well-informed man, no educated family, can afford to be without the Bible.   Better lose all other books from our family libraries, our schools, our colleges than this.

Blot it out of our literature, and blot all quotations from it and all references to it from other books, and our great libraries would be but hospitals for sick and wounded and mutilated books, entirely beyond the remedial resources of medical and surgical skill, and all the appliances of scientific laboratories, however thoroughly equipped.

I close with the following from a most distinguished pervert (or convert if you please) from the Church of England to the Church of Rome.

"Who will not say that the uncommon beauty and marvellous English of the Protestant Bible is one of the strongholds of heresy in England ?   It lives in the ear like music that can never be forgotten—like the sound of church bells which the convert hardly knows how he can forego : its felicities seem to be almost things instead of words ; it is a part of the national mind ; the anchor of national seriousness ; the memory of the dead passes into it ; the potent traditions of childhood are stereotyped in its verses ; the power of all the griefs and trials of a man is hidden beneath its words.   In the length and breadth of the land there is not a Protestant with one spark of religiousness about him whose spiritual biography is not in his Saxon Bible." *

---

* F. W. Faber.

14

XXVI.

The Young Man: What can He do? What shall He be?*

My first words are words of congratulation, and for these reasons :

First. Because you are young. And this means very much. You have an enormous advantage over people that are your seniors. Other things being equal, you will live longer ; and I assume, at the outset, that "life is worth living." Then you have the advantage of profiting by the mistakes committed by those who precede you, and, if you are not blind, you can avail yourselves of the successes they have achieved.

You have the freshness, the zest, of youth. You are full of courage and endurance. You can grapple with difficult subjects, and with a strong hand ; and, if you blunder, you have time to recover yourselves and start anew. In short, life is before you, and you look forward with the inspiration of hope and, it may be, also, of determination.

Second. I congratulate you, also, because you are poor. It is hardly likely that there are many sons of rich men here. As a rule they are not found in such places as this. They do not need the stimulus, the encouragement, of such gatherings and such counsel as may be expected here. Why should they? Their fortune is already made. Their bread and butter, their means of living, do not depend upon their own exertions : their necessities and comforts are already

---

* An address delivered before the Young Men's Christian Association, of Philadelphia, March 12, 1885.

provided for them. Why should they bother themselves about such subjects? You may find them this very evening at their clubs, or in other places, where they are not likely to learn much that is worth knowing. You need not envy them.

But you, I take it, are men who have your own way to make in the world. You know already that if you achieve success it must be because you exert yourselves to the very utmost. Indeed, you must depend upon yourselves, and this means that you must do everything in your power that is right to do, to help yourselves.

I am speaking, then, to men who thoroughly understand that there is no royal road to success any more than there is to learning, and that there is no time to trifle. If you were rich men's sons, these plain remarks would have no special pertinence, no importance.

My congratulations are quite in order, also, because very many of the high places in our country are held by those who once were poor lads.

Should you turn upon me and say, "Why, then, if one is to be congratulated on his poverty, do fathers toil early and late, denying themselves needed recreation, not ceasing when they have accumulated a good estate, almost selling their souls to become millionaires? why do they so much dread to leave their sons to struggle for a living?" More than one answer might be given to these questions. Some fathers have so little faith in God's providence that they forget his goodness, which now takes care of their families through the instrumentality of parents, and who can continue that care through other means just as well when the parents are gone ; and another reason is that they "who will be rich fall into temptations and snares," one of which is that the race for riches unfits the racer for all other pursuits and amusements, and he cannot stop his course ; he cannot change his habits ; he has no other mental resources ; he must work or perish.

Do not, then, let the fact that you are poor discourage you in the least : it is rather an advantage.

Third.   But again I congratulate you because your lot is cast in America.   It is a good thing to be born in this country, for, in all important respects, it is the most favored of all lands.   It is sometimes the fashion with certain people to disparage our Government and its institutions, and one must admit that, in some particulars, there might be improvement, and will be some day ; but, notwithstanding these defects, it is unquestionably true that it is the best Government on earth.   Is there any country where a poor young man has opportunities as good as he has here to get on in life?   Is there any obstacle or hindrance whatever, outside of himself, in the way of his success ?   If a young man has good health of mind and body, and a fair English education, and good manners, and will be honest and industrious, is he not much more certain to attain success, in one way or another, in this country than anywhere else?   You know he is.   Why? Because of equal rights under the law.   There is no caste here, that curse of monarchies.   There is no aristocracy in sentiment or in power, no House of Lords, no established church, no law of primogeniture.   One man is as good as another as long as he behaves himself.

If you want to consider this point further, let me commend to your careful consideration a most readable article by Matthew Arnold in the February number of the "Contemporary Review."   '

And, if you want further evidence, only look for a moment at the condition of the seething, surging masses of Europe, and the very alarming apprehensions of a general war. Before this year 1885 has run its course the United States may be almost the only country among the great powers that is not involved in war.

And, if further illustration were needed, let me point to that most extraordinary scene enacted in Washington one week ago yesterday. A great political party, which had held control of this Government nearly a quarter of a century, and which had exercised almost unlimited power, yields most quietly, most gracefully, all high places, all dignity, all honor and patronage, to the will of the people who have chosen a new administration. And everybody regards it as a matter of course. Was such a thing ever known before? And could such a thing occur anywhere else among the nations?

Having now spent quite as much time as I can afford in congratulating you generally, I proceed to the serious business before us.

Having shown you how favorable are the conditions which are about you, the next point is, what will you do with yourselves?

All of you who are not already engaged in business of some kind are expecting to be employed by somebody or engaged in some business. And I suppose you may be looking to me to give you some hints how to take care of yourselves, or how to behave in such relations.

I will try to do so plainly and faithfully.

I cannot absolutely promise you success. Indeed, it would be necessary first to define the word. And there are several definitions that might be given. One of the shortest and best might be in these words: "A life well spent." This definition shall be my model.

If you are at school, or in a commercial college, work hard at your lessons. Let your ambition be, not to get through quick, nor to go over much ground in text-books, but to master thoroughly everything before you. If you knew how little thorough instruction there is, you would regard this hint. There are so many half-educated people from schools and colleges that one cannot help believing that the terms of graduation are very easy. There have been, and are now, graduates of colleges who cannot add up a long column

of figures correctly, nor do an example in simple proportion, nor write a letter of four pages of note paper without mistakes of grammar and spelling and punctuation,
to say nothing of perspicuity and unity and general good
taste.

It is quite surprising to find how helpless some young men
are in the simple matter of writing letters : an art which, in
these days of cheap postage and cheap stationery, almost
everybody has something to do with.   If you doubt this, let
me ask you to try to-morrow to write a note of twenty lines
on any subject whatever, off-hand, and submit it for criticism
to an experienced writer.   Do you wonder, then, that an
employer, calling one of his young men, and directing him
to write a letter to one of his correspondents, saying such
and such things, and bring it to him for signature, is surprised and grieved to see that the letter is in such shape
that he cannot sign it and let it go out of his counting-
house ?

It is very true that letter-writing is not the chief business
of life, not the only thing of importance in a counting-
house ; but it is an elegant accomplishment, and most desirable of attainment.

In this connection let me say some words about short-hand
writing.   In this day of push and drive and hurry, when so
many things must be done at once, there is an increasing demand for short-hand writers.   In fact, business as now conducted cannot do without this help.   A principal in any
business cannot generally, or often, take the time to write
long letters.   Why should he ?   It does not pay to have one
that is occupied in governing and controlling great interests,
and in the receipt of a large salary, tied to a desk writing
letters or reports or statements of any kind.   He must "talk
off" these things : and he must be an educated man, whose
mind is so disciplined to terse and accurate expression that
his dictation may almost be taken to be final.   Yet it must

be brought to him for revision. He wants a clerk who can take down his words with literal accuracy, and who will be able to correct any errors that may have been spoken, and submit the complete paper to his chief for his signature. The demand for this kind of service is increasing every day, and some of you now listening to me will be so employed. See that you are ready for it when your opportunity comes.

If you are a clerk in a railroad office, or in an insurance company, or in a store, or in a bank, devote yourselves to your particular duties, whatever they may be. And do not be too particular as to what kind of work it is that falls to your lot. It may be work that you think belongs to your subordinate ; no matter if it is ; do it, and do it as well as he can, or even better.

Let none of you, therefore, think that anything you are likely to be called upon to do is beneath you. Do it, and do it in the best manner, and you may not have to do it for a long time.

Make yourself indispensable to your employer. You can do that ; it is quite within your power, and it may be that you may get to be an employer yourself ; indeed, it is more than probable ; but you must work for it.

Are you a Sunday-school teacher? Make your class the model class of the school : in the thoroughness of your preparation, the efficiency of your teaching, and in the admirable quality of the behavior of your pupils, and the last not the least of these items.

If you are a book-keeper in any counting-house or public institution, remember that you are in a position of trust and responsibility. When you make errors, do not erase the error ; draw faint red or black lines through it and write correct characters over the error. Do not hide your errors of any kind. Do not misstate anything in language or figures, spoken or written. Everybody makes errors at some time or other, but everybody does not admit and apologize for them. The honest man is he who does admit and apologize, and does so without waiting to be detected.

There have been of late some deplorable instances of betrayal of trust in our city; I may as well call it by its right name, stealing. The culprits are now suffering, in prison, the penalty for their crimes. While I am speaking to you there are men, young and not young, in our city who are now stealing, and who are falsifying their books in the vain hope that it may be kept secret; who are dreading the day when they will be caught; who cannot afford to take a holiday; who cannot afford to be sick lest absence for a single day may disclose their guilt. What a horrible condition of mind! It is hardly likely that such persons are in this audience, for such are not apt to find their way to such gatherings as this; but they are among us; they will go to their desks or their offices to-morrow morning not knowing but it may be their last day in that place.

And the day will come, most surely, when you will be tempted as these wretched ones have been tempted. In what shape the temptations may come, or when, no human being knows. The suggestion will be made, that by the use of a little money you may make a good deal; that the venture is perfectly safe; your broker tells you so, and points to this one, or that one, who has tried it and made money. It is only a little thing; you cannot lose much; you may make enough to pay for the cost of your summer holiday, or for your cigar bill, or your beer bill; or you will be able to smoke better cigars or drink better beer, or buy a gold watch, or a diamond ring, or pin, or anything else; you cannot lose much. You have no money of your own, it is true; but what is needed will not be missed if you take it out of the drawer, or withhold a credit of money. Shall you do it? No! Let nothing induce you to take the first dollar not your own. It is the first step that costs.

But suppose you do not care for this warning, or forget it? Suppose the time comes when you find that you have taken something that was not yours, and that it is lost, and that you cannot repay it, what then? Why, go at once to your chief; tell him the whole story; keep back nothing; throw yourself upon his mercy, and ask forgiveness. Better now than later. You will assuredly be caught. There is no possibility of continuous concealment. Tell it now before you are detected; and, if you must be disgraced, the sooner the better..

Am I too earnest about this? Am I saying too much? Oh, men, young men, if you knew the frightful danger that you may be in, some day, the subtle temptations that will beset you, the many instances of weakness about you, the shipwrecks of character, the utter ruin that comes to innocent wives and children by the crimes of husbands and fathers, as we who are older know, you would not wonder that I speak as I do.

Every case of breach of trust, every defalcation, weakens confidence in human character. For, every such instance of wrong-doing is a stab at your integrity if you are in a position of trust. Men of the fairest reputation, men who are trusted implicitly by their employers, men who are hedged about by the sacredness of domestic ties, on whom the happiness of helpless wives and innocent children depend, men who claim to be religious, such men (and you and I have known them) go astray, step by step, little by little; they defraud, steal, lie, try to cover up their tracks, cannot do it long, are caught, tried, convicted, sentenced, and imprisoned. Then the question may be asked about you or me: "How do we know that Mr. So-and-So is any better than those who have fallen?" Don't you see that these culprits are enemies of the public confidence, enemies of society, your enemies and mine?

If the names of those who are now serving out their

sentences in public prisons for stealing—not petty theft, but stealing and defrauding in large sums—could be published in to-morrow morning's papers, what a sad record it would be of dishonored names and blighted lives and ruined homes ; and how the memory would recall some whom we knew in early youth, the pride of their parents, or the idol of fond wives and lovely children ; and we should turn away with sickening horror from the record! But, if there should appear in the same papers the names of those who are now engaged in stealing and defrauding and falsifying entries, and holding back what is due, who are yet undetected, but who will, before this year is out, be caught and convicted and punished, what a horrible revelation that would be!

I would speak some words of encouragement to those among you who are without occupation. It may be that which you have tried has not suited you, or you have not succeeded in impressing your employer with a sense of your value.   Failure in something you have tried may mean only that you made a mistake in your calling. This is not uncommon.   It may mean also that you needed the discipline which you received in that mistaken occupation to fit you for a place which you are yet to fill. Men who have been trained as merchants, and have not been successful, have done admirably well at the head of institutions, and men who have not been skillful enough to take care of their own property have proved to be good care-takers of other people's property.

Men who have failed in one profession have become conspicuous in their successful prosecution of another.   A clerk in a dry-goods store may not become the head of the house, but he may get to be the head of something as important and profitable as a dry-goods store.

Changes are very common in our country, more so than anywhere else.   All the conditions of our American life favor change. Do not be discouraged, then, if you are obliged to change your occupation.

Whatever you are doing, let it be your best. All young lawyers cannot be judges; but is there any reason, my young friend, if you are reading law, why you should not be a judge ? At all events you can work up towards it. Clear, calm, dispassionate reasoning and judgment you will need, if you succeed at the bar, and these are the qualities we look for on the bench.

All physicians will not get to be professors in medical colleges ; but is this a reason why you should not reach that eminence ? Whether you seek that place or not, seek the qualities which will fit you for it, and you will make a family physician all the better qualified for such preparation.

All clerks in insurance companies and railroad offices and banks cannot become presidents ; but why should not you, young sir ? Whether you do or not, it is your duty to make the very best use of your opportunities. Don't you know that men in these conspicuous positions are dying off? Don't you know that, even now, boards of directors are looking about to find men who are qualified to succeed the present incumbents of such places? Do you think that anybody's eye is on you ? Somebody must fill these places. Will it be you ?

Do you know that much, very much, depends on yourself? Therefore, I say, do the best you can. So if a committee should inquire about you, and should even go so far as to seek a conference with you, they will depend very much upon what is said about you by those who know you best, as well as by what you say for yourself, and by your appearance and manners. And if they meet a man of untidy appearance and slouchy carriage and untidy habits, or in debt to his tailor and grocer, or landlady, they will pass him by, no matter what large promises he makes or others make for him. And remember that smartness, even to brilliant business talents, is not all that is wanted for men in upper places. High integrity, absolute incorruptibility, good manners, good education, pure morals, good habits, these are required of men who are to be the leaders in life and the chiefs in public institutions.

It was my purpose at the beginning of this address to give you some hints about reading—as to What to read and How to read ; but so much time has already been taken that I fear to detain you by any remarks at great length on this important subject. I cannot, however, let the occasion pass without saying something.

It would be very easy to give you a list of authors, or selections from their works, that may safely be read. But this has been already done by writers for young men. If it were safe and desirable, it would be well to give a list of books that ought not to be read. All I can do now is to say some things in a more general way.

Read no books but the best. I mean the best of their kind. You cannot afford to waste time over second-rate literature while that of a first-class character is equally within your reach.

Read what interests you. It is a poor use of time to read unattractive matter for the sake of mental discipline. You can get that discipline just as well with attractive reading.

Read in the line of your business, whatever that may be. If you are a mechanic or a scientist, read the "Scientific American," or something of that kind. If you are a bank clerk, there is a great variety of literature most practical.

Read for general culture. This is a wide field, and includes fiction, poetry, essays, etc.

Read for information. This means history and science, sacred and secular.

Read for entertainment. This means that sort of literature which may be read for amusement and recreation.

But remember you must have a purpose in it all. Not

until you are much farther on in life can you afford to take up a book to while away a weary hour or "kill time." The young have no time to kill.

How shall you read?

Read with care. If the book is your own property, read with a pencil in your hand, and make remarks in the margin, either of a general character, as implying that you may want to read certain passages again, or with certain marks, as signs, to indicate assent to or dissent from, the author's views. Todd, in his "Student's Manual," the best book of its kind ever written, gives a list of such marks, with their meaning, such as he was in the habit of using in his reading.

You will find, after reading in this way, that, on a second reading, you can go over a book in an hour or two, by way of review, and get all, or most, of what was specially valuable to you in the whole volume.

Then, if you want to get the most out of a book, and at the same time secure sound mental discipline, make a synopsis, or digest, of a specially important work now and then. But be sure you take the right kind of a book to begin with. I once tried to make a synopsis of Wayland's "Moral Science," but I had not gone far before I saw that the book was itself a digest of truth, and could not by me, at least, be made any more compact than it was already. But take Drummond's "Natural Law in the Spiritual World," and Canon Farrar's "Messages of the Books," and, when you shall have made an analysis, or synopsis, or digest of these two volumes, you will know more about theology and the structure of the New Testament than many graduates from theological seminaries.

Then, again, when a book has pleased you very much, write a short notice of it, as if you intended to send it to an editor (but don't send it), and, in your notice, state the general drift or purpose of the book, its style, etc., and whether

the author has succeeded in his purpose. Don't you see
that this will deepen the impression the book makes upon
you? If you say you can't read many books at this rate,
the reply is, it is not necessary that you should read many
books, but it is necessary that your reading should be
profitable.

I know we can't expect young people of our time to be
fascinated with the books which interested those of us who
were beginning to read fifty years ago. It was once a favorite
thought of mine to reproduce the literature of my early youth
for the young people about me ; and one book which had a
special charm for me, " Tales of the Castle," by Mad. de
Genlis, I was at great care and expense to obtain from London ; but, when obtained, it had no interest whatever for
those for whom I desired it, and, in fact, I could not read it
myself.

Now this is not to be deplored, for the literature of our
time for young people is immeasurably better than that
which was provided for them half a century ago.

The wide fields of Theology and History and Science and
Fiction and Poetry and Biography, never so attractive as
now, are open to all of you, and you may roam and browse
at your own will.

You must never be too busy to study. And, remember,
reading is not studying. Your education is going on all the
time. You are learning from books and papers every day.
Books, however, are the chief means of self-education.
Therefore choose the best, and read with a purpose and with
care. But don't have too much system or too many plans,
else you will tire yourself at the outset, be discouraged, and
break down and give it up.

As to newspapers, don't give too much time to them.
Don't let them take the place of books. Some people get
nearly all their reading from newspapers. This is not wise.

They have their purpose, and you know what it is ; keep them within that purpose.

"As to books of humor," as a distinguished writer has said, "especially those of American origin, they are to be carefully scrutinized and, at most, but tasted. Those of Lowell and Holmes are almost the only exceptions." This, however, is a narrow view.

And yet how strong is the tendency in the direction of extravagant caricature. Not long since there was a gathering of gentlemen at an evening party, at which were two most conspicuous men. One was Mark Hopkins, of Williams College, Massachusetts ; the other was Mark Twain. While many felt that it was no small privilege to talk with the modest and distinguished college president, and listen to his sound, grave and wholesome words, the stream of the guests was towards Mark Twain, who was the centre of an admiring group, convulsed with laughter at commonplace stories and jokes, which, if told by others, would have fallen flat, stale and unprofitable.

No modern book that cannot be read aloud in the presence of ladies ought to be read by young people. Let this be the test. I say modern book, because there are expressions in the plays of Shakespeare and in the Bible which one would not like to read aloud. But we must remember that Shakespeare was written, and the Bible was translated, two or three hundred years ago, when expressions were in common use which are now quite immodest. Such changes have been produced by culture and the varying customs of society, and changes in the use of the meaning of words. But no modern book, no book in general literature, printed in our day, ought to be read by the young, that would bring a blush to the cheek if read aloud in the presence of women.

One of the most pernicious habits is that of reading useless books and papers. I mean the weak and silly books and papers which are scattered in all directions. The most pop-

ular of all reading is fiction, not merely novels, but newspaper stories. The records of any public library will show
that more than three-fourths of all the books taken out are
novels. But there is a very large class of people who have
few or no books of their own, and who have not access to
any library, and who, therefore, depend on the weekly and
monthly papers for their reading. The number of such
papers is legion ; they are stuffed with stories ; there is little
else in them. Sometimes these papers are illustrated with
startling pictures, as extravagant in drawing as the text is in
description.

There was, some years ago, and may be now, a weekly
paper of flashy appearance, published in another city, but
scattered through our streets by the thousand, full of pictures
and high-seasoned stories, and every number of that paper
contained at least one picture representing a scene of vio-
lence, in which one or more of the characters had a pistol
pointed, or a club raised, or a dagger about to be thrust.
Can you wonder that the constant reading of such a paper
makes brutes and savages of the readers?

Young boys, errand boys, in street cars, take such papers
out of their pockets and forget everything in the reading.
And young girls, also, on their way to and from their
daily work in stores and mills and factories, are often absorbed in such papers. It is a fearful waste of time, yet
nobody has any time to waste. There is plenty of time with
most persons who have a taste for reading, to read what is
entertaining and suitable and edifying ; but nobody has time
to waste over such books and papers as these. Young boys,
at least, have no time for this. I would not, if I could, keep
you from reading stories. I am fond of them myself. I
have read many of them. I have gained great advantage
from them. As long as I am able to read anything at all, I
expect to read fiction ; but I do not read ,that which appears
in the weekly flashy story papers, for it is generally of the

weakest and poorest description. You can learn nothing good from it ; it is an utter waste of time. But this is not all. Such reading is weakening and debasing to the mind. You read of improbable scenes ; nothing like them ever occurred in human experience. Improbable characters are described ; nothing like such men and women have you ever seen or heard of, except in such stories. They move in society which is not to be found anywhere. They are surrounded by impossible circumstances. There is no description of life or character that is worth a straw ; no duty presented ; no laudable ambition excited. What possible good can come from such reading? Can it be in any sense a preparation for the real life that is before you—a life which, to most of you, must be one of trial and hardship and struggle?

There is an abundance of attractive and instructive reading which is within the reach of you all. There are novels, plenty of them, which no one will object to your reading. They are pure, elevating, wholesome. Even some which seem to have been written with the sole purpose of amusement are not without merit. Some of the finest delineations of human character ever made by an uninspired pen are found in novels ; they are profound studies. Some of the most thrilling and accurate descriptions of battle-scenes ever written are to be found in novels. Some of the finest specimens of Christian life and activity, of self-denial and suffering, and of true courage and manliness, are found in novels. The highest, the brightest humor, the deepest pathos, the profoundest philosophy, are found in novels. Some of the best sermons, some of the sweetest hymns, the most fervent prayers, are to be found in novels. Some of the finest, the best minds that have appeared within this century, have been devoted to teaching practical and religious truth and duty through the thin veil of fiction. All the recreation that you need, that you ought to have in what is called light reading, you can get in novels.

15

But who shall choose the books? Is it safe for you to do it? No! No!

Why? You lack experience. You should seek the advice of others older and wiser than you are. He or she, of whom you make the inquiry, ought to know you, and ought to know what books will suit you best. It is a great thing to have such a friend or teacher. I once had such a friend, a gentleman of extensive reading and large knowledge of human nature, and, whenever I wanted a book on some special point for myself or for another, I went to him and was never disappointed. You ought not, while young, to read any novel, unless one universally approved, without asking the advice of some intelligent friend. Remember that you have much to learn.

After a while, even if you do not already know it, you will be surprised to find how little you know. I have read many books, but almost every day I am impressed with the conviction that I know so little. Oh, if I could live my life over again, with the advantages you have, I would be more careful of what I read.

A fine literary taste is often formed and cultivated by the use of reading-books in school. If they were a trifle heavy a half century ago, they contained the gems of the language. The sources of supply were the English classics and translations from the Latin and Greek, and they were read over and over again until they were imbedded in the memory.

Professor Jowett, the Master of Balliol, speaking in Westminster Abbey over the grave of Bulwer, said: "It is difficult to estimate works of fiction by a moral or religious standard, but we must admit that novels exercise a wonderful influence over us, greater probably in the present age than in any other, and that they form in literature a new element, which was unknown to the ancients. They not only add to the stock of harmless amusement (which is no light matter), but, when the work of a great writer, they may justly be considered as one of the ties which bind us to each other, lowering or elevating the taste of a nation, enlarging our knowledge of human nature, and showing the world to us in many new lights and effects."

I would say a brief word about music : its most wholesome effect upon the character of the young, especially when cultivated as an art, in the concert, the oratorio or the opera. More particularly is the effect of the oratorio most healthful.

What shall I say about recreations ? For recreation is absolutely necessary to a well-developed life. What shall I say about billiards, and cards, and the theatre, and boating, and base-ball, and tennis, etc. ?

This I say in general. As to the first-named, the evil is chiefly in the associations which surround them. In themselves they may be perfectly innocent. Billiards and cards and theatricals in a private house are no more to be discouraged than chess, checkers, dominoes, nor the reading of Shakespeare, in parts, in a private house ; but don't go to public places to play billiards or cards ; and, if you will go to the theatre, always take with you your mother or your sister, or some other lady for whom you have high respect. And don't go very often, under any circumstances.

Do you think that any business house or corporation would give you employment if it were known that you were in the habit of going to the theatre, or to billiard rooms or card parties, or that you feel it necessary to smoke incessantly?

I am not opposed to simple and pure recreations. I approve of them heartily. Macaulay says of the Puritan, that he did not object to bear-baiting so much because it gave pain to the bear, but because it gave pleasure to the spectator. I am not of that way of thinking. Only I do not want any of you to be so much devoted to amusements, while others turn aside and seize the prizes of life.

Something must be said of the danger of evil company— a danger to which you are especially exposed.

The desire for companionship sometimes leads people, and especially young people, into company which is wicked and vile. A boy finds himself associated with a schoolmate, or a fellow-apprentice, or a fellow-clerk, who is attractive in manners, full of gayety and fun, but who is not what he ought to be in character.

No one is entirely bad. Many persons of bad character have some points that are not repulsive, and sometimes are attractive in some respects. A comparatively innocent boy is thrown into such company and, at first, he sees nothing in the conduct of his new friends which is particularly out of the way. The conversation is somewhat guarded, the jokes and stories are not specially bad, and, for a time, nothing occurs to shock his feelings ; but, after a while, the mask is thrown off and the true character is revealed. Then very soon the mind of the pure, innocent boy receives impressions that corrupt and defile it. All that is polluting in talk and story and song is poured out. Books and papers, so vile that it is a breach of law to sell them, are read and quoted without bringing a blush to the cheek, and, before his parents are aware of the danger, the mind and the heart of their son are so polluted and depraved that no human power can save him.

I very well remember a boy who, early in life, gave himself up to vile company and vile books and vile habits, and who, long ago—almost as soon as he had reached an early manhood—sunk, under the weight of his sinful habits, into a dishonored grave, but not until he had defiled and depraved many a boy who came under his influence. Better would it have been for his companions, if their daily walks and play-grounds had been infested with venomous serpents, to bite and sting their bare feet, than to associate with a boy whose heart was full of all uncleanness.

I want you to believe that it is dangerous to associate with the wicked. Circumstances may throw us among them, the providence of God may send us there, but we ought never to seek such company, except for good purposes. What I mean is that we ought not to seek such associations, however agreeable they may be in other respects, and not to remain among them except for their good.

There are wicked people, in every community, of all ages. We cannot altogether avoid contact with them. We find them in the walks of business and among our schoolmates.

Many a young man, many a boy, has been forever ruined by evil companions. A corrupt literature is bad enough, . but evil companions are more numerous and, if possible, more fatal. Bad books and papers have slain their thousands; bad companions have slain their ten thousands. I can recall the names of many who were led away, step by step, down the broad road that leads to destruction, by companions genial, attractive, but corrupt.

There are some companions from whom you cannot separate yourselves. They are with you continually ; at home and abroad, in school or at play, by day and by night, asleep and awake, they are always with you. There is no solitude so deep that they cannot find you, no crowd so great that they will lose you. No matter who else is with you, they will not—cannot—be kept away. I mean your own thoughts, your bosom companions. Shall they be evil companions or good? Ah! you know who, and who only, can answer this question.

I once went through a Monastery in the old çity of Florence. It was a retreat for men who were tired of the world, or who felt so unequal to the strife and conflict of life in the world, that they supposed that peace could be found only in retirement. The house was of the order of St. Francis. One of the monks took me into his cell, and I sat down and talked with him. It was a very small room—one door, one window, bare walls, a small table, two wooden chairs, a few books, a crucifix, a washstand, with three or four pieces of crockery, and that was all.   Here he lived, and, except his calls to the chapel, just across the corridor, and his walks in the cloisters for exercise, here he expected to die.   It seemed very dreary and lonely to me.   But I thought, if this were a certain and sure way of escaping from evil thoughts, and the only way, men may well submit to the confinement, the solitude, the monotony, the dreariness, and the horror, of this way of life. But, alas! it is not so.   No close and narrow cell, no iron doors, no bolts and bars, can shut out our thoughts, for they are a part of ourselves ; they are ourselves ; for, "as a man thinketh in his heart, so is he."

I say these things to you because there never was a time when so much was required of young men in order to achieve success as now.   There is the keenest, the fiercest, competition on all sides.   Our schools are sending out every year, thousands of candidates more or less thoroughly equipped for employment in the various walks of life ; and thousands of sturdy boys are coming here from the country every year determined to contest with city boys the right to the best places.   You see, then, that it is no child's play to get ahead or keep ahead of this vast throng.   It will task all your energies and demand the very highest qualifications to maintain such a position.

I believe that a merchant or mechanic, an officer of an institution, or a clerk, is just as much called by divine providence to that position as the minister of the gospel is called, and that he can just as reasonably claim the protection and help of Almighty God.

I believe that all work has a religious, as well as a secular, character.   I was once turning over the leaves of a large book, which was a register of credits, when a gentleman came into my office and asked me if I read my Bible as carefully as I was reading that book.   I replied that I believed it was just as much my duty to read that book carefully, and to remember the contents of it accurately, as if I were reading my Bible ; not meaning in the least to disparage the importance of the daily reading of the Holy Scriptures.

If you have no plan in life, if you have not yet chosen your business, your profession, or your calling, if it seems to you that there are no providential indications as to what you are to do, it is very probable that the very circumstances which surround you will help you to determine your lot, and these are providential.

The temptations that beset a young man in a great city are innumerable and frightful. Many of them are utterly unknown to those who live in the country. Here you are beset at every corner, and I do not know of any place more dangerous or more fatal to the character of young men than the streets of a great city at night ; and those of you who are in boarding houses, where you have not the comforts and conveniences of a home, who do not like to be alone in your bedroom, or whose bedrooms are so uncomfortable as to ren- der them unsuitable for sitting-rooms, who have few or no comforts, who are often found on the street at night with no special aim or purpose, are most particularly in danger.

A young man who is fond of reading, who can go to the public library and find pleasant associates and good books, and who has the judgment and the taste to make good use of them, is highly favored. It was not so forty years ago. There were no places accessible to young men, strangers from the country, where they could spend their evenings in safety, when I was a youth, and the consequence was that very many such young men, thus withdrawn from the restraints of their homes, became an easy prey to the dangers that be- set them in the public streets. You cannot even go from this hall to your homes or your lodgings to-night, without being confronted with some of the perils to which I have alluded. Some of you, it may be, will yield ; perhaps you have yielded before ; if so, it will be easier for you to yield again, and you

may go even from this place of warning and instruction to
places and associations that are utterly destructive to your
moral nature.   Let me say to such of you as are accountants,
who know something of book-keeping, that every credit
must have a corresponding debit, and you well know what
that means.   " Whatsoever a man soweth, that shall he
reap."   If you do a wrong to yourself, or to any one that
falls in your way, or who has the right to look to you for
help and protection, you may depend upon it that sooner or
later you must pay for it.   You cannot do a wrong thing
without punishment.   It will assuredly come ; if not now,
at some time in the future.   And I give you this warning in
all earnestness, beseeching you to take it to heart, and to
see to it that, for your own sakes, for your hopes of happiness in this life and hereafter, for the sake of those who may
fall within your influence, or who may be connected in any
way with you, and who will be rejoiced at your success or
overwhelmed at your failure, I beseech you, for the sake of
all such, and because of the recollections which will come to
you from the future, when you look back upon this scene
and these warnings, to take heed, and to walk in that
straight path of truth and soberness and righteousness which
will end in peace.

The dangers that beset you in the streets are of two kinds. .
First, there is the temptation to go to places where liquors
are sold.   It is very easy to step into these places.   The
doors are never barred ; the lights are always bright ; the
pictures on the walls are attractive ; in cold weather the fires
are always comfortable ; the company is apt to be what is
called jolly ; you are sure of a hearty welcome ; and the in-
ducements to stay late are many.   But remember that you
cannot touch pitch without soiling your hands ; you cannot
take fire in your hands without being burned.   And remember, too, that it is easier to go the second time than the first,
and that, if you do go more than once or twice, it is very

likely to be all over with you for this life.   Oh ! if you could
see the ruined families, the wretched wives, and more
wretched children, .made so by these dreadful places, you
would pause before your feet pass for the first time the doors
of these houses of death.

The other danger is one of which I cannot speak in language sufficiently plain.   I will only say to any man in this
audience who has, or who ever had, a pure mother or sister,
that these pitiful and lost creatures who meet you in the
streets once were as pure, perhaps, as those whom you love
so much ; and that they have been brought to that lost and
pitiful condition by such as you, if you are without principle ; and that hereafter, when we shall be called to account
for our doings, to Him who knoweth all things, it will be
asked why we did such things?   Think of any man doing
to one whom you love what you are tempted to do to these
helpless ones !

Professor Thompson, of the University of Pennsylvania,
once said in a baccalaureate sermon that the two things most
dreaded by young men are Poverty and Obscurity.   I have
tried to show you that poverty, at the outset at least, is not
to be seriously dreaded ; and, while no one willingly accepts
either of these as his lot in life, it is well to know that there
are conditions in life much more to be dreaded.   Riches do
not always or often make the possessor happy, nor are the
conspicuous always the most favored.   That which is most
to be dreaded of all human calamities is crime—self-com-
mitted crime—and this is altogether gratuitous, unnecessary.
To this you are all exposed, although you may now say, in
your virtuous indignation, "What, is thy servant a dog that
he should do this thing?"

I was invited here to speak to young men and to say
earnest and serious things to you.   I determined to do my
duty while here, as I try to do wherever I am.   I have seen
life in various aspects, very much that is bright and happy ;

but, alas! much, also, that is sad; and among the saddest
things that I have seen is the destruction of human character.   So I warn you against some evils, the fatal consequences of which I have seen in many young men with as
fair prospects as you have.

Daniel Webster was once with a company of gentlemen at
dinner. He had just come from a journey and seemed weary;
he talked but little, and presently sank into a reverie. All
attempts at conversation failing, a gentleman put to him this
abrupt question : " Mr. Webster, will you tell me what was
the most important thought that ever occupied your mind?"
Mr. Webster slowly passed his hand over his forehead and
said : " The most important thought that ever occupied my
mind was that of my individual responsibility to God."   I
do not know how much of the great man's thoughts was
given to this overwhelming subject, but I commend the
thought to you, young friends, and urge you to consider it
seriously.   Nothing is of so much consequence to you.

Life to me is very grand, and it grows immeasurably in
importance as I approach its close.   I said, in the beginning,
that " Life is worth living."   I repeat it at the conclusion.

A third of a century ago a vessel brought from St. Helena
the dust of a man who had been the terror of Europe, who
had desolated more homes, and broken more hearts, than
any man who ever lived. They buried him in Paris, in a
splendid temple erected for that sole purpose, and all France
wept over the tomb.

Was his life worth living?

On the banks of the Potomac, in a marble sarcophagus, in
a very simple enclosure, are the remains of a man whose
name stands higher in American history than any other;
who, although a soldier, became such in defence of his
country ; who cared nothing for "the pride, pomp and circumstance of glorious war;" who made his country independent, and in this had his reward ; who lived long enough

to see it established among the nations of the earth ; whose
death plunged all the people in mourning, and against
whose memory no man living, even at this day, dares utter
· a word.

Was his life worth living?

> Work away ;
> For the Father's eye is on us,
> Never off us, still upon us ;
> Night and day
> Work and pray.
>
> Pray, and work will be completer ;
> Work, and prayer will be the sweeter ;
> Love, and prayer and work the fleeter,
> Will ascend upon their way.
>
> Live in future as in present ;
> Work for both while yet the day
> Is our own ; for Lord and peasant,
> Long and bright as summer's day,
> Cometh,—yet more sure, more pleasant,
> Cometh soon our holiday ;
> Work away.

XXVII

The Uneducated Employed.*

A DISTINGUISHED Jurist of our city delivered, last summer, an address before one of the societies in the venerable University of Harvard, choosing for his subject, "The Case of the Educated Unemployed." With an intimate knowledge of his subject, and with rare felicity of thought and expression, he set before his audience, most of whom were either in the learned professions or preparing to enter them, the over-crowded condition of those professions, especially that of the Law, a preparation for which is supposed to imply a more or less thorough academic or collegiate education.

I have set myself to a widely different task ; for I would speak to the UNEDUCATED EMPLOYED, I would show the importance of education to the workers with the hand, whether in the mills, the shops, or among the various trades and occupations ; who live in the small but comfortable homes which make our city the pride of all who value the well-being and good living of the plain and hard-working classes. By education I do not mean that of the colleges, or of the common schools merely, but also that which is acquired sometimes without the advantage of any schools. And I particularly desire to show that an uneducated worker, whatever be his work, is at an immense disadvantage with one

---

* Address before the Y. M. C. A., Kensington (a manufacturing district), Nov. 30, 1885.

who is engaged in the same kind of work, or any other, and who is more or less educated.

A mechanic may be well trained in his work ; may have more than his share of brains ; may be highly successful in his business ; indeed, may have acquired a large property, and have very high credit, and may hardly know how to write his name. A man may have scores or hundreds of men in his employment, and be conducting business on a very large scale, indeed, and yet be so ignorant of accounts that he is entirely at the mercy of his book-keeper, and may be so defrauded as to be on the very brink of ruin and not know it until it is almost too late. In the course of a long business life, more than one such case has come under my observation. A man may be partially educated, able to cast up accounts, able to keep books by double entry (and no other kind of book-keeping is worthy of the name), and yet not be able to write a simple agreement in good English, nor understand clearly the meaning of such a paper when written by another.

Very many of the business failures that occur are due to the fact that the person or firm did not know how to keep accounts. This is not confined to people of small business. How often after a failure are we told "that the man was very much surprised at his condition ; he thought he was all right ; he could not account for his failure, and that in a short time he would have his books in such a shape that he would be able to make a statement to his creditors and ask their advice. It would require ten days or so, however, before he could tell how he stood." Why, if the man had been an educated business man, and an honest man, he would have known in twenty-four hours how he stood.

The great majority of people who are employed are not educated. They do not know how to do in the best manner that which they have to do. Perhaps a good definition of education, as the word is applied to a working-man, may be that *he knows how to do that which he has to do, in the very best way.*

Education may be of three kinds, viz.:

1. That of the *schools.*
2. *Self-education,* which may be *incidental* or *direct.*
3. That of *trade* or *business.*

That of the schools. And this is the best of all ; for the whole of one's time is given to it, and if the means of your parents or guardians permit, and you are so inclined, you may go through the whole course, as provided in our public schools. And the entire course means very much ; not merely the rudiments, such as reading, writing, arithmetic, grammar, geography ; but it means history, science, the higher mathematics, and even one or more of the modern languages. And all this with text-books, instruments and other appliances, absolutely free of cost to the pupil. A boy, therefore, who passes through the entire course of study in our public schools, which includes the Boys' High School, has excellent opportunities of acquiring a most substantial education. Whether the system of common schools, now established by law, originally contemplated the higher branches of study, or was intended to supply the means of education to the rich, or well-to-do families, are questions which may demand a full discussion some day ; but while the present system is in operation, its fine privileges are within the reach of all who persistently seek them.

Certainly the education of the schools is the best of all; and if any of *you* are still in the schools, let me urge you with all seriousness to make the best use of your opportunities. You can never learn as easily as now. You are young. You are not burdened with cares. Do not relax your efforts in the least; do not yield to weariness; do not think you know enough already; do not be impatient lest others of your own age, who have already left school to go to work, get ahead of you in trade or any kind of business; if they have the start of you, they may not be able to keep it; and depend upon it, in the long run you will overtake and pass them, other things being equal, if you have a better school education than they have. When you are told that young men who are well educated are thereby unfitted or unwilling to take the lowest places in trade or business, do not believe it. I know to the contrary. The better the school education you have, and the more you know, the more valuable you will be to your employer.

Another kind of education is called, but most inaccurately, SELF-EDUCATION. All that I mean by it is, that education which one acquires between the school and the trade or business. As so defined, it may be divided into two parts, viz.: the incidental and the direct.

Let me speak first of the *incidental.*

I mean by this that education that comes to us from the *church* and from *society.*

If it is your good fortune, my young friend, to go to a church where there is an educated minister, who knows not only how to explain the Holy Scriptures, and apply skillfully and faithfully their gracious teachings to the minds and consciences of his hearers, but who is also a man of high cultivation in general literature, and who brings out from his treasures, things new and old; thank God for the great privilege. I shall never forget, nor can I over-estimate the great advantages that I enjoyed in this respect, when a young man, I came to this great city. I learned to study the Scriptures, not only from the two or three sermons of every Sunday, but the one or two every week between the Sundays. And this preaching was of the most interesting and instructive character. The pure, strong Saxon-English of the sermons and prayers was a continual model set before me. The rich stores of sacred and secular learning were a constant stimulus to quicken my desire to know and study. For some four years I enjoyed this great privilege, and its effect upon

me was something like that of a college course. Most of
you either have already, or can have, some such advantage
as this, if you are desirous of a higher cultivation; and
I can assure you that a pure style of speaking, even in
common conversation; and of writing, if only a letter of
friendship, are not without value to one who has to make
his way in the world as a mechanic, or as any other business
man.

Another means of incidental education is in *society*. You
cannot live alone, and you ought not if you could. You
seek companions, or other persons will seek you. Let your
chosen associates be those whose friendship will be an instruction to you, rather than simply a means of social enjoyment. There are young people of both sexes who, without
being vicious, are utterly weak and foolish, idle and listless,
drifting along a current, the end of which they do not care
to think of. They are living for this life alone, with no
thought of the future, no ambition, mere butterflies, who
float in the sunshine when the sun *is* shining, but who, in a
dark and cloudy day, are bored and miserable, and utterly
useless. Sometimes they are pleasant enough to chat with
for a few minutes, but to be shut up to such companionship
as this, would be intolerable. Society has a large element
of this description, and you are likely to see much of it in
your daily life.

But this is not the worst phase of life among the young
people with whom you may be thrown. There are worse
elements than this. There are those who are depraved to a
degree quite beyond their age; who have given themselves
up to work all uncleanness with greediness; who put no re-
straint on their inclinations; in whose eyes nothing is pure
or sacred; who have no respect for that which is wholesome
or decent; who are the devil's own children, and who are
not ashamed of their parentage. And to such baleful, deadly
influences and associations will you be exposed, my young

friend; and you may not be apprised of their true character until it is too late to be delivered.

But there are *direct* means of education, so called.

1. The first of these which I mention is the use of books. This is unquestionably the best means to use. I am supposing that you have some taste for reading; if you have not, it is hardly worth while for me to speak, or for you to listen. I know some people who rarely read a book, and I pity them. They seem to think that all that is necessary to read is the daily newspaper. I do not say that such persons are necessarily very ignorant, for very much may be learned from the daily paper. But the newspaper does not pretend to supply all that you need, to fit you for a life of business, either as a dealer in merchandise or as a mechanic. No, you must read books, not only for entertainment and recreation, but for information and culture which you can obtain nowhere else. If there is no public library within your reach, seek out some kind-hearted man or woman who has books, and who will be willing to lend them to one who is in search of knowledge. I well remember a gentleman in my early life here, who did this kind office for me before I was able to buy books, and there are such men now who will do the same for you.

If you have little knowledge of books you ought to ask the advice of some practical friend to point out such books as you may most safely and properly read. For if left to your own judgment or taste, you will probably waste valuable time, or be discouraged by an attempt to read something not immediately necessary or appropriate. But do not attempt to follow an elaborate plan of reading such as you will find detailed in some books, for you are very likely to be discouraged by the greatness of the task. Such lists, I fancy, are made out by scholars who have read almost everything, and to whom reading is no task whatever, and who have plenty of time. Do not attempt to read too many books,

16

nor too much at a time, and do not be disappointed or discouraged if you are not able to remember or put to good
account all that you read. You cannot always know what
particular kind of food has afforded you the most nourish-
ment. You may rest assured, however, that as every morsel
of food that you take and are able to digest, does something
to build up and develop your system, or repair its waste, so
every book or paper that you read that is wholesome, does
something, you may not know how much, to strengthen or
develop your mind.

There are books that you read for entertainment or recreation, and that are written for that purpose only. You may
read such; indeed, you ought to read them, for you need, as
everybody else needs, recreation and amusement, and there
is much of the purest and best of this that you can get from
books. But you must not make the mistake of supposing
that most, or even a very large proportion of your reading,
can be of this character. You would not think of making
your daily meals of the articles of food that you enjoy as the
sweets of your meals. You would not think of living on
sponge cake and ice cream for a regular diet. You might as
well do so, as to read only the light and humorous matter
that was never intended for the mental diet of the working
man. No! If you would attain the real object of reading
and study, you must read and study books and papers that
tax the full powers of your mind to understand them. This
will soon strengthen the quality of your mind, even as the
exercise of your muscles in work or play will develop a
strength of body, that the idle or lazy youth knows nothing
of.

If you would know how to make yourself master of any
book that you read, form the habit, if the book is your own,
of making notes with a pencil in the margin of the pages;
but if the book is not your property, or if it is, take a sheet
of paper and write at the end of every chapter, full questions

on the matter discussed; and the answers to such questions will probably bring out the author's meaning so fully that you will have *absorbed* the book and made it your own; for as an eminent American author has said, "thought is the property of whoever can entertain it."

I said just now that the daily newspaper does not pretend to supply all that you need to fit you for a life of business, either as a dealer in goods, or as a mechanic. But the daily paper is a most important means of education; so important that no one can afford to ignore it. I hesitate not to say that every young man, every head of a family, ought to take a daily newspaper, which should be his own; that is if he has not the use of one taken by another. Nowadays one cannot be well informed who does not read a newspaper. The whole world is brought before us every morning and evening, and if we do not read the news as it comes, we shall not know what we ought to know. It is not necessary to read everything in a daily paper, there are some things that it will be better for you not to read. It is not necessary even to read all the editorials, brilliant as some of them are, for sometimes they discuss subjects that are not at all interesting nor useful to you. Of the newspapers from which I make the most clippings, there is one which is the fullest of advertisements, but which sometimes has nothing whatever in it that I read. But when it does discuss a subject of interest, it is apt to leave nothing further to be said.

But to read with the most advantage one ought to have within easy reach a dictionary, an atlas, and, if possible, an encyclopedia. Then you can read with profit, and the mere outlines which the newspaper gives can be filled up by reference to books which give more or less complete histories.

I think it may be said that the political articles, which appear in the height of a campaign, are hardly worth reading, unless you think of entering politics as a money-making business, which I sincerely hope none of you are thinking of doing. And I am sure that the articles giving full accounts of crime, and especially the details of police reports, and criminal trials, you will do well to pass by and not read. I really believe that a familiarity with these details prepares the way in many instances for the commission of crime, just as the reading of accounts of suicide sometimes leads to the act itself.

Some of the best minds in our country, and in the world, are now employed in writing for the periodicals and magazines. No one can be well informed without reading something of the vast amount of matter, which is thus poured out before him. I have not named the newspapers, nor the magazines which you may read with the most profit; but any of your friends who has any acquaintance with the subject can advise you what to read. Rather is it important for you to know what *not* to read. Many of the most popular and the most useful books that have been published within the last quarter of a century have first appeared in the pages of a daily or weekly or monthly paper. The best thoughts of the best thinkers first see the light in such pages.

Besides the newspaper and the literary magazine, there are scientific periodicals, which are of essential value to a worker who wishes to be well informed in any of the mechanical arts. The *Scientific American* is perhaps the best of this class, both in the beauty of its illustrations and in the high quality of its contributions. The *Popular Science Monthly* is a periodical of a wider range, and more diversified character, though not always of as sound and wholesome material. These periodicals, if you are not able to subscribe for them as individuals or in clubs, you may find in the public library. But let me urge you to turn away from what is called the Dime Novels. Not because they are cheap, but because they are often unwholesome and immoral. The vile, fiery, poisonous whiskey which so many wretched creatures drink until the coatings of the stomach are destroyed, and the brain is on fire, is not more fatal to the health and life than is the immoral literature I speak of, to the mind and soul of him who reads. There is an abundance of good literature that is cheap—do not read the bad.

Having now spoken of the education you may get in the *schools*, and that which you may acquire for *yourselves*, if you have the pluck to strive for it, either incidentally in the *church* under an *educated ministry*, or in the *society* which you cultivate, or more directly from books, whether read as an entertainment and recreation, or better still by careful study; or through the daily newspaper, or the periodical, whether literary or scientific, or what is best of all, that which is decidedly religious, I turn now to the *education* which you acquire as you are working day by day at your daily trade or business.

Let me beg you to consider the great value of truthfulness in all your training. Hardly anything will help you more to reach up towards the top. And when you are at the head of an establishment, your own or somebody else's (and I take it for granted you *will* be at the head some day), whether it be a workshop, or a factory of any kind, or a store, no matter what, a fixed habit of keeping your word, of not promising unless you are certain of keeping your promise, will almost insure your success if you are a good workman. How many good mechanics have utterly failed of success because they have not cared to keep their promises? A firm of high reputation agrees to supply certain articles of furniture at a time fixed by themselves. The time comes, but the articles do not come. A call of inquiry is made, and new promises are made, only to be broken. Excuses are offered and more promises given ; then incompetent workmen are sent ; then more delays ; until, when patience is nearly exhausted, the work is finished. Then comes the bill, and there is a mistake in it. The whole affair is a series of disappointments and misunderstandings. Will you ever incline to go to that place again?

It is usual for miners of coal to place their sons, as they become ten or twelve years of age, at the foot of the great breakers to watch the coal, as it comes rattling and broken down the great wire screens, and to catch the pieces of slate and throw them to one side, and they allow only the pure coal to pass down into the huge bins from which it is dropped into the cars and taken to market. To an uneducated eye there is hardly any perceptible difference between the coal and the slate. But these little fellows soon become so quick in the education of the eye, that they can tell in an instant the difference. When the boy grows older he graduates to the place of a mule driver, and has his car and mule, which he drives day by day from the mouth of the mine to the breaker. Then when he begins to be of age, he fixes his little oil lamp in the front of his cap, and goes down into the mines with his pick, and becomes a miner of coal. It seems a dreary life to spend most of one's time under the ground shut out from the sunshine and from the pure air. And most of these men having no education, and never having been urged to seek one, are content to spend all their days in this manner. But occasionally there is one who feels that he is capable of better things than this. And I know one, at least, who began his work at the foot of a coal breaker, and worked his way up through all these stages, as I have told you, and who determined to do something better for himself. So he gave much of his leisure (and everybody has some leisure) to study; nor was he discouraged by the difficulties in his way. He persevered. He rose to be a foreman among the men; then having saved some money, instead of wasting it at the tavern, he bought his teams, and then bought an interest in a coal mine, and became a miner of his own coal, and had his men under him, and has grown to be a rich man, and is not ashamed of his small beginnings nor of his hard work. This is only one instance of success in rising from a low position to a high one.

The same thing is going on all around us, and we see it every day. In a public talk like this it would hardly be proper to give you names, but I could tell you of many within my own knowledge who, from positions of extremely hard labor and plain living, have risen to be the head men in shops and other places, which they entered at the lowest places. Such changes are continually occurring. And there is no reason whatever, except your indifference, which prevents many a one of you, my friends, from becoming, if God gives you continued health, the head men in the places where you are now working as subordinates or in very low positions; or if not where you now are, at least in other places. And I have come to tell you what you know already, that there is plenty of room for advancement. It is the lowest places that are full to overflowing. Who ever heard of a strike among the *chiefs* of any industry? No, indeed! They have made themselves indispensable to their employers and they don't need to strike. And there is hardly a young man here who cannot, by strict attention to business and conscientious devotion to the interests of his employer, make himself so invaluable that he need not join any trades union for protection. Do the vast army of clerks in the various corporations, or in the great commercial houses, or in the public service, or in the army and navy,—do these people ever band themselves in any associations like the trades unions? They know better than that, they accomplish their purposes in better ways. If the working classes, so called, were better educated, they would not suffer themselves to be led by the nose by people who will not themselves work, who will not touch even with their little fingers, the burdens which are crushing the life out of the deluded ones whom they are leading to folly. It is a true education that is needed, a true conscience that must be cultivated, to enable men to do their own thinking, and determine for themselves what are their truest and best interests.

I urge you all to seek that higher and better education which will make you true men. Even if you have not now, nor ever have had, the great advantage of the education of the schools, it is by no means too late to make up, in part at least, for that want. I have tried to indicate several means by which you may make up for what you have lost. Some one or more of these means is within the reach of every one who hears me to-night. I have tried very simply, but not the less earnestly, to show you how you can fit yourselves for higher places than you now hold. It is for you to say whether you will avail yourselves of these plain hints. No earthly power can force you to do that which you will not do. You may lead a horse to a brimming fountain of water, but if he is not thirsty, no coaxing nor threatening nor beating can make him drink. I may show you to demonstration, the abundant fountains of learning, but I can't make you drink, or even stoop to taste the stream, if you are not thirsty. I can't make you study, however great the advantage to you, or however much they who are interested in you, desire that you should.

Every year this question which I have been pressing upon you becomes more and more important. The great colleges of the country are graduating their thousands of students, many of whom will compete with you for the high places in the mechanic arts. So are the public schools of the country sending out hundreds of thousands, many of them having the same aim. Technical schools, teaching the mechanic arts, are multiplying. Great changes have been made in our own city recently in this respect. The Spring Garden Institute is doing a noble work in this way. The Girard College is moving in the same direction, and soon it will be sending out its hundreds every year to compete with you, for places in the shops, with this great advantage over you, that these Girard boys have a school education,—the best that they are able to receive,—while you, many of you at least, have hardly any education at all. Do you suppose that you can keep up with them? They will go ahead of you just as certainly as a trained race horse will outrun a draft horse, whose work has been to draw heavy loads very slowly over these rough pavements.

Look at the poor ignorant people from abroad who sweep our streets,—look at the stevedores who load and unload the ships,—look at the men who carry the hod of mortar or bricks up the high and steep ladders,—look at the drivers and the conductors on our street cars, the most hard worked and poorly paid people among us, and are you not sure that most of these people are *un*educated? No one wants to be at the bottom all the time. We may have been there at the first ; but those who have made the most progress are generally those who have had the best education. I know that education is not a sure guarantee of success ; many other things enter into the consideration of the question ; but I am saying that, other things being equal, *he who knows the most will do the best.* There are, alas, many instances of the · sons of the rich who have been well educated, who have everything provided for them, who have no stimulus, no spur, who have no regular occupation, and need not have any ; many of whom sink into idleness and dissipation, and their fine education goes for nothing. But you are not of this class. You are men who have to make your way in the world by your own exertions.

Now as I am urging upon you the necessity of seeking a better education, do not put me off by saying that you have no time, that after working all day you have a right to your evenings, that you must have some fun, that you are not going to make a slave of yourself for the mere chance of getting ahead faster, that there is no certainty about it anyhow ; these are all chaff, and utterly unworthy of a young Amer-

ican.   Why can't you deny yourself for the sake of the advantage it will be to you hereafter?

Think of the long winter evenings that are before you.
The most hard worked among you gets through the day's
work at six o'clock.   Take an hour to wash up and get your
supper, and you have three hours before bed-time.   What
will you do with these three hours every day?   If you wish to
know what can be done under the most unfavorable circumstances, let me tell you of William Cobbett, one of the most
vigorous and most voluminous of English writers on political economy.   I do not quote him because there is anything to be admired in his views on other, and especially on
sacred subjects, but to show what a man of determined will
can do.

"I learned Grammar," said he, "when I was a private
soldier on the pay of six pence a day.   The edge of my
berth or my guard bed was my seat to study in ; my knap-
sack was my book-case ; a bit of card board lying on my lap
was my writing table ; and the task did not require a year of
my life.   I had no money to purchase candles or oil ; in
·winter time it was very rare that I could get any evening
light but that of the fire ; and only my turn even of that.
And if I, under such circumstances, and without parent or
friend to advise or encourage me, accomplished this undertaking, what excuse can there be for any youth, however
poor, however pressed with business, or however circum-
stanced, as to room or other conveniences?   To buy a pen
or sheet of paper I was compelled to forego some article of
food, though in a state of half starvation.   I had no moment
of time that I could call my own ; and I had to read and
write amidst the talking, laughing, singing, whistling and
brawling of at least half-a-score of the most thoughtless of
men, and that, too, in the hours of their freedom from all
control.   Think not lightly of the farthing that I had to give
now and then for pen, ink and paper.   That farthing was,

alas, a great sum to me. I was as tall as I am now ; I had great health and great exercise. The whole of the money not expended for use at market was two pence a week for each man. I remember, and well I may, that on one occasion, I, after all necessary expenses, had, on a Friday, made shifts to have a half-penny in reserve, which I had destined for the purchase of a red herring in the morning ; but when I pulled off my clothes at night, so hungry then as to be hardly able to endure life, I found I had lost my half-penny. I buried my head under the wretched sheet and rug and cried like a child. And again I say, if I, under circumstances like these, could encounter and overcome this task, is there, can there be, in the whole world, a youth to find an excuse for not learning that which is necessary for him to know?"

But we need not go to England for noted examples of this kind. The man who acquired more languages than any other man in the world probably, was Elihu Burritt, an American blacksmith ; and he worked regularly at his trade until he could afford to leave it and give himself entirely to study. That man knew as many as fifty languages well enough to read their literature. And I have heard him when he held an audience of some two thousand people spellbound, while he talked to them on the same general subject that I am now presenting to you.

I shall fail of my duty if I do not say some words to a class of persons—some of whom I hope have found their way to this room to-night. I refer to such young men and boys as sometimes stand at the corners of the streets in large and small companies, and amuse themselves by smoking and chewing tobacco, telling bad stories and making remarks upon those who pass by. I am sure much of this arises from thoughtlessness ; but I wish to point out the exceeding impropriety of this behavior. I have known ladies to cross the street and go quite out of their way and at much inconvenience, rather than pass within hearing of these boys and young men. And what right has any one to make the streets disagreeable to any passenger? And what right have you, young man, you, boy, whoever you may be, to block up the way or make loose or rude remarks, or spit your tobacco on the pavement over which I walk? You have no more right to the streets than I have, and you ought not to annoy me as I go to and fro on my lawful business.

All this is a most serious waste of time, and you are wasting it probably because no one has particularly called your attention to it. The time may come when you will recall the words of advice which you hear to-night, and you will regret when it is too late, that you turned a deaf ear to what was said.

I have now tried at some length, and as much in detail as the time will permit, to show the importance of such education as will enable you to rise in your trade or business, whatever it may be, to the upper places ; and I have tried to show that a true ambition leads one to strive to be chief rather than a subordinate, to be a foreman rather than a journeyman.

But, after all, everything will depend upon yourselves. There is no Royal road to education ; the very meaning of the word shows this ; the mind must be drawn out, worked over, developed, rounded, hammered, somewhat as a black-smith puts a piece of rough iron in the coals, keeps it there until it is red-hot, then draws it out, lays it upon his anvil, and hammers it, turning it over and over, striking it first on this side and then on that, rounding it off, then when it cools, thrusting it among the coals again, then hammering away again until he has brought the rough piece of iron to the size and shape he wishes, when he allows it to cool and harden. Now if you are willing to work your mind (as the smith works the iron) into the shape you want it, you will surely bring yourself to the front among active, ingenious and successful men.   But this means hard work, and work all the time.

Now if you really mean to avail yourselves of any of the hints which I have given you, or which others may give you ; if you really mean to succeed ; if you are not content to be a worker low down in the scale of industry ; if you mean to be a boss rather than a common worker, a head man in the mills or in the shops ; if you mean to rise rather than to be obscure ; if you intend to be well-to-do, instead of living from hand to mouth ; if you wish to keep your wives from being household drudges ; if you wish to give your children the advantage of a fair education, as many of you had not, you must grapple with the subject with all your might and keep at it all the time.   And you must keep out of the streets at night, away from the taverns, and from the low theatres, and from gambling dens, and from other places which I will not name ; and, in short, you must be true Americans, no matter what your fathers were, for there is no truer type of manhood in all the world than a real American ; and nowhere else in all the world has a poor man so good an opportunity to be and do, all this, as in our own good city of Philadelphia.

XXVIII.

SOME PRINCIPLES OF SAFE BANKING.*

I THINK it well to turn aside from the great principles of Finance and Banking, which have been, or will yet be, discussed by other members of this convention, and devote the time before me to some observations on a few of the more simple and homely features of the business in which we are all engaged.

Until quite lately we thought it worth while to have our own views of legal tender notes as one of the factors in the currency ; and some of us held this short theory, that if Congress had the right to issue legal tender notes in time of peace, there could be no need for any other currency ; but that if Congress had not this right, then the only circulating notes should be those issued by the national banks. This latter view we thought to be sound, but all our cherished views on the subject are of no practical value whatever in the light of the recent decision of the Supreme Court ; and all our big talk about the dishonest silver dollar which Congress creates at the rate of two millions per month, and makes us take at the value of one hundred cents in gold, goes for nothing ; for our masters at Washington are not likely to be affected in any way by anything we say or do on the subject.

It seems hardly worth while therefore to vex ourselves about things so entirely beyond our reach. Let us address ourselves to something which we can control.

---

*An Address before the American Bankers' Association, at Saratoga, August 13, 1884.

(254)

If we do not learn some useful lessons from the sad experience of the last three months, it will surely be because we are not willing to learn. The teacher is stern, exacting, inexorable; and if the pupils are not made wiser they should be expelled from school, and seek other means of education, or other occupations.

What are some of these obvious lessons? One is that there appear to be some persons engaged in managing banks who have very inadequate ideas of the gravity and responsibility of their calling. They are inexperienced, and so at the mercy of unprincipled men; or filled with conceits, and so unteachable; or so inordinately greedy of profit that they will carry more sail than they can safely do, intending to hold out signals of distress to stronger vessels in the fleet, under the hope which ripens into assurance that they will not be suffered to go down.

The cause of the disastrous occurrences within the last three months in one of our cities, and which have been mainly limited to that city, is not far to seek. When the National Banking Act was enacted the banks in the Atlantic cities were most unjustly obliged to redeem their circulating notes in the city of New York. Protests against this arbitrary feature were unavailing; but, as a compensation for the wrong, such banks were allowed to keep one-half of the reserve required by law in the banks of that city and count it as cash. This opened a door of profit within the law: a tempting bait indeed to banks, who could thus make one-half of their reserve interest-bearing. This has gone on until the banks in the city referred to came to hold the reserve of nearly all the banks in the country; a fund of many millions of dollars, most of it presumably on instant call. It needs no discussion to show that this became a condition of extreme peril; for every one knows that call money cannot safely be invested in time-paper. What then? Why this call-money must be lent on call to bankers, brokers and stock gamblers (the distinction is clear between these three classes), and on pledges of such stocks and other securities as have an apparent market value.

It is very well known that "call-loans," no matter how good the security pledged for them, do not always prove to be call-loans. It is within bounds to say that, ordinarily, they do not yield more than half their amount. For all banks resort to them for investments of what is called "minute-money," and in time of need, all are likely to call at once ; and, even if they are responded to promptly, it will be found that certain deposits, not apparently connected with the borrower, and which had been counted on as somewhat permanent, have melted under the appeal ; and about one-half the call, or the enrichment to come from the call, has been discounted !

The banks in the city referred to have become pretty thoroughly aroused as to the dangers of their position, and through their very able Clearing House Committee have grappled with the subject. Their arguments for the abolition of interest on deposits are very forcible, and sound principles of banking are on that side ; but some of us who live outside of that charmed circle have doubts that the revolution (for it is a revolution) will be successful.

There is a better way than this to meet the question, and a much more simple way. The redemption of notes is now effected by the treasury at Washington, and by the issuing bank at its own counter. Thus a gratuitous wrong has been righted. Now let the National Banking Act be so amended that a bank shall not be permitted to count as a part of its reserve any cash outside of its own vaults ; except where the associated banks in a city make one of their own number a depository for the common use of all, and where such deposits are represented by Clearing-house certificates.

If this association could be induced to adopt a resolution calling upon Congress to pass such an amendment to the act, the question of allowing interest on bank balances would shrink to insignificance, and might be left to settle itself.

Let the honor of moving such a resolution be enjoyed by some representative of that city which has received the greatest benefit from that feature of the law, and which has suffered most in consequence ; and I call upon you, gentlemen, brethren in a good cause, to adopt such a resolution in this convention. Let us commit ourselves to the *right* in this most serious question ; then shall capital, which has been forcibly diverted or enticed from its home, flow back into its true channels, and the national banking system, which, in most respects, if not in all, is the best the world has ever known, be strengthened at its sources in the several banks. A good so great as this is worth a sacrifice to secure ; for it is a well-known fact that any great force disturbed in its natural functions becomes an element of real danger ; and hired capital or call-money as a basis of business is most uncertain.

Here is another very brief suggestion in the line of sound banking.

Let a credit ledger be opened in the Clearing-house of any city, in which shall be kept a record of the names of payers and endorsers, amounts and maturities, of all notes of $1000 and upwards held by the various banks, which have been bought from brokers. Reports of such paper to be made to the Clearing-house anonymously, and information concerning such names to be given only to members of the Clearing-house. Large sums of money may be saved to banks by this means of information.

We who have charge of the banks in this growing country control an enormous power ; but unless we can work in harmony our forces are greatly crippled. We do not see enough of each other ; the opportunities of meeting are too

17

rare.　We are good men and true, else we should be out of place where we are.

For some years past the Scripture saying that "the borrower is servant to the lender" has been reversed, and the lender has been servant to the borrower.　The banker has been servant to the merchant or the broker, and has been treated as servants generally are treated, obliged to accept such terms as were offered ; but it looks a little as if our turn had come round again, and as if we might state our terms once more.　Do not let us delude ourselves and get proud ; for this reason, among others, that this condition of things may not continue.

We are not titled men.　We wear no stars nor epaulettes on our shoulders—no laurel wreaths on our brows.　There are no Doctors in finance.　We are not counted among the learned professions.　In fact, we are not counted a profession at all—only tradespeople.

But we have been of some service to the state.　We contributed a fair share of officers and men, who went to the support of the government in the dark days of the war ; and those of us who did not go to swell the ranks stayed by the stuff.　We had charge of the *sinews of war;* but for which, the war could not have been prosecuted as it was. First we gave our capital ; that is, the money of our stockholders ; and when that was all gone, we gave our depositors' money also.　And no better work was ever done.

Was not this heroic?　And we never speak of ourselves as heroes, but only as trustees—a most self-denying and poorly appreciated class of men, trying to make money for other people.

There are few positions of trust where the temptations are greater to use other people's money improperly than among bank officers and clerks ; yet, when we remember that among the scores of thousands of such trusted people, there is here and there only one who betrays his trust—not enough in number to make an appreciable percentage—it may well be asked whether men in the professions so called, or in any other business, can show a cleaner record.

We live in times when to be a bank officer is to be an object of suspicion or apprehension. And we ought to be men of clean hands. No temptation to enrich ourselves by the use of other people's money ought to be listened to for a moment. No speculation in stocks, even with our own money, ought to be entered into. If we must operate or speculate in stocks, let us get out of the positions of bank officers and go on the street as private capitalists.

A bank may be said to be in good condition when it has an adequate capital (not too large) ; a contingent fund at least half as large (and no suspended debt or over-due paper) ; when its deposits are free of interest and three or four times the amount of its capital ; when its dealers supply it with business paper to the extent of its needs ; when liberal salaries are paid to its officers and clerks ; when there is a trained man in reserve for every position that may become vacant ; when there is a pension fund adequate to the comfortable support of its worn-out clerks ; when it has a Board of Directors who are not content to be mere figure-heads, but who understand their business and remember their qualification oaths ; directors who count the cash frequently, and without notice to anybody ; who insist that every person employed in the bank shall take a vacation of at least two weeks every year, at which time another person shall do his work, and who believe in this dogma, that " nothing is good enough that can be made better."

I know something of a bank that has lived eighty years, and has paid to its stockholders an average of more than nine per cent. per annum during all that time ; that has accumulated a profit and loss account of about two-thirds of its capital ; that has provided an adequate pension fund for its superannuated clerks ; that has never been behind its neighbors in matters of great public interest ; that has graduated in a single generation, from its staff of clerks, nearly twenty persons to high positions in its own or other institutions, four of whom became bank *presidents* and nine became bank *cashiers ;* the others being secretaries and treasurers of large corporations, and one into the Christian ministry.   I think this is a record that she may well be proud of.*

There are two kinds of government for a chartered bank.

1. *Personal government* or government by the president, who manages the bank as if it were his personal property ; making loans and discounts according to his judgment, and reporting to his colleagues of the board just as much as he pleases and no more.

2. The other kind is *representative government*, where the president is the executive officer, carrying out, as far as he is able, between boards, the wishes of his colleagues, and reporting faithfully to them at their stated meetings all that he has done.

---

* I venture the suggestion that a bank is created and sustained not merely for the purpose of making money and paying large dividends to the owners of its shares ; as it is not the chief end of the individual man to make money and become rich.   It is eminently proper that a merchant, manufacturer, mechanic, railroad manager or farmer should conduct his business on high principles, dealing justly with his competitors, taking no unfair advantage of the ignorance of others, requiring faithful service and giving just remuneration ; and it is the office of a well-managed bank so to administer its affairs with reference to the well being of others, that it shall always be ready to aid, within proper limits, legitimate enterprises for the public good ; not overworking or underpaying its employés, nor retaining in its employment persons of unworthy character, but holding up before the community in which it is located, a model bank in all its features.   The community has a right to claim this of all its citizens, and it has an equal right to claim it of all banks and other financial institutions ; for all the money in the country except what is in the Treasury of the United States or in the pockets of the people, is in the custody of banks, trust companies or bankers, by whatever name they may be called, and it is of the utmost importance that the business of such institutions should be conducted by men of high personal character.

There are two principles of management of the current business of a bank.

One is *strength*, which, under all circumstances, is to be the first consideration. By this is meant that no greed of gain, no desire for large dividends, no ambition to put up the price of the stock, shall induce the management to lose sight of the cardinal principle that in *strength* only is safety.

The other is *profit*. As a rule, the inexperienced men are those who are most anxious for large immediate profit. They cannot wait. Not content with the golden egg every day, they want to draw on the goose sometimes for two or three eggs a day, and—you know the fable.

I submit these two principles of government, and these two methods of daily management, most respectfully to your consideration, gentlemen ; well assured that you will agree with me that a *government of directors*, with *strength* as the cardinal principle, is the best for a chartered bank.

XXIX

A National Bank Currency without the Security of United States Bonds.[*]

THE silver question has absorbed so much attention lately that there is some danger of overlooking another question also of great importance. This is the rapid reduction of the volume of National Bank notes. The frequent calls for payment of bonds held as security for this circulation, the very high price of the bonds which must be bought to replace them, the inclination of many banks in the large cities to withdraw their circulation, the very small profit in this feature of banking, will, at no distant day, unless some change in the law is made, practically blot out the National Bank notes.

Whether the community will willingly part with this representative of money, which for more than twenty years has proved itself to be the best kind of bank circulation ever devised, is a question not very easily answered.

The subject must be considered in its broadest sense, and not as one pertaining to the banks only. It is well understood that the banks do not derive much profit from their circulation. Some of the most successful banks are State Banks, which have no circulation, and can have none ; and many of the National Banks have withdrawn their circulation.

Certain it is that the country must have a paper circula-

---

[*] A paper read before the American Bankers' Association, in Boston, 1886.

(262)

tion ; and this ought to be redeemable in coin at the pleasure of the holder.

The question is, shall that circulation consist of legal tender notes, National Bank notes, or both? Or shall it be gold Treasury notes, or silver Treasury notes, representing coin or bullion, dollar for dollar deposited in the Treasury?

The National Bank Act was passed to make a market for Government bonds. That purpose was most successfully accomplished. If the National Banks are to continue to supply the currency for the people, some important changes must be made. The following suggestions are offered, some of which may be worth consideration :

1. Free banking, *i. e.*, free to any number of persons, with not less than fifty thousand dollars capital each for banks in small towns, and two hundred thousand dollars each for banks in cities.

2. The stockholders of these banks to be liable in double the amount of their capital, *pro rata*, at par, for the redemption of the circulation (the note holders being involuntary creditors), and to an amount equal to the par of their stock for their deposits (depositors being voluntary creditors).

3. Such banks to be allowed to issue circulation through the Comptroller at Washington equal to each bank's capital and surplus, provided that the circulation of any bank shall not exceed twice the amount of its capital.

4. This circulation to be redeemed at the counter of the bank, and at the Treasury in Washington in lawful money.

5. The 5 per cent. deposit for the redemption fund at Washington to be continued, and counted as part of the required lawful reserve.

6. Banks in the sixteen cities named in Section 5191 Revised Statutes, United States, to be required to keep not less than 25 per cent. of their deposits and circulation in lawful money in their own vaults or in the vaults of a common depository, certificates for which may be used and

counted as money in settling balances between each other, and banks in all other places to keep not less than 15 per cent. under same conditions.

7. When a bank fails and is unable to pay its circulation from the Redemption Fund in Washington, or from its own assets, or from the assets of its stockholders, the Comptroller of the Currency shall redeem it, and he shall be reimbursed by a *pro rata* assessment on all the National Banks in the State in which the insolvent bank is located.

8. The legal tender notes to be retired in sums not exceeding in any three months the issue of the new National Bank notes. This will dispose of the United States legal tender note question. There is no contraction in this, and the one hundred million gold reserve will, of course, go into circulation gradually.

9. The new National Bank circulation to have all the functions that the present bank notes have.

10. The United States Treasury may issue notes of the denominations of one, two, five, ten, twenty, fifty, one hundred, five hundred and one thousand dollars, on the deposit of gold coin or bullion of standard fineness and weight ; such deposits to be held for their redemption only ; the Treasury may also issue silver notes of the same denominations on the deposits of silver dollars or silver bullion, both of equal intrinsic value as the gold coin ; such deposits to be held for the redemption of such notes only. All these Treasury notes to be full legal tender.

11. The cost of printing and issuing new National Bank notes, and the destruction of the old and worn out ones, and the Government examination of all banks of issue, to be divided into two equal parts, one-half to be charged directly to the banks *pro rata*, the other half to be charged to United States Treasury against the taxes already collected on National Bank circulation.

12. The new circulation to be taxed at the rate of one per

cent. per annum until a redemption fund of 25 per cent. on the circulation of each bank shall have been accumulated, after which there shall be no tax on circulation.

13. Three-fourths of the reserve fund shall be invested in United States bonds or other securities to be approved by the Secretary of the Treasury and the interest added to the fund.

14. No other security for circulating notes to be required, and all banks to be permitted to withdraw the bonds now deposited with Treasurer of the United States as security for circulation.

It is the conviction of many people that the legal tender money, although justified by the exigencies of the war, should have been called in and extinguished as soon after the war ended as possible. It has been a disturbing element in our finances ever since ; it will continue to be, until redeemed.

If it is right to have National Bank notes, there should be no other kind of paper circulation, except gold and silver Treasury notes, representing the deposit of coin or bullion of equal value in the Treasury to redeem them.

Why is it not right to have legal tender notes? Because there is nothing but the faith of the Government to redeem them. Because Congress, with the concurrence of the President, can make money scarce or plenty as they choose. The legal tender circulation now is, say three hundred and fifty millions. If it is right to keep out this amount, why not double it? Who shall say what is the proper amount?

XXX.

How to Treat Your Banker.

SOME years ago I wrote and sent to the *Public Ledger*, the leading financial paper in Philadelphia, the following : "Hints to Those who Keep Accounts in Banks." The editor published them with these preliminary words :

" It is the belief of many observant philosophic persons who are well on their way through life that if people generally knew more they would behave better, though few if any of them believe that knowledge and morality are synonymous terms. Acting on this conviction, the following 'Hints to those who keep bank accounts' have been suggested by a gentleman well qualified by general intelligence and long practical experience to advise the young and untaught of the several matters whereof he writes. We give the seventeen 'Hints' in the order furnished, and recommend our readers to cut the article out of the *Ledger* and post it up in some conspicuous position in the counting-house or other place of business, or on the inside back of the day-book or ledger, where it may be in constant view of all, from the apprentice boy to the chief of the house."

Eleven years after this the same paper republished the "Hints" with the following introduction :

" The gentleman who suggested these 'Hints' is to-day in active business, directing one of our foremost financial institutions, and endorses all the 'Hints' as having stood the full test of the experience of the eleven years since they were first prepared and published. Now it happens that a prominent bank in Europe, having found these 'Hints' floating

(266)

about the world, and liking them, has issued an elaborate New Year's Circular, which is sent over here with the 'Compliments of the Season,' reprinting all the 'Hints,' and saying, 'We take the liberty of drawing your attention to the annexed circular ; owing to the excellent counsel tendered therein to bank clients and the public in general we trust you will have no objection to exhibit it at some conspicuous place in your office.' Thus requested from abroad, we again corral the waif of many years and reproduce the article as giving wise advice and information to all who have dealings at bank.''

HINTS ABOUT BANK ACCOUNTS.

1. If you wish to open an account with a bank provide yourself with a proper introduction. Well-managed banks do not open accounts with strangers.

2. Do not draw a check unless you have the money in bank or in your possession to deposit. Do not test the courage or generosity of your bank by presenting, or allowing to be presented, your check for a larger sum than your balance.

3. Do not draw a check and send it to a person out of the city, expecting to make it good before it can possibly get back. Sometimes telegraphic advice is asked about such checks.

4. Do not exchange checks with anybody. This is soon discovered by your bank ; it does your friend no good and discredits you.

5. Do not give your check to a friend with the condition that he is not to use it until a certain time. He is sure to betray you, for obvious reasons. Do not take an out-of-town check from a neighbor, pass it through your bank without charge and give him your check for it. You are sure to get caught.

6. Do not give your check to a stranger. This is an open

door for fraud, and if your bank loses through you, it will not feel kindly to you.

7. When you send your check out of the city to pay bills write the name and residence of your payee, thus—pay to Jno. Smith & Co. of Boston. This will put your bank on its guard if presented at the counter.

8. Do not commit the folly of supposing that because you trust the bank with your money the bank ought to trust you by paying your overdrafts.

9. Do not suppose you can behave badly in one bank and stand well with the others. You forget there is a Clearing House.

10. Do not quarrel with your bank. If you are not treated well go somewhere else, but do not go and leave your discount line unprotected. Do not think it is unreasonable if your bank declines to discount an accommodation note. Have a clear definition of an accommodation note : in the meaning of a bank it is a note for which no value has passed from the endorser to the drawer.

11. If you want an accommodation note discounted tell your bank frankly that it is not, in their definition, a business note. If you take a note from a debtor with an agreement, verbal or written, that it is to be renewed in whole or part, and if you get that note discounted and then ask to have a new one discounted to take up the old one, tell your bank all about it.

12. Do not commit the folly of saying that you will "guarantee the payment" of a note which you have already endorsed.

13. Give your bank credit for being intelligent generally and understanding its own business particularly. It is much better informed, probably, than you suppose.

14. Do not try to convince your bank that the paper or security which has already been declined is better than the bank supposes. This is only chaff.

15. Do not quarrel with a teller because he does not pay you in money exactly as you wish. As a rule, he does the best he can.

16. In all your intercourse with bank officers treat them with the same courtesy and candor that you would expect and desire if the situations were reversed.

17. Do not send ignorant and stupid messengers to bank to transact your business.

XXXI.

The Merchants' Fund.*

It is one of the glories of our American life that we have no aristocracy. There is no royal family among us, no dukes and earls and lords, no privileged class, and no titles except official designations. We have our Doctors of Divinity, of Medicine, of Laws and of Music; our Generals and Captains in the army; our Admirals and Commodores in the navy, and it is also true that our Judges and members of Congress have the prefix "Honorable" to their names; but this term as well as that of the doctorate is now-a-days so generally and sometimes loosely applied, that it comes to mean little more than the plain Mr. or Esquire, one or the other of which every man claims; but which really only distinguishes the *sex* of the person referred to.

There is, however, a class of men among us, as there is in all cities—in fact, they *build* the cities,—a class undistinguished by any title or uniform dress, whom we have the best authority for calling by a name second only to that of a Monarch. For the old Hebrew prophet Isaiah writing of a city (Tyre) that was at that early day mistress of the Levant, calls her the *crowning* city, crowning herself and others as if she were mistress of all the world, and he calls her merchants Princes.

The term merchant, though meaning originally one who

---

* Address before the Merchants' Fund, Academy of Music, January 31, 1874.

(270)

imports and exports various articles of merchandise and sells by wholesale, has by popular use come to include almost all who trade, whether in domestic or foreign goods, whether in large quantities or by retail.

Between the producer and the consumer, the worker and the capitalist, the man who works with his hands and the man who works with his brains ; between these two classes, that ought never to have opposing interests, but who, by designing men, are often made to appear in conflict with each other, there is a wide, it may be said, an immense field occupied, and necessarily occupied, by those who exchange commodities.

The farmer who produces grains, vegetables and fruits ; the miner who digs in the earth for his minerals and ships them to a market ; the manufacturer who reduces crude elements to the materials and the implements that wait upon the wants of man ; the grazier who rears the cattle upon a thousand hills ; the fisherman who makes the sea give up her treasure ; the axemen who level the forests, all these need the offices of those who are trained to the business of exchanging these commodities with each other in barter, or for money, in the shortest possible time and in the least expensive way.

The men who organize and control the immensely varied and complicated machinery of commerce are merchants. They are not often called to fill the highest places in the councils of the nation. There is a popular notion that a man cannot be a statesman unless he has been bred to the law, but I ask you what would our National Legislature be without merchants? What Secretary of the Treasury ever submitted a report to Congress worth reading, who was not materially aided in its preparation by the merchant? And what tariff law was ever framed which met in any proper degree the wants of the people and the wants of the Government, that did not owe all its details and much of its scope

and grasp to the convenient and ready suggestions of the
merchant?

And in the darkest hour of our late war, when the fate of
the nation hung trembling in the balance, when the Government was utterly at a loss where to turn for help, the Secretary of the Treasury sought and found help, and adequate
help, from the bank presidents of the three great cities, nearly
all of whom were or had been merchants.

And so our great railroads, hugging and binding the con-
tinent with their iron arms ; our canals, running like arteries
through the land, carrying the life from the centre through
the whole system ; our telegraphic wires, the nerves of
thought and intelligence, thrilling the world ; our ships
bridging the ocean with an almost continuous ferriage ; all
our appliances of steam on the land and the sea ; all are the
creatures of commerce, without which society would stag-
nate or go back to its original elements of families and tribes,
and life would no longer be worth preserving and devel-
oping.

If you ask me whether the mercantile calling is a *profession*, I may not be able to prove to you that it is, but it can
be proved that there were merchants before there were lawyers, or even physicians.

The lawyers may go back as far as Moses, for aught I know,
who was the greatest law-giver of all, and we read much of
them in the New Testament, though not always in the best
connections ; the physicians, it would seem, must have lived
as far back as men lived who needed the healing art, though
there is no trace of them in history until we read that when
old Jacob died in Egypt, "the physicians embalmed Israel,"
and we know that science had reached a high degree of cultivation there ; but the merchant goes back to the days of
Abraham, and it would seem, even far beyond that, for we
read that that venerable patriarch, from whom the Christian
as well as the Jewish Church has sprung, on the death of

Sarah, though he had been a wanderer and dwelling in tents, desired to purchase a place of final rest for his beloved wife. He opened negotiations with the owner of a certain field for its purchase. The bargain seems to have been made in a public place, and in the presence of a number of people. Ephron, the proprietor, either affected with the grief of the patriarch, or desiring to conciliate the good offices of a powerful chieftain, offered the land as a gift, but the rich and independent Hebrew was too proud to accept as a gift that which he was able to pay for, and he refused the freely offered donation. The land was then said to be worth four hundred shekels of silver (our English word *shilling* is derived from this), and Abraham closed with the first offer, and weighed to Ephron the amount, four hundred shekels of silver *current money* of the *merchant*. This implies, of course, that merchants were a class in that early day, and a class long enough and well enough established to regulate the money of trade and commerce, and possibly some of you will agree with me, when I say that if merchants in our time instead of the politicians, had more to do with the regulation of the money of trade and commerce, it might be better for us all.

The silver in that early day was weighed, for coins among the Hebrews were unknown until the captivity. Nowadays we coin it, and you cannot have forgotten the tremendous effort made by one high in authority only two or three months ago, to turn by a gradual though *slow* process all our greenbacks into silver, *five dollars at a time!*

Oh, if our admirable system of paper money had only been in vogue in the days of the patriarchs, Abraham might have floated up and down the land of Palestine, and even into Egypt, on the broad bosom of an inflated currency.

If I am bound to admit, however, that the merchant of that day was a *travelling* merchant, I hope you will not insist on calling him a *peddler*.

The brilliant author of Caxtoniana, in an essay "on the
18

management of money "—an essay which might well be printed in letters of light, and hung in the counting-house of every merchant, and in the bed-room of every merchant's clerk, says: "*Money is character*—money is also power. I have power not in proportion to the money I spend on myself, but in proportion to the money I can, if I please, give away to another. . . . Talk of the power of *knowledge!* What can knowledge invent that money cannot purchase? Money, it is true, cannot give you the brain of the philosopher, the eye of the painter, the ear of the musician, nor that inner sixth sense of beauty and truth, by which the poet unites in himself philosopher, painter, musician; but money can refine and exalt your existence with all that the philosopher, painter, musician, poet, accomplish. That which they *are*, your wealth cannot make *you ;* but that which they do, is at the command of your wealth. You may collect in your libraries all thoughts which all thinkers have confided to books; your galleries may teem with the treasures of art ; the air that you breathe may be vocal with music ; and better than all, when you summon the Graces, they can come to your call in their sweet name of Charities. You can build asylums for age and academies for youth. Pining merit may spring to Hope, to your voice, and Poverty grow cheerful in your sight. Money, well managed, deserves indeed the apotheosis to which she was raised by her Latin adorers ; she is *Diva Moneta*—a goddess."

The desire to possess money is well nigh universal. Whether it be the pleasurable excitement in acquiring it, or the power to give it away, or to exchange it for articles of use or enjoyment, or for the grosser pleasure of heaping it up and adding hoards to hoards; whatever be the motive, we are all striving for possession. It is this which makes the merchant ; it is this which brings the boy from the country, where he has lived as untrained and unshackled as a wild colt, and makes him submit to the restraints of business habits ; makes him willing to be shut up in a "close and dusky counting-house."

As we look out on the surface of society, we see that there is a race going on continually—that race is for riches—and who shall win? And so universal is this pursuit, that one of the sacred writers has expressed the sentiment in a passage which we would refuse to. believe if it were not in the Bible ; a passage which is rarely if ever preached from in our days—for reasons which are most apparent, "the *love* of *money* is a root of all kinds of evil."

But, like other pursuits in life, that of the merchant is not always successful ; in fact, the disappointments are more numerous than the successes. The best educated, the best trained, the wisest men, fall into errors of judgment ; make mistakes in their calculations ; stretch out their hands to help a friend or a neighbor a *little too far*—lose their balance and fall.

It seems impossible to avoid these mishaps. And it will not do to make provisions against such misfortunes in the way of private settlements on the members of one's family. The high-minded, honorable merchant cannot so provide against possible or probable days of darkness ; for while he continues in business, his creditors, and the public generally, consider that his whole estate is liable for the payment of his obligations, and in the event of insolvency, he cannot *enjoy*, without harsh criticism, any provision which, in the days of successful business, he may have made for his declining years, and for his dependent family.

You know, you all know, by observation or experience, how sad it is to see a man who has spent the best years of his life in mercantile pursuits, who has held up his head among the highest and the best, in the consciousness of a success and an integrity of his own creation ; you know how sad it is to see such a man overtaken and overwhelmed by misfortune, not always the result of his own mismanagement, plunged into the depths of poverty, hiding himself from the gaze of his fellow-men, and reduced to such deplorable extremity, as to suffer for the actual necessities of life. I need not, I cannot dwell on this picture. Your own imagination can fill up the outlines and make the application.

Now I tell you nothing new when I say that the object of THE MERCHANTS' FUND is to provide for just such cases.

Some of the best men have found themselves in this condition. They are too old to work, they cannot beg—I dare not suggest the other alternative, and they come to be wholly, or in part, dependent on this Fund. It is one of the most delicate and graceful of all charities. The giver and the receiver never meet—they are unknown to each other ; and the pain of obligation is removed as far as it can possibly be.

There must be, in this audience, many who can help this Fund. Quite recently, as you have heard, a *princely* gift has been made by a retired merchant (in fact princes rarely make gifts so munificent !), a man whose name will be cherished in profound respect and gratitude by coming generations, as it is here and now—a man who, in the light of the highest and best example, is going about doing good—seeking objects on which to bestow his large benevolence. He has realized in his own experience that saying of our blessed Lord which, though not found in any of the Gospels, has been preserved in the memory of one of his Apostles, that " it is more blessed to give than to receive."

Not many are able to make contributions so large—but very many, almost all, in this assembly can do something, however small, for so good an object. The largest benevolence ever manifested in our world by any human being, in the way of pecuniary charity, was represented by the lowest possible sum—*two mites !*

When a rich man dies, we read with much interest that part of his will which recites his bequests to benevolent institutions ; how much he gave to this and that cherished object, and we rejoice to learn that his executors will have the honor of distributing these sums in the directions indicated ; but I can tell you of a better thing than this : *Be your own executor.* Take the satisfaction of giving with your own hand these sums, and enjoy with an excusable selfishness, the only selfishness that *is* excusable, the great pleasure of making others happy.

You need not fear that the sacred trust will be betrayed. The names of the officers and managers of this Fund are a sufficient guarantee that your contributions and your bequests will be faithfully guarded. Some of the very best names in our city are here, and they are as familiar to you as household words.

I trust you will not think me invidious, and I know you will excuse me when I say that there is one name high in the list of officers of this MERCHANTS' FUND— a gentleman who sits on this platform to-night—whose long life, spent in the midst of you, is an illustration of the highest, purest integrity, whose venerable head, white as snow, has never been bowed in shame or grief, unless it be for the faults or misfortunes of others, who gave up the career of an honorable merchant more than twenty years ago to take the charge of a large moneyed institution, which he guides and controls with an intelligent judgment worthy of the very highest praise.

It is to men of this character that you commit the almost sacred ministrations of your MERCHANTS' FUND.

www.ingramcontent.com/pod-product-compliance
Lightning Source LLC
Chambersburg PA
CBHW020844020726
47497CB00005B/1244